Nothing to Lose

Nothing to Lose

a novel
Jim Sanderson

Jim Sanderson
5/3/14

For Ana
I hope that
you don't think that
you lose anything
in this book

TCU PRESS

Fort Worth, Texas

Copyright © 2014 by Jim Sanderson

Library of Congress Cataloging-in-Publication Data

Sanderson, Jim, 1953-
 Nothing to lose : a novel / by Jim Sanderson.
   pages cm
 ISBN 978-0-87565-578-9 (alk. paper)
 1. Private investigators--Texas--Beaumont--Fiction. 2. Murder--Texas--Beaumont--Investigation--Fiction. 3. Bars (Drinking establishments)--Texas--Beaumont--Fiction. 4. Beaumont (Tex.)--Fiction. I. Title.
 PS3569.A5146N68 2013
 813'.54--dc23
                            2014042131

TCU Press
TCU Box 298300
Fort Worth, Texas 76129
817.257.7822
www.prs.tcu.edu

To order books: 1.800.826.8911

Cover design by Barbara Whitehead

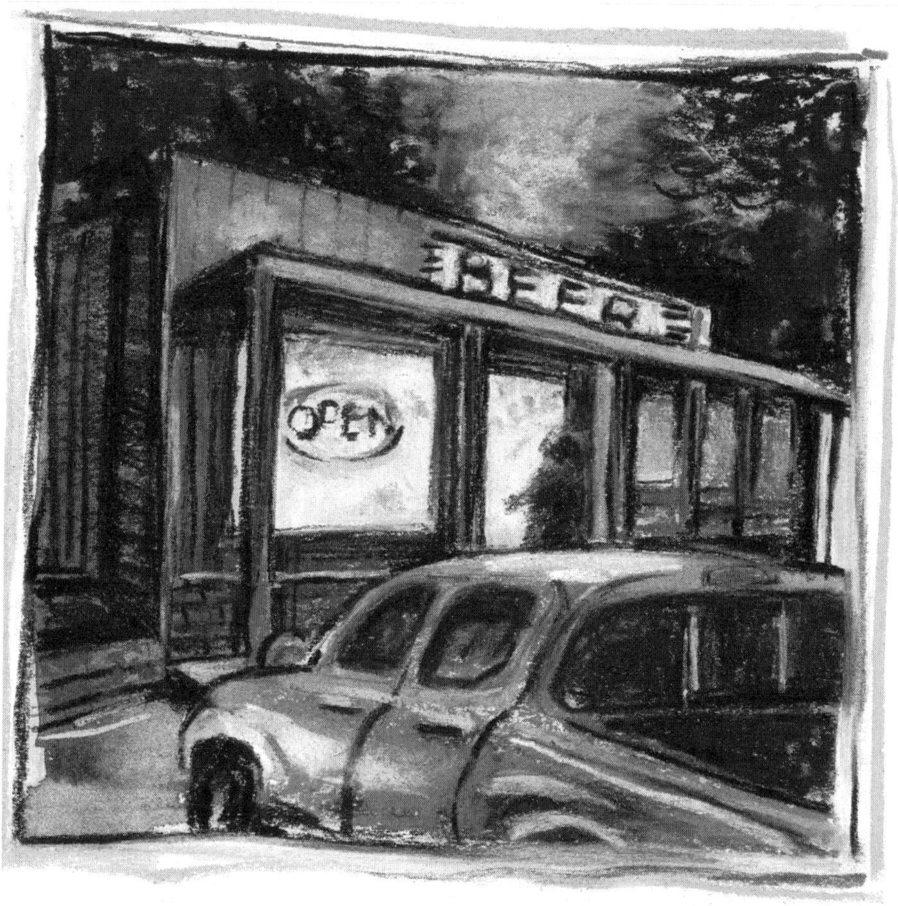
OPEN

ONE

The good thing about Beaumont in September is that it isn't Beaumont in August. September is mostly hot and muggy with air so thick you almost have to shove it up your nose with your thumb. August makes you wish you were dead, makes you forget what it is like to wear a clean, dry shirt, makes you believe that the true son of God is Willis Carrier, the man who invented practical air-conditioning. July is just as bad. June, May, September, and October are just miserable, not unbearable.

I live on the southeastern edge of Texas's Pine Curtain, in Beaumont. In my house, near Jefferson County's northern line, I am surrounded by pines. If I drive just a little south, down state Highway 69, the Eastex Freeway, I am in marshland and former rice fields. The pines give up, as though this soil is just too soft, porous, and damp to support a sizeable tree.

In Jefferson and Orange Counties the humidity soaks through everything, never lets up, never truly lets the sun in to dry things out. So the people living behind the Pine Curtain live in claustrophobic damp, dark, smelly tunnels carved under the trees and through undergrowth, mud, mush, and swamps. Texans have an Aggie joke. An Aggie takes his girl out parking. They get passionate. She tells the Aggie that she wants him to kiss her someplace dark, smelly, and wet. So he drives her to Beaumont.

But we had made it partially through September without a hurricane, fall was coming, and I had money in my pocket. I had been on a good gig. Denny's management claimed that a late-night shift worker was running her hands through the till and taking some home with her in the early mornings. Management paid me to take photos of her leaving the shift and to follow her for a while. I was hoping for her to escape prosecution—whether she was stealing or not. Whatever happened to her, I had gotten paid well. And then a chemical engineer in midcounty, Cody Hudson, paid me to take photos of his wife's affair with an aging ex-hippie named Harry Krammer. I figured I deserved to cool down just as the summer was starting to.

So I was jogging along one of my usual routes: one of the drainage canals that cross Tram Road. And the jogging, on that September day, felt almost good. A late morning summer shower caught me, and though sloshing through mud, I was cooled. I hurried because soon the sun would come out and turn the banks of the canal into a sauna.

I passed the upside down tallow trees, the ones bent over by Hurricane Rita so that they were growing in the wrong direction, but still growing, seething, disgustingly refusing to die with dignity. Tallows are trash trees. Like the hyacinth plants, nutria rats, and fire ants, tallow trees were imported (for decoration or by accident), so like the fire ant, nutria rats, and hyacinth, the tallow trees have no real deterrents to their quests to dominate the area.

Stepping fast instead of actually running as I used to do, I passed the "blue roofs" with their blue shards that waved to me in the slight breezes. In my neighborhood, on the southern tip of the Big Thicket, and thus the edge of the meth labs and small marijuana plant gardens, the people were poor. Those that stayed took advantage of the government supplied temporary roofing as long as they could.

To mark the millennium, God sent his wrath upon Southeast Texas in the form of Hurricane Rita. People died, not in the midst of God's wrath, but in escaping it—old folks and the infirm dying in buses caught in the evacuation route traffic jams. God's wrath damaged most of the buildings. One movie theater and the airport terminal took two years to recover.

For years, in and around town, we still saw blue roofs. The temporary tarps that the government provided stayed on poor people's roofs until the blue dissolved or shredded. With the roofs gone, the buildings soon disintegrated. So God with his hurricane solved the social problems that government never could fix. When the un- or under-employed left, they didn't come back. And when their buildings fell in on them, the persistently poor just left.

Jogging was penance for the night before. Jogging hurt. It made me feel every one of my fifty-some-odd-mostly-misspent years. But it felt good when I finished—just like penance. And sometimes, the jogging, like the penance, felt good in and of itself. And sometimes, after I finished, I felt like I had learned something since I myself had given up on being upwardly mobile.

That's right, I'm nearly spooky religious. You see, the pines have a natural swamp gas sifting around their bases, roiling around at night. The timber treatment plant and the gas and oil refineries add their rotten-egg and sour smells. You can see all of these smells. They are gray with a tint of greenish-blue mixed in. Living in the pine swamps, the people just naturally have visions and want to kiss snakes. No matter what their beliefs, they become Pentecostals. Or they hide from what they know and become Baptists. One way or the other, we're all religious down in these swamps. The area behind and near Texas's Pine Curtain is governed by three *P*s: pine, petroleum, and Pentecostals.

I had just stepped off the canal, and was baby-stepping, like an old man jogs, down Tram, toward my house. I ran into traffic, and out of the corner of my eye I saw a Jefferson County Sheriff's car slow down in the opposite lane. I slowed down. The car pulled as far off the road as it could, and Deputy Sheriff Emily Nguyen stepped out of the driver's side. I stopped jogging, and Emily and I stared across the road. Emily was just barely taller than the roof of the car. The Jefferson County Sheriff's department uniform just didn't look right on her. It gave her no authority. Thank God, she knew enough about how she looked to wear a baseball-style cap instead of the cowboy hat most deputy sheriffs wore. "Get in," she said.

"I'm jogging."

"You're getting too old for jogging. It's bad on your joints," Emily yelled at me. "Get in," she said. She could never stay away from her point for long.

I walked across the road. "Somebody shot and killed Harry Krammer," Emily said.

"What's that got to do with me?"

"The crime scene investigators found some of your photos in the house." While my mind was whirring to try to keep my mouth from getting me in trouble, I said, "How do they know the pictures are mine?"

"Who else's would they be?"

"How the hell did they get in his house?"

"That's what I was wondering."

"Can't I take a shower?"

"No. I'm not supposed to know anything. Get in the car."

I circled around the car to the passenger's side and got in. When Emily climbed in and buckled up, the faint stink of my sweat and leftover cigarette smoke that had soaked into my hair and skin the night before filled the car.

Stink, though, besides making my head hurt and besides making me thirsty, makes my mind work. I didn't think, which I should have, but I remembered.

Three weeks before, I rang Cody Hudson's doorbell to deliver the photos he had hired me to take of his wife and Harry Krammer. It was the first time I had met him. We had done our business over the phone. Cody answered the door, pulled it open, and looked down at my shorts. "It's hot. Private investigators don't have dress codes," I said.

"I thought you guys wore trench coats?"

"It's Beaumont, dude," I said.

He let me in. He was dressed in a white shirt and tie. I could see his hard hat and his goggles lying on the dining room table. "So let's have it. I took a couple of hours off, but I have to get back to the plant."

Cody flipped through my photos. "Oh my God," he said. The one he saw was of Jessica and Harry kissing as she left his house early one morning. After I had taken that photo, an elderly lady in color-coordinated purple and blue jogging tights banged on my side window and wanted to know what I was doing in the neighborhood. I drove away with her memorizing my license plate and threatening to call the police. She did call. And for the umpteenth time the Beaumont Police Department called me and told me to be more discreet.

"I have a list of where they were for the past two weeks. I can give you an estimate of how much time he spent with her, when they turned in, when she left. I have more photos, same as those."

"Who is this son of a bitch?" Cody asked.

"He's a social worker. From what I can tell, a lot of people speak very highly of him, from his clients to his friends. He's got a master's degree. He's a gentle sort. A nice guy, with a few past addictions, a few too many ex-girlfriends. You need some more?"

"What's that got to do with my wife?"

"It just shows I'm thorough. I try to give you your money's worth."

"I'm not sure that I want my money's worth."

We were still standing next to the front door. Oblivious to me, Cody turned from me and plodded into his living room. "So what am I going to do?" he mumbled.

I stepped in, not wanting to comment, but wanting my check. "I generally find . . ."

"What did I do wrong?"

"In my business, and in my general observations, I find it best not to question. If you could . . ."

"How could she just turn her back?"

"Mr. Hudson, perhaps if you look at this as a step forward. This does not have to be the end of anything, but maybe a beginning, no matter what happens. We can all adapt and adjust and move forward." Of course, I really didn't believe what I was saying. I really didn't believe I was saying it. But I had found that if I listened to Oprah or Dr. Phil and remembered those clichés, those same clichés could calm my clients and get me my check a lot faster. And if I got the check and could excuse myself before things got really nasty, I could avoid the truth: which was the yelling and the screaming and the accusations and then the divorce.

"But how could she? Didn't I give her everything?" He paced to think. "When did she have the time?" I didn't answer. He looked at me, and the way his brows knit together told me that I owed him an explanation.

"She'd usually meet him after school. And at nights, when you were away, she'd telephone the sitters, and well. . . . It's never really that hard—if you want to," and here, out of meanness or spite, I said, "and she wanted to."

"What do I do?"

"I don't know. That's not my job."

Cody came toward me shaking his head. "I've got to get back to work," he said.

"Mr. Hudson, just one more thing, if you could." He straightened, I dropped my head, "My second check."

✦

Emily got on 69, exited on Dowlen, drove past the mall and the franchise stores sprouting up and down Dowlen and thus creating traffic jams, and pulled into Beaumont's latest addition to its cultural growth: the new Krispy Kreme doughnut shop. Emily and I sat across from each other with my coffee and water in front of me and Emily's coffee in front of her, and three disgusting doughnuts in the middle of the plastic table. She finally reached and grabbed a doughnut while I sipped my water.

"I'm not supposed to know about this. The Beaumont Police Department is handling it. But since I'm one of the few cops in this town who like you, I thought I'd better warn you about what's coming your way." Emily didn't look at me but at her doughnut.

"Emily, you're still doing the work of three white men."

Emily smiled, "Stop your redneck act. You're not as backward as you like to pretend."

"If they knew I was smart, they'd try harder to fuck me."

"You do good enough fucking yourself."

"What's coming my way?"

"Somebody is going to question you. Maybe if you just voluntarily showed up at the police station, you'd be forgiven rather quickly."

"You're an angel, Emily."

Emily munched the doughnut as methodically as she did everything else. Then she looked down at the half still between her fingers. "You know these suck. They're just nothing but sugar."

"You can have mine," I said.

After we finished at the doughnut shop, instead of driving back down Dowlen to 69, Emily pulled into the Walmart Supercenter. "What are we doing?"

"I'm going to buy you a towel and a T-shirt. You're starting to stink. Then we're going to go by the crime scene. I think I can get you past the yellow tape."

✦

Old Town Beaumont used to be all old rich. But it had become some old rich, some new rich, and some crack houses. It was full of gays, transvestites, drug dealers, theatrical types, poor students—those folks trying to escape overpriced rent in suave apartment complexes by living in older homes. Harry fit right in. He lived in what would have been called a bungalow if it had been built in Southern California in the thirties instead of in Beaumont. It was a modest cottage stuck between what had been near mansions.

As Emily and I walked across the yard, the neighbors gawked at the yellow tape decorating Harry's porch. They gawked at me, too, as Emily led me up to the cop guarding the crime scene. "Nobody is allowed inside the tape," he said.

"I've got permission," Emily said.

"Nobody," the cop said, then looked at me. "Seen any good pictures?" he asked me. I recognized him. He was in a couple of my photos.

Emily tried again. "Look, Arthur knows me..."

"Nobody goes past the tape." Several elderly people gathered behind us. They started asking us what had happened in whispers.

"Shit," Emily said and ducked under the tape. "Come on, Roger," she said.

The cop just smirked. "So you recognized me?" I asked.

"Every cop recognizes you. Even in your underwear." I glanced down at my jogging shorts. "If you ain't already figured it out, you better be real careful."

When I stepped into the house, I heard, "Get the hell out of my investigation." We adjusted our eyes to the dark and looked around. I saw Arthur Solieu eating a tuna sandwich. Arthur was a fat man, and his fat, unwrinkled fingers looked like two Vienna sausages joined by a knuckle, and a half Vienna sausage attached to the last knuckle. He sucked the mayonnaise off one of his fingers. "You two sightseers back your asses on out of here."

"Hello, Arthur," Emily said.

"Emily Nguyen, this is a city matter. Keep the county in its usual indifferent position."

"Hello, Arthur," I said.

"Who are you?" Arthur said as he munched a potato chip.

"I'm Roger Jackson."

"I heard of you. In fact, don't you go nowhere. You're a suspect."

I looked over at Emily as if to blame her, and she just shook her head, as though she were disappointed in Arthur.

Arthur carefully laid his quarter of a sandwich on a plate and walked to us, wiping his hand on his shirttail. "Glad you could dress for the occasion," Arthur said and shook my hand with the one he had just wiped on his shirt.

"So what do you know, Arthur?" Emily asked.

"This your typical dress?" Arthur asked me.

"Emily stopped me jogging. I usually put on a nicer pair of shorts."

"I thought it was me, or the remnants of old Harry, that was getting gamey."

"Do you recognize anything?" Emily asked me. I looked around. Harry decorated his apartment in early destitute bachelor, sort of like me. Secondhand furniture, the end table and coffee table had glass stains, chips, and buckles in the wood. The sofa used to have blue and green stripes, but the fabric had faded into a dark mint green. No ashtrays. No pictures or photos on the wall. Shoes were scattered throughout the place. He had probably come home, shucked off his shoes, and then flopped onto his sofa for a microwave dinner and then some TV, probably baseball or football. The only expensive thing in the room was the thirty-two-inch flat screen. My eyes stopped on a bookcase. It was crammed with books, mostly paperbacks, most new—not leftover college textbooks. College graduation was the time most people stopped reading. I stepped to the bookshelf and pulled out a novel.

"Hey, don't touch that," Arthur said. It was recently published. Emily and Arthur followed me into the bedroom. Same story: magazines, books, shoes, underwear, dirty clothes. Almost as though displayed, a flat football was on his dresser. The bedroom had photos. One was of a young Harry in what looked like a soccer uniform with his arm around a black teammate. "That fellow is now vice principal at Main High School," Arthur said. Another photo was of an attractive lady in her fifties or sixties. She was thin, almost gaunt, so wrinkles showed in her face, but she had a youthful gleam in her eye. She would probably have been too old for Harry, not for me.

Arthur slipped on some rubber gloves and pushed open the bathroom door. I stepped in. It was where he had been killed. "Blood scares me.

Makes me want to hurl," I said and stepped out, and Emily and Arthur followed me into the living room.

For Harry Krammer, his cheap rental house was just a place to sleep, watch TV, and read, and then it occurred to me that to Harry it was also the place to consummate his affair with Jessica Hudson, and maybe with the older lady in the photo. "So how's the crime scene analysis coming?"

"Oh just fine," Arthur said. "Soon as I get all the hairs and fingernail slivers and such scraped off and sent to the Beaumont PD lab; then they'll run it through the electro-proton calimeter and figure out the DNA, the exact minute the murder took place, and who the murderer's daddy is. Just like on that TV show."

Emily started to chuckle, but before she could speak, I asked, "And why am I here?"

"I'm trying to help a friend . . ." Emily said.

"Me or Arthur?" Emily hung her head as though I was scolding her. "Look, I wouldn't be here from the middle of my jog unless you two wanted me here."

Arthur held out a thumb as though counting, "Number one you are a suspect."

"How did you figure that out?"

"They're your photos."

"Oh, Jesus."

"You show them to him. You get in an argument. You, you . . ."

"You're slowing down, Arthur."

Emily spoke out. "They're your photos. We can figure out who that woman is in the photo with Harry, and since she legally lives in Nederland, out of Arthur's jurisdiction, I'm here. Now, we were hoping you might be able to explain just a little before we ask more questions." Her voice was strong enough to scare me.

"Were you taking the photos for him?" Arthur asked.

"I don't kiss and tell."

"Then number one suspect is you," Arthur with his fingers again. "Number two is that woman, or her husband, or both of them. You want to elaborate any?" Arthur stood in front of me with his fat Vienna-sausage-length thumb sticking out of his fist and his two-Vienna-sausage-length forefinger sticking out of his fist.

"I took the photos and delivered them three weeks ago."

"Husband pay good?" Arthur asked.

"They're usually the ones with the money," Emily said. They waited but I didn't say anything.

Arthur held out his middle finger. "Number three is the cocaine supplier."

"The who?" I asked, and both Emily and I looked at Arthur.

"I snooped around and found a little tiny baggy. The lab people told me that, even without testing it, they knew it was really bad, nasty stuff—low-grade shit. Probably cut once or twice in Houston, once more here in Beaumont. Then probably some way down-and-out dealer cut it another time or two. I mean, look around. Has Harry got the dough to get good cocaine? I mean, who did he know could have got him anything better, even if he had the money? From the sleazy dives he hangs out in, as evidenced by those photos of yours, he's gonna meet the talcum powder and baking soda people."

"So are the papers gonna say that one doper shot another?" I asked.

Arthur shrugged his shoulders. "Unless you can tell me how mad the husband was."

"Or her," Emily said.

"Or them," Arthur said.

"Or the guy he, she, or they hired," Emily said.

I closed my eyes. I felt the air push in on me. I almost choked on its thickness. "I don't want to be a part of this. I don't want to go with you. I'm off the case. I'm just the guy who took the pictures. Maybe I'm not an innocent, but I am a bystander. Uh uh, no way. I ain't helping."

Emily said, "We know that it was premeditated. Got to be."

Arthur was next to me. "But the stupid fucker was not a pro. We got the gun. Of course, it'll be registered to some guy in Ohio, and there's no prints on the gun. Shooter probably followed him into the bathroom and shot him. That didn't do the trick, so they shot him again. And from the looks of it, whoever shot him, shot him just as he was taking a pee."

Emily looked at me. "Harry didn't know me," I said. "You don't just get up and go take a pee in front of somebody you don't know. It had to be somebody he trusted, not me," I said.

"All we got is your word you don't know him," Arthur said.

I looked at Emily; Emily looked at Arthur and said, "Come on, Arthur. Quit picking on Roger."

"Could it have been a robbery?" I asked.

Emily shrugged. "Harry didn't have any money. He could've stiffed the guy. He could have just been in over his head," Emily said. "Whatever, he ran into a real fuckup of a drug dealer, hit man, or robber."

"Couldn't y'all have waited until I finished my jog and took a shower?"

"We like you in those cute shorts," Arthur said.

"What do you want me to do?"

"Be a buddy. You know, you might have access to some things," Arthur said. "And you know," he pointed one of his Vienna sausage fingers at me, "that photo business of yours is real close to extortion. You 'remember' anything, you call me, huh?"

On the way back to my house and my shower, Emily apologized for sucker punching me. Once Arthur called her, it was probably all her idea. She was a lot smarter than Arthur.

I got out of Emily's patrol car and let her kick up some gravel as she backed out of my driveway. In my shower, I realized that Arthur and Emily could win all sorts of brownie points for closing the case as quickly as possible. They were playing me to see where I flinched, so they could know what to use on me. So they got me early, during my jog, nursing a hangover. Hell of a lot to brag on. It was not that hard to make me flinch. I prided myself on flinching. I was thinking about running away. But the phone rang.

Slopping water across my bathroom and into my bedroom, I caught my phone. Cody Hudson wanted to see me as soon as possible. Some Beaumont detective had come to see him. I wanted to give him a chance to calm down and me a chance to eat some lunch and cool off. I wished that I had some pot, but I was even more glad that I'd stopped smoking it. Alcohol may be immoral, but at least it was legal, at least in some spots in some counties behind the Pine Curtain.

TWO 2

I live in a lease-to-own A-frame house down a road off Tram Road, then down another dirt road off that road. With the rain in Beaumont, I never had a hard time finding mud to camouflage my Toyota truck. And several times a year, with the dirt road in front of my house, I was just mudded in. I'd sip my own whiskey and listen to the rain falling through the pines to my tin roof. My frame house got a mildew smell, and used to, twice a year, I'd squirt bleach on it, then hose it down. After a while I just got used to the mildew.

When I returned from my Hurricane Rita evacuation to Austin, I had to park my pickup off of Tram Road, in the sloping drainage ditch, and walk over and through the broken trees that clogged the landscape. It was as though the hurricane (or the tornados it stirred) had just sheared the trees midway up their trunks with a giant Weed Eater. Shredded wood was everywhere. Without electricity and the necessary air-conditioning, I sat in my A-frame and ate Vienna sausages and drank warm beer and whiskey while I slapped at mosquitoes and our large mutant love bugs and gnats, and I constantly blew the assorted bugs out of my mouth and blinked my eyes against them. When the power came on, I didn't run to the TV to check up on civilization but simply stood in front of the air conditioner. Gradually, stores opened, trash was picked up (though the piles of trashed trees and wood stayed for months), people returned, lights came on at night, and first Beaumont, then my neighborhood became a part of modern America again.

My landlady, a widowed Jehovah's Witness who evacuated all the way to Springfield, Missouri, before she returned, has a special agreement with me, and I may actually own my A-frame house if I ever care to press charges. I send in my minuscule rent/mortgage, and my landlord pays the taxes while she looks for eligible men she meets in church and on the Internet. Behind the Pine Curtain, if you say you're a Christian, that statement verifies you as honest, solvent, trustworthy, loving, sensitive, and prime marriage material. My landlady says that she is a Christian in the daytime, but at night she drinks in many of the same bars as I do. Bless her though, she has promised me that if she dies or if she finds a nice, solvent Christian gentleman, I get the house outright.

I changed into one of my best pairs of shorts, some old jogging shoes, and a Hawaiian shirt for my meeting with Cody Hudson. I figured that I didn't want to be too formal, nor too casual. And I wanted to be cool.

As I drove south on 69 to Nederland in my brand-new Toyota full-sized crew truck, trying to make my mind concentrate on work, it kept returning to pleasure: the powerful air-conditioning, the room, the armrest, and the CD changer in my new Toyota truck. When I began investigating my own divorce, and then got a job investigating other people's divorces, back in Austin, twenty years ago, I bought a brand-new Toyota pickup. Now Toyotas were all I bought, in honor of my first one.

As I passed the stretches of federal and state prisons and the county jail holding units just south of Beaumont on 69, I came back to work. Ten years before, when Texas was intent on putting as much of its population in prison as it could, say as many prisoners as students, Beaumont's sly politicians got a whole series of prisons located in Beaumont. So now committing a crime in Texas is good business for Beaumont.

Nederland, my destination, was created by old Dutch settlers. They had the misfortune of settling right in between the oil boom at Spindletop, at the southern end of Beaumont, and just north of the refineries that started in Port Arthur. From Port Arthur, the refineries could get their processed oil to Lake Sabine and then to the world. But the refineries eventually followed the Neches River up from Lake Sabine and on into Beaumont. So Nederland had refineries and then jobs and then a high rate of cancer.

What Nederland didn't have was black people. So when the federal government told Port Arthur and then Beaumont to start desegregation, the white population moved to Nederland and other blue-collar towns. Better to live with cancer, rednecks, turbo-Christians, and school principals trying to resurrect the 1950s than to allow your kids to go to school with Negroes. Nederland had a prohibition against selling liquor by the drink, which kept the white trash from congregating, and good Christian values to coax the skilled workers and the white-collar engineers to move to the area.

Cody Hudson had started out poor but proper, studied hard, and after getting his degree from Lamar University, on the south end of Beaumont, he became a respected chemical engineer raising a Christian-Baptist family in Nederland.

Cody Hudson was rich enough from refinery money to have a house tucked away from the rest of the suburban tract lots. The original well-to-do builders of the neo-Victorian houses in Cody's area, to extend their property and to further separate themselves from their neighbors, bought property right up to the refineries' property lines. So from the back of their houses, they had a magnificent view of the refinery smokestacks that stayed lit and often belched out black, gray, or yellow-tinted smoke. Since the hurricane, the Hudsons also had a view of twisted tallow trees and bulldozed wood and brush that made high-rise critter condos.

Engineers offer a certain comfort as clients. They aren't like the politicians, social do-gooders, and reformers that I had in Austin. They aren't histrionic. They don't gush emotions. They don't weep, condemn, or cuss. They simply figure out a formula for what went wrong, and then concoct a new one to fix the faulty valves in the marriage.

Cody Hudson answered the door, scowling at me like I had murdered Harry Krammer. Cody was an engineer, but he wasn't a numbers nerd. His hair was styled, shirts and slacks matched, glasses contemporary. But he had some Beaumont redneck left in him. He stared at his feet like he was asking them whether or not they should kick the shit out of me. After several uncomfortable, twitching moments, he finally asked, "So what can you tell me?"

"I can tell you Harry's dead."

He turned away from me, and I guessed that I was supposed to follow him in. He looked over his shoulder at me as I followed. "Don't you own any long pants?"

I wondered why my legs offended everybody. They were hairy, but taut from jogging, and didn't have the varicose veins people my age get. Still, everyone in this subtropical climate wondered why I wore short pants.

I just followed him through his house, tastefully decorated, not that I'd know what tasteful was, but I just noticed the blended colors, the placements of non-distinct, decorative paintings, the draperies and blinds. Cody let me outside to the glassed-in patio. A breeze was blowing, and Cody and Jessica were enjoying the view from their porch and sharing a pitcher of martinis. Beyond their yard was a vacant field with several large piles of scooped Rita tree damage. A neighbor was driving golf balls toward the refinery welling up farther beyond him.

Cody motioned toward Jessica and introduced me. If I thought Cody had scowled, I now stood corrected. Jessica just curled up in her chair, turned her head away from me to watch the golfer take another swing and send a ball toward the refinery. She sipped her martini. Cody sat beside her, took her hand, then patted it. He looked at me as if to say, "See what you've done?"

Jessica twisted in her chair to look at me. "I had cops in my school. I had police interfering with my class. Here's a bunch of second graders, children. And my principal comes to the door and calls me out into the hall. Little children are peeking out the door to see me talking to a cop. Well, a detective. He wasn't in uniform. So maybe they couldn't tell he was a cop." Her face had the blank look of a newly spayed dog. She just knew she had done something wrong, but she couldn't figure out what, so she begged with her eyes for me to fix it and make the hurting go away.

Cody stood up. "And I had the same guy in my office. Some obnoxious man, trying to be polite, but making all sorts of accusations." Neither had offered me a chair or a drink. So I sat down myself and stared at the pitcher of martinis.

Finally, Cody said, "Have a drink." As I poured a martini, the golfer sliced, kicked the ground, and cussed. They were vodka martinis. Stoli or Grey Goose, only the best for the Hudsons.

"You took those pictures," Jessica's face gained a little color. "You followed me around, after school, and you saw me go to Harry's house." She sniffed and daintily lifted a finger to her nose. She was elementary-school-teacher cute. Hair cut short, but just long enough to have a pony tail and bow. Like Cody, she was midthirties and radiated pleasant wealth. Harry Krammer, from his job to his appearance, radiated poverty. I wondered how she had ever met him.

"Jessica was so upset I had to take the kids to her mother's. They asked what was wrong with mommy. She's been crying for days. And now this." He extended his hand. Jessica took it. I felt like downing the martini because my mouth was about to give a really harsh critique of the play I was getting. I wanted to ask how much Jessica cried when Cody showed her my pictures. I sipped the vodka, felt its warmth, and thought with my stomach instead of my mouth. I looked at the golfer, his back to me, walking toward the refinery.

"How could this happen?" Jessica said and stared at me. What it was about her eyes was that her lids stayed open. She never lowered them; she didn't blink; she sniffed and raised her forefinger to her nose. The cocaine would have caused the sniffing, but not the unblinking eyes. "How can you do what you do?"

I was tired of this game of shoot-the-messenger. "Because your husband paid me very well." Jessica tried to recoil from me, but her mind and body were moving in slow motion.

Cody stepped forward. "That was uncalled for." Jessica switched her blank look from me to him. Cody swung his head between the two of us: "We're going to fix it. We're doing everything right. We're going to Wednesday Bible study. We're going to church more. We've got an appointment with a marriage counselor." So they *were* Baptist.

Cody squatted next to Jessica so that he could wrap his arm around her and stroke her opposite shoulder. She stared at me, the blankness now anger, one little tear in her wide-open Orphan Annie eyes. "What was that policeman thinking? I teach children for God-sake. I'm creative and artistic. I've been to college."

"What do you want? What do you want me to do?"

"Fix it. Just fix it," Cody said.

"How do I fix it? What's done is done. Bad timing, bad luck, bad evidence? What?"

"Find the killer. Find whoever shot Harry. Get the cops away from us." Cody straightened. The martini pitcher was three-fourths empty. Jessica held a glass, and so did I. There was one more empty martini glass. . . . Cody apparently had not had a drink. I looked at Jessica. She scratched her teeth with her forefinger. Harry's grade of drugs was not good enough for Jessica. I wondered where she found her drugs—especially before she met Harry. . . . Or were the drugs the reason she met Harry?

Cody went on. "I don't trust the cops. But find somebody, so they get him, not us."

"Could have been a woman who shot Harry."

"Whoever. Jessica and I can deal with our, our problems. I'm fixing those. But it's unfair for us to have to deal with our own problems and the police, too." I supposed that Cody considered Harry lucky. Or inconsequential. I wondered where Jessica's grief for Harry was. I wondered how Harry could have been so stupid. Then I thought about my own life. I wondered how I could be so stupid.

"Look," I said to shift my thoughts from my stomach and mouth to the discreet, deferential side of my mind, if there was such a side. "Unless they find somebody in a few days, this becomes a cold case. Harry's not important enough to keep investigating. At that point, they probably find nothing. For me to keep looking will get expensive."

"You've got a big chunk of my money now," Cody said. "But we've got some savings. . . ." He squatted by Jessica again, squeezed her arm, and looked at her as though to get her permission to spend their savings on me. "So I figure that I can afford your salary and your expenses for a week."

"As you know, my expenses are pretty cheap. But I'll tell you what, I'll charge a set fee. My salary for a week, and I'll work until I find out something. I'll try to let you know what the police think, whom they suspect. And I'll try to find out what I can." I kind of liked the idea of Cody paying me for what the police were going to make me do.

Cody squeezed Jessica's arm again. She turned to look at him, and they nearly bumped noses. He pulled himself away and looked at her unblinking eyes. "Okay, honey?" she asked.

Cody just nodded. I held my hand out, and he shook it. Then I held my hand out to Jessica. She folded her fingers over my hand, shook it, then turned away from me. "Now to start off, just two questions. Mrs. Hudson . . ." Jessica turned to me. "How did those photos end up at Harry's house?"

Something besides anger and confusion fluttered behind her unblinking eyes. "I showed him the pictures to explain why I was going to recommit myself to my husband." And good-goddamn-holy-sickening-shit, Cody kissed her.

"What do you know about Harry's cocaine?"

Again she turned on that flicker behind her eyes to think: "Nothing."

"The cops found some."

"I wouldn't know about that." Cody kissed her again.

I nodded and thanked them. On the way out of their suburb, I wondered if Jessica hadn't left the cocaine at Harry's house.

THREE 3

As I pulled out of the Hudsons' guarded community, I got a call from Amber's principal. Amber was in the third grade and had just whipped some fourth-grade boy's ass. Poor Amber was about to be suspended. Her school had a "zero tolerance" policy. Amber had requested that the principal call me instead of her mother.

I had been falling out of a relationship with her mother, Rachel Gutierrez, for about a month. Rachel was not a bad person, and I didn't think that I was, despite the flaws that Rachel always found in my character. We were both middle-aged scared that the other one might be our last chance. Except for being romantically desperate, Rachel was cocksure. I think I was with her because she was everything I once wished I would be: successful, reputable, cocksure. Rachel was what I had a chance of becoming before I started fucking up.

I found my way to Dishman Elementary, a newly designed school, the newest in town, and placed myself in a chair in front of the principal's desk. The principal sat in front of me with her fingers interlaced, staring a hole through my forehead. Standing in back of the principal was Amber's teacher. She shook her head on cue from the principal. To the other side of the principal, sitting in a chair more appropriate to her size, was Amber. Amber hung her head and fought tears.

The principal had told me that normally only the parent could intervene in such cases, but since Amber had listed me as a person to call in case of emergency, we could all make an exception. Further, Rachel was apparently caught up in a court case and the school secretary had to leave a message.

The indictment against Amber was that, during recess, Amber had tackled a boy bigger and older than she, somehow gotten on top of him, rubbed his face in the mud, then punched him on the back of the head. She had also ruined his white-shirt-and-khaki-pants school uniform.

The principal's retelling of the sordid tale was as much meant for my information as for Amber's further embarrassment. "Did anyone ask Amber why she did that?" I asked.

Because she had followed rules, the teacher behind the principal smiled as the principal explained. "We've found that it is best not to even ask. We try to encourage zero tolerance for any violence."

"Maybe something upset Amber. Maybe we ought to listen to her side."

"We had to pull her off of the boy," the teacher said.

"Even a prisoner gets a confession," I said. Amber lifted her head and smiled at me. Without permission, I said, "So does the accused want to tell me what happened?" Amber and I both looked at the principal. She scowled. "Let's just consider this a private conversation, the one I would have heard as soon as I got her in the car," I said to the principal.

Amber blurted, "That boy called me a *mulatto*."

"Do you know what a mulatto is?"

"My friend said it was like a stray cat or dog."

"Well, that's not so bad," I said.

"It was the way he said it. I wasn't going to hit him," she looked around at all of us. We could all see that she was fighting to keep from crying. "But then he said I was *trash*. That my mother was trash. He said his father had heard about her." Amber had tears in her eyes, but she also had an icy anger behind them. I didn't know if she was fighting the boy for Rachel's sake, or for her poor, lost biological mother's sake, or for both. "He said I had a whole bunch of mothers and that this one's boyfriend took dirty pictures." I wanted to beat the hell out of the little snot now.

I straightened in my chair to look at the principal and the teacher. "Well, there you have it. She was defending her mother's honor."

"That's the reason but not the justification," the principal said. "We have zero tolerance, and this is a second offense, so Amber has a two-day suspension."

"The only reason she's getting suspended is that she got the jump on the little bastard. Sounds like to me there were all sorts of extenuating circumstances." Just as I finished, the door to the office swung open, and

Rachel stepped fully and forcefully into the room, her taut legs spread out shoulder width, her skirt rising above her knee. It was her lawyer stance, ready to kick ass and take names.

"This is a learning tool. We want to teach her to avoid violence," the principal said.

"Jesus," I said. "She'd have a fairer hearing if she were facing criminal prosecution." I thought that Rachel would like that statement, so I checked behind me. She let her mouth fall slightly open as she stared at me. That was also one of her lawyer looks.

Amber's teacher saw her chance. "Amber, what did you say to that boy when we pulled you off of him?"

Amber hung her head. Her tears came back. "I called him a fucker."

Immediately, there was a chorus of "Amber!" The principal's came out as a scolding. Rachel's came out as a surprise. Mine came out with a bit of a laugh. The teacher smiled. "Roger" came out of Rachel's mouth as a scolding. It accompanied the scowl on her face.

—✦—

Since Amber's legal guardian had at last appeared, I left. As I walked out of the shining new school to the circular port where parents and buses could pick up kids, I felt that I had deserted Amber. Child custody services had taken her away from her real mother when Amber was almost a year old. The teenager admitted that she couldn't handle a child. Amber stayed in a series of foster homes, earning her foster parents some miserly state pittance, until Rachel found her.

Rachel was a good liberal with a cause. She was not from the area, but at least she was from South Texas. A smart Chicana, she pushed her way through law school, graduate school, and equality with men and Anglo women. She was a prosecutor, then a liability lawyer. She had earned her place. But she had heard her biological clock ticking, so she adopted Amber. Amber was not the newborn that Rachel wanted, but there was no waiting list for a Mexican child nearly three years old. Amber's eyes just melted Rachel's heart. Presently, feeling more confident in her ability to influence not just her children but the future, Rachel had started proceedings to adopt six-month-old Ralphie, a black child. She planned to make him into what he could be, just as she was doing with her first adopted child.

I stepped from the shade into the sun when Rachel came out of the school leading Amber by her hand. When they got close, I said, "So let's go out to eat tonight. And let's let Amber choose."

"No," Rachel said. "I'd prefer to keep things just as they are, for right now." She ducked her head.

"I haven't been over for two weeks." I turned to Amber. "What do you say, Amber? You want some Mexican food? Some pizza?"

"I want Chinese," Amber said. "An egg roll."

I turned back to Amber's mother. "See there?"

Rachel grabbed Amber and pulled her in front of her. "Stop pandering to her."

"This hasn't been easy for Amber. Let's treat her to something."

"This is not the time to reward Amber. She needs to control these impulses," Rachel said and pulled Amber along with her as she marched toward the parking area. I saw her profile, the straight well-formed nose, the flip of her shoulder-length hair on the left side of her face.

"Wait, wait," I said.

I ran to them and grabbed Rachel's arm. She swung around, swished Amber to one side, spread her feet and squared her shoulders, and looked at me with her stern, lawyer gaze. The day's humidity and dirty air pushed in on my chest, and I couldn't get words out through my throat.

Rachel crossed her arms. Forty-six-year-old Rachel didn't have laugh lines; hers were all from worry. But I liked the character they added to her face—and the contrast to her smooth, young-looking, pampered body. I could do no better than Rachel.

I looked down at Amber. She looked at her mother and copied the same stance. Then she ducked her head, so she didn't have to look at me. "What is this? What's going on here?" I asked.

Rachel dropped her arms. "Don't you understand the severity?" She jerked her head toward Amber, and a strand of black hair, caused by the flip, covered her left eye. She pushed the strand of hair back.

"She's a kid. And the other kids tease her."

She looked down at my legs. "You showed up in shorts? How does that look?"

"I was working."

"Looks like you work at relaxing. What's that going to look like to Amber's principal? What's Amber's principal going to think of her guardians if you show up at her school for an important conference with no regard for propriety?"

I looked down at my legs. "Are my legs that bad?"

Rachel growled. "You know exactly what I'm talking about."

"I'm honest. You said you like honesty. Said you didn't want any games."

"But *everything* is a game with you, including this incident." She looked down at my bare legs. "Can't you just try a little tact once in a while?" She stared at me for a moment, then sighed. "At least you wore a decent shirt and tucked it in."

Amber giggled. She pulled her hand away from her mother, took a step toward me, then shifted her gaze between the two of us. "I'm sorry," she said, to me, then once again to her mother.

Rachel knelt beside her daughter and hugged her and said, "Oh baby, just don't fight anymore." She looked up at me, then said to Amber, "Run on to the car, be careful crossing the pickup area. I'll be there in just a moment."

Amber trotted away, but after several yards, stopped, and turned around to watch. Rachel rose and crossed her arms. "Amber wanted to talk to you, not me. And you showed up first, not me."

"Don't worry," I said and stepped forward to hug her and to stop this conversation from going where it usually did. We'd been there too many times already. Rachel almost did hug me. But then she stepped back. She wasn't through with her summary. "Where does she get that language? That attitude?"

"Good God," I said. "They're only words."

"They're not very appropriate words for children."

"What do those empty-headed educationalists know? They took those everybody-feel-good education courses they make them take in college. How can they understand Amber?"

"But Amber has to adjust. Like I had to. Like you refuse to do." Heat was radiating up from the asphalt under our feet. I felt my shirt sticking to my body. I felt my sweat weight my jockey shorts and twist them around my crotch. "And look at what you do for a living," she went on.

23

"Look at the people you hang out with. Look at that bar where you hang out."

"You're a personal injury lawyer, for Christ's sake," I answered. She turned away from me to go back to Amber.

But Rachel stopped. I saw her shoulders heave as she breathed in. She turned back to me. I waited for this conversation to go down that road we'd been on before. "You know I *did* love you, Roger."

I waited for the *but*. But *but* didn't come.

I stepped toward her. "I know." I hugged her, and I was surprised that she let me.

After we had both caught some grateful breath, she turned away from me and walked to her daughter. I watched the muscles of her calves flex, watched her ass move under her skirt. She grabbed Amber's arm and tugged on it.

For only a second, Amber tugged back, swiveled her head around to see me, and said, "Bye, Roger. Thanks for coming to get me." I watched her leave as I stewed in my own sweat.

I looked at Rachel's retreating back.

"Ambulance chaser!" I said, under my breath. In truth, Rachel was everything I wished I had become.

Since early July, I'd been wrestling with a memory. With Amber acclimating to other girls at a friend's slumber party, Rachel spent the weekend in my house, seeing if we could live together. During the night, out of need, comfort, relief, or just reaching, we ended up in each others' arms and woke that way. We stayed that way because the closeness felt good. But Rachel had thoughts. "I can't trust this," she said.

"What's to lose?"

"Nothing for you, but I've got Amber." Cheek to cheek with me, she said, "I don't want you to become too much of a daddy." As Rachel ended our affair with this excuse, I wondered if a child adopted so long after her birth could really have a daddy, or a mother.

FOUR

Coming back from Amber's school, I got caught in a traffic jam on College Street. It was an area of decent Mexican and Vietnamese restaurants, groceries, video stores, body shops, and used-tire stores in deserted service stations—and of course, now, blue roofs and hurricane damaged, deserted ex-businesses. Off College Street were several once-stately old houses that had fallen into deep disrepair. The traffic jam was caused by a twenty-year-old car that had given out at a traffic light. In front of me was a pickup truck with *Jesus* printed all the way across the rear window. Underneath *Jesus* was an *I support Beaumont Blue* bumper sticker. The driver got out with his cell phone to help. He wore a T-shirt with "I got mine" printed on the front with the silhouette of a pistol beneath the printing. On the back was the silhouette of what looked like a burglar holding a gun, with circle around it and a line through it. The guy was probably a security cop with a gun permit or a concealed weapons license.

I drove straight to Nothing To Lose and had a Slim Jim and bag of chips for supper.

The Nothing To Lose bar was named to honor Janis Joplin, from a time when the Port Arthur native, despite her fame, was still considered trashy in Southeast Texas. But the owners loved her songs, and so named the bar after "Me and Bobby McGee" to honor her, even though they never knew that Kris Kristofferson wrote the lyrics, and they didn't quite get those lyrics right.

Nothing to Lose (opened before that monumental date in 1971 when Texas approved liquor-by-the-drink) was, for years, a setup bar: bring your liquor and pay for ice and cokes. It had gotten a liquor license, hired a three-piece country band of locals on Friday and Saturday nights, and generally let in any clientele who could walk in under their own power.

Nothing To Lose was close to my house. I could walk home from it if I needed to, and two or three times a year, especially after a particularly disturbing case, I needed to. Tonight promised to become one of those nights.

Nothing To Lose, like my rented house, was just off of Tram Road, on the very north end of Beaumont's city limits—in fact about thirty feet beyond it, so we dealt mainly with the Jefferson County deputy sheriffs, and they remained mostly indifferent to us. Geographically, Nothing To Lose and my rented house were just a few feet behind the Pine Curtain. North of the bar lay the vast pine forests; south of it lay mostly marshy Jefferson County.

That night was the type that I liked at Nothing To Lose. A slight thunderstorm had burst through in late afternoon, just before dark, so the pines were drooping with rain. I liked the sound of rain on the tin roof, but even more, I liked to step out the back door onto the deck and feel the slight spray from the drooping boughs of the pines and the muffled creak of the boughs sagging from the moisture. Sometimes, I'd opened my mouth and hold out my tongue to collect some of the acid rain caused by the refineries. That night, I knew that I would stay until closing, so I hunkered at my reserved spot at the horseshoe-shaped bar. From this spot, I could lean against the wall and have a fair view of who was walking in to torment or amuse me.

Lynette, the bartender doing a good country-girl job of fighting middle age, asked if I *wanted* another drink and then asked if I really *needed* another drink and then asked if she *ought* to serve me another drink. I should have worked on convincing myself that Lynette would be a good woman for me; instead I was hoping for someone just a little more cleaned up. God, I wanted a Baptist! The jukebox was screaming out the redneck rock or country that had become popular because no one ever listened to the lyrics that made fun of the people listening to them. I alone heard the moisture falling on the tin roof.

"Maybe if you eased off just a bit," Lynette said.

"Eased off of what?" I smiled and reached toward her hand.

"Eased off of me, you horny old goat."

"You know with another two drinks and two Viagras, I could show you a wonderful time."

"You'd show me how to pass out and use your stiff pecker to keep you from rolling out of bed."

No sooner had she said the words than Bruce was beside me with an arm around me. I hadn't seen the self-appointed fashion plate of Nothing To Lose come in. "You scored some yet, you horny old goat?"

"You know Lynette. I ain't scoring."

Bruce was a small man with no particular talents or abilities. He tried to be cool. And since "cool" changed, Bruce tried to change. He took up muscle building when that became popular. He got the no-neck, thick-shouldered, puffed-out look of a muscle builder, but he could not sculpt his beer belly into a six-pack. Even so, he started wearing those stretchy, too-tight T-shirts and tank tops (wife-beaters, the young people said) that the muscle-heads liked to wear. His beer belly stretched his shirts out more than his chest did. He grew his curly red hair long, then put it in dredlocks, then in cornrows, and finally just shaved all the expensive styling away. Then he started filling himself up with tattoos, then with piercing. So far he had three or four rings in each ear, something shiny and gold on the side of one nostril, and a horseshoe-shaped golden hook in one eyebrow.

"You know Horny Goat Weed is a new aphrodisiac they sell at truck stops. I think it's got ginseng or something in it. You can get it off the Internet too," Bruce said. "Want to buy some at discount prices? Special price just for you!"

"I got nothing nor no one to be horny for," I said.

"What about me?" Lynette asked.

"You just talk a good game."

"Someday, if you cleaned up and treated me half decent, you might be surprised."

"Like I said," Bruce said, "need some Horny Goat Weed?" His tongue stud clicked against the back of his teeth. Lately, like most of the rest of Beaumont, Bruce was trying to be a biker. He'd had three wrecks in the six months he'd had his Harley.

I could have afforded a better bar that might have offered a little better conversation. After all, I had an education and a law degree behind me, way behind me. But the better conversations usually came with some degree of pretension, mostly some plagiarized rant from a screaming right-wing talk-radio nut. But then, I had my own pretensions. When I bought my new Toyota crew cab, I drove it around town. Then I drove it home, got out a crowbar, and put a few dents in it. Then I drove around in some mud. Camouflage. First thing people notice is a shiny new car.

"So Roger," Bruce started, "you got any good pictures?" If I weren't scared of him, I'd have told him to shut the fuck up. He was just a bit too skittish—a grown teenager frightened by the world—and since he couldn't reason his way too far, only copy other people, he was dangerous.

"At least Roger's got a job," Lynette said.

"I got a real job. I work in day care." Bruce wasn't lying. He was good with kids and old people. Before his stint at kids, he worked in a retirement home. The same insecure, nervous temperament that made him dangerous made him gentle around people who couldn't physically harm him.

Cody Hudson, on the other hand, had his shit together and the world by the balls. Cody Hudson was a local boy who got his degree, married an unassuming, nice, local girl with her own low-level ambitions, and thus both had wrapped themselves in the comforts that the local area provided. Jessica dedicated herself to children and spoke to her colleagues about family values; meanwhile, something in her loin and mind had yearned for that desire, that knowledge, that pleasure, that exoticness, that escape from local intellectual and spiritual suppression. Poor Harry seemed the answer. Maybe he was.

Cody, the engineer, had no concept of want beyond what he could see in front of him. Life was circumscribed. It was easy. He had done the calculations. He had figured and married well and right at the right time. He was an engineer, a Republican (no matter how he voted), and a Baptist (no matter where he did or didn't go to church). The world dare not turn against him. So how could Jessica?

Bruce was beside me and guzzling a beer as David Allen Coe sang the perfect country western song. Meanwhile, Lynette, cautioning me about drinking too much, poured me another straight bourbon. We were worse off socially and financially than those with aspirations and money in the west end of Beaumont, or in south Jefferson County, or those out in the west part of the county, acting like they were living in the country, or those just north of us, in dry, ultra-Baptist Lumberton. We were running defensive maneuvers to try to gain some time on the inevitable. But at least we knew that the inevitable and the unplanned were waiting for us out there in the dripping pine forest. We were Pentecostals; they were Baptists.

Bruce's attention span drifted and so did he. I was glad. On the other side of the bar were Ridley and Edmore, already in their leather. They used to be members of the only all-black Harley riders' group in Beaumont, but the all-black group merged with an all-white group to form a truly mixed-race Harley riders' group. Ridley and Edmore were now actively recruiting Hispanics and Asians.

Soon Leroy, a used-car salesman with several loan sharks looking for him, sat within a bar stool of Ridley and Edmore, and everyone nodded. Shirley came in and sat in between Ridley and Edmore and Leroy. Shirley, who worked as a waitress at a Mexican food restaurant, was about six-four and emotionally or mentally challenged. She was mostly quiet and reserved, but sometimes, she just got hyper; sometimes she got sexually hyper. That night she went from chatty, to slurring, to kissing, so Leroy, sensing this was a sexually hyper night, was buying her drinks and hugging her.

Midway through Lynette's shift, Zia, the condom salesman, showed up and immediately annoyed everyone with his salesmanship. An Iranian by birth, Zia got to this country with some of his father's money, but then when the Shah was deposed, he had to stay here or risk getting shot at home. Now he had citizenship and a sales route where he stocked the restrooms of sleazier bars with condoms and sex novelties.

He sat by me. "Hey, you want nasty key fobs? I got nasty key fobs. I give you one." And he handed me a plastic toy with a lever that you pulled and two people started fucking. It had an attachment so that I could attach it to my key ring. "Hey, Roger, you like sexy movie? Glow in the dark rubbers? I got glow in the dark rubbers and nasty movies in my car. You pick out the ones you want. Discount for you." I told him that I didn't want the movies. "How about books? I got fuck books. Some with pictures, some with just words." Zia told me the plots of several of his fuck books. When I still refused to buy one, he left to stock condom and sex novelty machines in the men's and ladies' rooms.

But Zia got me thinking about plots. I told Lynette about the novel I had most recently read, Billy Lee Brammer's *The Gay Place*. I had a taste for serious literature, no cop novels for me. I had this deep need to discuss something with weight or heft beyond lawsuits, murders, illicit fucking, drinking, or puking.

"Why are you reading a book about queers?" Lynette, of course, asked. I found the novel in the religious/inspiration/self-help section of the local Books-A-Million, shelved next to books on alternative lifestyles. Of course, I explained that it was about Texas politics in the late '50s. She pooh-poohed that by asking what was so exciting about Texas politics. I didn't get to explain much more.

"You know, I bet I could write a book," Lynette said. Yeah, and I could probably do brain surgery, I mumbled under my breath. "With my experiences, I bet it would be a best seller." Like most people, Lynette had the hard part down— the experiences and the idea. The actual writing was the easy part. "If I just found the time. And you know I'm artistic and creative. I worked for a while at a flower shop and then I was a hairstylist. Then I got part ownership in this bar."

"The world has enough writers. What it needs is another bartender," I said.

"Yeah, you're right," Lynette said.

In our world today, cosmeticians, beauticians, and barbers all claim to be *artists*. The *Beaumont Enterprise* even lumps them under the term *artist* in the want ads. As with Jessica Hudson, elementary schoolteachers claim to be *creative* because kids are supposedly creative. Like Leroy, local salespeople and advertisers, especially those people selling advertising, claim to be *intellectual*. If those words could help people with self-esteem, why should I argue? I should start claiming to be a marriage counselor. Private investigators who take compromising photos have no self-esteem-boosting euphemisms and clichés. I was at least partially responsible for a decent guy's death. I needed more of an ego boost than what Lynette and bourbon could give me.

FIVE

Every year, I claim several professional expenses on my income taxes, but I rarely get more than the standard deduction. If I developed a little more interest in equipment, I might get some more deductions, but my computer and my digital camera were as high tech as I got. My living room served as my office. I needed my truck, of course. If I had to meet a client, it was usually at his or her house or in my truck, or I was taking pictures of him or her—from my truck. No tracking devices, bugs, recorders, or high security equipment.

I bought a Baretta upon the advice of a cop, and I joined the line of applicants waiting to get a license to pack. But I never actually packed the gun. I forgot I even had it. I just stashed it away under some old clothes. I figured that if I was in a situation where I needed a gun, I'd try bluffing, begging, or running away. So I decided that I didn't need equipment. People hired me for my mind. What I do is observe people, and then act accordingly. That's what I learned in college when I was trying to be a hippie radical in a Texas town that was not yet ready to be liberalized. That's what I learned when I was studying to be a lawyer. That's why Emily and Arthur wanted me to investigate.

A funeral is a good place to observe. I didn't bother studying the mourners in the first reserved pew at the funeral for Harry Krammer. I didn't watch them either when they gathered under the canopy at the graveyard. Relatives rarely gave me much information. Instead I looked for friends, the mourners who sat midway down one side of the chapel and lost against tears or tried to look stoic; the ones who stood in the hot sun outside the canopy and stared at their shoes, and lingered just a bit as the family was escorted back to the limo. I hung back a little. Deputy Sheriff Emily Nguyen watched me. She recognized me even in long pants and sweat-stained jacket.

I was trying to fit in, but it was an odd crowd. What was particularly peculiar about the mourners were young black and white women with babies. They held the infants' heads to their shoulders, stared stoically, and finally gave in to crying. At the service, there were five of these women. At the burial plot, four more showed up. My mind told me I was stupid. Harry was a social worker. These were his clients.

As Harry's funeral broke up, I saw three obvious friends of his who reacted as though they truly regretted Harry's demise: the vice-principal, the lean older woman with a graceful walk, and the pert and pretty woman in her late thirties. I knew where I could find the vice-principal, but I wasn't sure about the other two ladies. I adjusted my tie, rolled my shoulders under my sport coat, and approached the pretty woman first.

"This is a terrible time, I know, but if I could just have a word with you." The lady stopped, looked around to see if anybody saw me, then tried to walk past me. "Please, Miss." She stopped. I held out my hand, but she didn't take it. "I'm Roger Jackson, a friend of sorts of Harry's, and I'm trying to help the police put some kind of reason together for why this horrible thing happened."

"I have nothing to say," the woman said. Clouds had mostly covered the sky, but the sun poked shafts through the clouds. The humidity was melting the woman's hair, and she had tiny, dry riverbeds cut into her makeup, made by her evaporating tears. I felt like my sport coat was biting my armpits.

"Please, if this isn't convenient, then call me. I can be very discreet." I pulled a card out of my pocket and handed it to her.

She looked at my card and smirked. "Roger Jackson, investigating services. You might have once followed me and Harry. I don't want you following me anymore. I've got a husband and a job. Now leave me alone." She handed the card back to me.

"Please."

She stared at me a second, as if considering her options. "If you want someone who will talk, go see that lady." She pointed to the middle-aged lady gliding toward the line of parked cars. "You can catch her if you hurry. Tell her Stacy sent you."

I hesitated a moment, then ran for the older woman. From behind her, I noticed that her upper body was graceful because she sort of swayed from side to side. Her toes pointed outward, like a ballet dancer's. Her dress, or costume, whatever it was, looked like veils that seemed to flow behind her. She had one of those old-style women's hats, the practical kind, with a brim that spread over the lady's face. "Ms. Ms.," I yelled. The woman kept walking. Either she was hard of hearing or wanted nothing to do with me. Finally, she turned around.

I squared my shoulders, fingered a card, and started: "This is a terrible time, I know, but . . ."

She held up her hand at a ninety-degree angle and all but whispered, "Stop." I stopped. "Are you with the police?"

I thought. "Well, sort of." She twirled away from me. Her veils or gossamer or whatever followed her twirl, just a second or two after her. "And sort of not." She stopped, and her veils floated past her, then lightly floated to their proper drape around her lean body. "I'm trying to figure out what happened to Harry. . . ."

"Of course you are. Now let me see a card or something." I pulled my sport coat down by its pockets to give my armpits a rest; then I reached into its inner pocket and pulled my card out and handed it to her. She held it away from her at arm's length. I pulled my reading glasses out of my pocket and held them toward her. "That's actually a charming thing to do, Mr. Jackson." She took my glasses and read my card. She looked familiar. I was trying to figure out where I had seen her before.

"Stacy said to tell you that she sent me."

"I spotted you annoying her. Believe me, she won't talk to you. She's rather defiant about cutting herself off from Harry." The lady deftly opened her purse and dug in it with one hand while she held my card with the other. She produced a pen, let the purse slide down her forearm on its straps, and wrote on the back of my card. "Cocktails start at three. I took the day off." She handed my card back. Her address and the phone number were on the back. Then she twirled, swirled, and floated away from me.

It dawned on me that I had seen her picture at Harry Krammer's house.

When I got back to my truck, Emily Nguyen was leaning against the fender. She looked like a child. "So what are you doing?"

"Paying my respects to Harry."

"Look, this is a big case for me. Arthur's letting me in on it. We're cooperating. Don't fuck it up for me."

"Why would I fuck it up for you?"

"I don't know about *why*, but the *how* is trying to do your own investigation."

"Emily, I respect you too much to . . ."

"Cut the bullshit. I'm just telling you that, if I hear that you're out trying to beat us to something, I'll pull you in for questioning every thirty minutes."

"As Burt Reynolds said in one of his movies, 'Ain't nothing scares me but women and the police.' And you're both." I walked to my cab hoping that Emily wouldn't hit me with her gat.

—✦—

Main High was the oldest high school in Beaumont. *Main* was old-fashioned; it sounded old. So Main High had become Jesse Jackson Learning Center to disguise the fact that nobody was learning very much. The halls at Jesse Jackson Learning Center were a prime example of the dismal state of our education system. It looked about like one of the many prisons in midcounty. Security guards roamed the halls, steel gates clanged shut, teachers yelled at mostly black students to slow down, tuck in shirts, get rid of the gum. Public school education was actually good training for life in the US prison system. Yet instead of the mean looks and the shuffling or strutting of prisoners, there was youthful insouciance. Girls galloped uncontrollably down the hall with their tits and dreadlocks bouncing. Boys couldn't keep their hands from their crotches and couldn't keep from walking to some communally heard beat. You could practically smell the hormones. They were still kids, though. Sometimes a clutch of girls or boys would just burst into giggling, jumping, punching, or screaming. Pent-up youth was exploding all around me in this prison. Some things don't change.

In the midst of the swarming, mostly black bodies was Vice-Principal and former coach Greg Giddings. His suit coat strained to contain his large shoulders. His shaved head glowed with sweat and reflected the midafternoon light. He shouted orders, cautioned, laughed, high-fived, patted backs, shook his forefinger. For a moment I stood back and watched this warden. He was well suited for this job. From these confused, wayward, unsure teenagers, he commanded respect, fear, and, if they admitted it, just a little admiration. As the mass of young adults—dangerous because they were still just children—drained from the hall, Greg Giddings walked to the main office, then into his office. I followed him right into the main office, walked past the secretaries and clerks, opened the door to his office, and went in.

He looked up from his desk, shocked to see me. "How did you get in here?"

"Walked right in."

"After all those security training seminars we sent the staff to. And you just waltz in here." He dropped his head, then shook it. "Are you a parent? Who are you here about?"

"I'm here about Harry Krammer."

"Are you another cop?"

I guessed at the right answer. "No, I'm a friend."

He motioned for me to have a seat across from his desk. "I'm one chapter away from my dissertation at the University of Houston. I'm telling my committee, I'm saying 'Look you fuckers, this is the way it's gonna be. No more fucking around,' and suddenly Harry's dead. How did I know that he has this photo of me and him on his mantel? So cops are thinking I know all about his death." He reached up with one hand and rubbed the sweat off the top of his slickly shaved pate. He loosened his tie, then struggled out of his jacket. I shrugged off mine.

He eyed me for a moment longer, then started again: "The cops are asking me about any sort of drug habits and affairs that Harry had. They showed me some pictures of Harry and this woman."

"I took the photos. What I want to do is find Harry's murderer."

"Who's paying you to look?"

"That's confidential."

"Then you might as well ask the police about what I said." He stood and motioned for me to leave.

My mind jumped around, but I made it be still long enough to say, "My client's paying me to find the truth. That's what I intend to do. What happens with that truth and who gets it is not my concern."

Greg circled behind me, then back to his desk, sat down, put his hands behind his head, leaned back in his chair, and smiled. "There's this old, flat football in Harry's living room. You think you can get the cops to let me have it?"

"Let things cool down, and I'll ask. I'm owed a few favors."

I'm not sure if it was me or just the timing, but something twisted a pressure valve on Greg. He sighed loudly and seemed to sag a little in his chair, his face relaxing into something that looked like resignation. "We met in college. I was one of the few black students who actually chose to go to Southwest Texas State. I ended up on an intramural football team with Harry—the Black Mollies." He twisted his head to look at me. "You look old enough to know what that means."

"I'm old enough to have gone to Southwest Texas State and helped start the Black Mollies. I thought of the name to spite the local rednecks."

"No shit?" Greg pulled up. "You were one of the mollies?"

"In the early seventies. I stuck to pot and booze, but the others liked whatever they could get their hands on. Plus they could sell their extra pills to kids cramming for finals. The funny part was that those Black Mollies guys were all good athletes."

"Harry and I got there a little later. They were already established as an intramural team. Harry didn't even play in high school. But that white boy could hum a football. I was this black kid from Beaumont thought he could play college ball and was flunking both school and football. But both Harry and I straightened out. Our senior year, we were playing for the intramural championship. I mean the championship at the fourth best party school in America." Greg stopped to look around, then lowered his voice. "I mean there was pussy, beer, and money on this game."

A wave of nostalgia hit me, although my memories were slightly different. As the editor of a radical newspaper, I got my Volkswagen bus firebombed, but the pussy and beer part sounded familiar. "The good old days."

Greg smiled. "In this game though, we were behind. On what was to be the last play. I broke out in the opening. I left this white fraternity boy staring at his jock dropped around his knees, and I was down the sideline. I'm thinking that I better slow down, ease up. Ain't nobody can heave a football that far. But here it comes. Harry chunked that pillar perfect. I had to speed up. That ball was a step away from my fingers. I reached, but some soft mud or something gave way, and I was falling. Reaching and falling, for like minutes. I hit the ground just as that ball hit my fingers. I got it. Tight. But then it hits the ground." Greg looked at me like he might cry. "And the ball goes bouncing away."

"And that's that football?"

"Yeah, but it doesn't just represent some old-timey college days. When Harry was all bent out of shape by that Stacy chick..."

"Who?"

"You don't miss much. The one you tried to talk to at the funeral."

"What about her?"

"Nothing about her for now. But when he was bent out of shape over her, and my life was about over because my wife was leaving me, Harry convinced me to go to California with him. I found this hot young white girl, drifted off with her, and gradually made my way back to Beaumont, as did Harry. But see, he still had that ball."

Greg Giddings was smiling at the memories in his head. Then he gave his head a little shake, as if realizing he had given me too much of himself.

"So of course you want Harry to have a clean death. You want the truth."

Greg scowled. "Don't push, man. Harry and I were buddies. I'm a native Beaumonter, and I got called an Oreo because of my friendship with Harry. But I told those folks to fuck off." Greg looked out the window and shook his head. "And Harry, he told me he envied me. That's rich. A black man, in a predominately black school, and me with a past and history here. He said I had more respect, authority, and class than he ever did. How about that? How the fuck about that? And then the stupid fucker gets himself shot over some pussy." Greg hit the table. He had tears in his eyes.

"Tell me about Harry and women."

"Harry always had these great women. But they always had complications. Usually that they were married."

"Like the one in the photos?"

Greg suddenly grew serious. He leaned across his desk on his elbows. "You're not official. You can know something and shut the fuck up about it, right?"

"I'm private."

"Okay, you answer me a question on the up and up. Did the cops find cocaine at Harry's place?"

I didn't hesitate. "Yes," I said.

"Harry was a social worker, worked for the state, same as me. No way he was going to have cocaine around. Hell, he even quit smoking pot. But that woman. I did a little research in Beaumont ISD files. She's too good to live in town, but she's not too good to work here. And she's had a few late days and reprimands and difficulties. You getting my drift?"

"It was her cocaine?"

"You going now."

"Or it was planted as an excuse?"

"Now you're really going."

"What do I do?"

"Have you talked to Lee Tomlinson?"

I started to ask who Lee was, but then I pulled the card out of my pocket. Lee Tomlinson had invited me for cocktails at three. "I'm going to meet her."

"She has the story. She can tell you more than me. I don't want to get anybody in BISD in trouble. But if I tell you and you tell the cops, well then..."

I nodded and pushed myself up to leave. "No, no. You got to understand here," he said. "You a fellow Bobcat, man. SWT! A man been hurt, killed. And the only thing can make up for that is truth, man. The fucker deserves the truth. A black man in Beaumont, I don't trust Beaumont cops to find shit because Harry ain't that important. So I'm taking a big-ass leap of fucking faith here and begging your scrawny white ass for some of that truth. And if SWT and my begging ain't enough, I got some money and Lee Tomlinson's got some money, and we'll pay your ass for just a dose of the truth. And if that ain't enough, I want you to remember that you took the photos got him killed."

I felt like that last speech had been planned and waiting for me. I squirmed. "My job, man."

"Yeah, you didn't think I knew about the photos. So you owe me now."

I nodded and said, "Here's to truth, then. I may like a little of that money. Go Bobcats!" We nodded at each other, and I was alarmed when I felt a tear of sympathy for Harry and Greg and my own lost youth at SWT. Maybe our pasts were really lost. Southwest Texas State had even changed its name to Texas State in order to fool Yankees into believing it was some traditional, prestigious school, not an infamous party school for forty years.

As I started out, I heard Greg call after me, "Hey." I turned around. "Integration, huh? I was in the first group of black kids to ever really get integrated in this town. Been integrating all my life. And now look at me, look where I'm at." He chuckled and shook his head, "You saw all those black faces in this school. Tell me what good it's all done."

"Probably none," I said. "But it seemed to have helped you and Harry." He nodded thoughtfully. "Yeah. Go Bobcats."

On the way out, I congratulated myself for possibly having two people pay me for what the cops were making me do. But I had this feeling that I had stumbled into doing just what they wanted me to do.

By three, the gray day had grown darker, storm clouds had bunched up, and I could see the rain coming from the north. It was still oppressively humid, but the norther was pushing cool rain toward Beaumont, so instead of shorts I pulled on a pair of stiff jeans, the first time since April.

I drove to the address that Lee Tomlinson had given to me and found myself in Old Town in front of an iron gate with a run-down ex-mansion behind it. I looked for some way to get through the gate, and finally found a buzzer. When I buzzed, the gate opened. The house had once been green but the dried, peeling paint had turned the color of a crumpled, used pastel tissue.

I heard toenails click on cement, then a low growl. I froze in time to see an enormous mutt walk toward me. I didn't know mutts could get that big. I thought only a purposefully bred dog could get that size. He walked toward me drooling and growling. He had gray around his face, and he would have run toward me, he was trying to run, but his muscles just wouldn't work. Then I heard, "Balanchine, shush." Lee Tomlinson in a pair of very tight shorts showing off her shapely legs stepped out from the back of the house with a tall, cloudy tonic glass in her one hand and a cigarette in the other. Her feet still pointed out like a ballet dancer's. "This way, Mr. Jackson. This way. Don't mind Balanchine."

In fact Balanchine stopped his growling, looked up at me, drooled, and wagged his tail. When I rubbed the top of his head, he drooled some more and vigorously wagged his tail. He then followed me to Lee. Lee sniffed the air. Then Balanchine stopped sniffing me to sniff the air.

"The rain. You can smell it coming," Lee said.

I looked over my left shoulder to the north. "You can see it coming, too."

"The rain and the feel of it coming and going is one of the things that makes this area delightful."

"Yeah, I guess," I said.

"Oh, Mr. Jackson, I know most people don't like the humidity, but it makes the air seem soft. It surrounds you and massages you. Keeps your skin moist, too," she said and opened her back door. She stepped into a screened porch. She had a small wicker table set up with gin, tonic water, a bucket of ice, and freshly cut mint. She sat in one wicker chair and motioned for me to sit in the other one. "I thought that we could chat outside and enjoy the coming rain." I wished that I had worn shorts. "Besides, my house is mostly a wreck. My house remains a wreck. I've been fixing it and redecorating for years, but my salary doesn't match my plans."

Balanchine pressed his nose against the screen door, and Lee jumped up and let him in. He immediately hobbled over to me, put his head in my lap, and drooled. "Push him out of the way when you get tired of him." I wanted to get more of her confidence before I pushed her dog's head out of my lap. Lee slumped into her chair, crossed one bare leg over the other, and dangled her sandal from her toes. "Make yourself a drink," she said. She took a long drag on her cigarette, then crushed it out in the ashtray on the table. "I don't really smoke. Just one a day. That's all. A reward." She returned to her cross-legged, sandal-dangling slouch, and I made myself a very stiff gin.

"Greg Giddings said that you and he might like to hire me to find out who killed Harry."

"Right to the chase, huh, Mr. Jackson? But not so fast. Let's get to know each other." Balanchine and I exchanged mournful looks. "I work at St. Elizabeth's recreation center as a fitness director. I used to be an aerobics instructor. Well, sometimes I teach water aerobics. But really, I'm a dancer." I looked down at Balanchine. "I know what you're thinking, and yes, I stripped, but I was a real dancer too, mostly modern dance. I did several touring musicals. I choreographed my own sequence for a show in St. Louis. But age doesn't let you stay a dancer. So as I aged, I worked as a stripper at several gentlemen's clubs in Oklahoma City and Houston. But age won't let you stay a stripper either. So here I am. Now, tell me something about yourself."

I looked at Balanchine for advice. Lee had taken the interviewing away from me. "I got married, dropped out of law school to take care of my wife's ailing father. When he died, she divorced me, and I tried to be a lawyer. I wasn't doing so good as a lawyer, so I started investigating for a divorce lawyer. So here I am."

"Now we know some little inkling about each other. I need to trust you." She sipped her drink, uncurled from her position, put her elbows on her knees and faced me. "If you go to a gentleman's club and buy a girl a drink and ask about what she does, she'll tell you that the other girls are just *titty floppers* but that she's a *dancer*." Lee held her arms out like she was posing. Balanchine's sad eyes and drool gave me no hints about where this information was going. "We all yearn to be dancers, Mr. Jackson. But most of us never get to be more than titty floppers." She dropped her pose and looked almost sad. "I can say that I'm a dancer. Harry was a dancer. What about you, Mr. Jackson?"

"I feel like I've been stripping but nobody's been watching, or caring."

Her eyes looked as soulfoul as Balanchine's. "Greg Giddings called me and said that he had talked to you. Greg and I have been talking quite a bit about Harry's murder. Harry was dear to both Greg and me. If you knew Harry, you knew Greg and you knew me, so Greg and I are compatriots of sorts. But our positions don't allow us to follow through on our suppositions. That's all we have right now are suppositions."

"I think I'm working for one of your suppositions. I'm not sure that I want to work for you, too."

The ice in my glass clinked. The gin cooled the back of my throat and made me want another drink even before I finished the one I had. I pushed Balanchine's head out of my lap, and he limped to Lee and put his head on her thigh. Her eyes sparkled from her chiseled face. She had been more beautiful and had worked hard to rescue what beauty she could from her life, years, and vices. "Greg and I just want you to do the same job, only for us, too. All we want is the truth. And you should want the truth, too . . . to appease your guilt for taking those photos."

She and Greg Giddings had gone through this. I wondered if perhaps they hadn't entered into some conspiracy with Cody Hudson and Arthur Solieau. I considered running out of the house. "What do you think that the truth is?"

Lee curled herself back into her wicker chair. I sensed another long comment trailing off in several directions, so I downed my drink and mixed myself another while Lee talked. "When Stacy, the woman you met this morning, broke up with Harry so that she could stay married to her husband, Don, I comforted her." Lee hesitated but smiled. "Maybe I comforted her a little too closely." Now Lee smiled at me, and I felt like she was digging through my pockets. "I met Harry through her. Then I met Greg. And since a man doesn't cry on the shoulder of another guy, and because Harry was continually getting dumped by married women, I became something of his adviser and confidant. Stacy won't talk to you because she wants Harry and me to stay out of her present life. But she's not a bad sort. She feels bad enough about Harry's murder and wants to help enough to put up some money— if need be." Was nothing simple with these people? Was Lee's story just a performance? Was it a conspiracy against me? Or Maybe Harry just had a lot of friends— and bad luck with women, just like a lot of us.

"Should we start talking about how much money?" I asked.

"Come on, Mr. Jackson. Don't spoil your thus-far charm."

"Let's not talk about money."

Lee politely nodded and continued her story. "So he moved on to Jessica Hudson. He couldn't see the shipwreck that Jessica could become. He asked me where he could get some cocaine for his new lady. I refused to help. He must have gone to somebody else. Eventually the name *Bruce* came up. Some guy who worked with kids." I damn near sucked an ice cube down my throat. "You know Bruce?" Lee asked.

"No."

"Greg and Stacy and I think that this Bruce might lead you to the killer."

"Are you sure about all of this? Have you told the police?"

"The police are rather slow. And I don't trust them."

"I'm sorry, but I don't trust that answer."

Lee pushed Balanchine's face off of her lap, stood, crossed to me, knelt in front of me, and took the hand that didn't hold my drink. "I'm going to send a gentleman friend of mine to see you. Where should he look you up?"

"I don't know if I want him to look me up." I tried to pull my hand away from her. She held on tightly. Balanchine joined her, and together they begged me with their eyes.

I jerked my hand away, put my glass on the table, and stood. "Ms. Tomlinson, I don't mind taking your money. But normal people go to the police with this sort of information."

"Make another drink, Mr. Jackson."

"Give me another story."

Lee Tomlinson freshened my drink and then handed my glass back to me. "My gentleman friend is not *normal people*. And your clients, the Hudsons, only appear to be normal people. The police came to them. They didn't go to the police."

She stood up right in front of me, and I saw that she was as tall as I was. I looked down at her ballet dancer's feet, then back at her face and saw that I was dealing with a formidable woman. "Goddamn it, Roger." Lee threw her hands in the air and waved them. "You're making me become dramatic."

I shrugged my shoulders. "Sorry."

She tried to laugh but caught herself. "To tell you the truth, I don't think the police are going to do shit. Oh, they'll arrest someone and prosecute him, but they'll just stop there. End of case. I want to know what really happened. So I started my own investigation as soon as I heard Harry got murdered. I asked my friend for help. And he agreed. But he *can't* use the police. Greg Giddings is a principal and doesn't want to tell all that he knows about Harry. Stacy is married and has a child. She doesn't want any investigation going on around her. But we all want to know what happened to Harry. My friend and you seem to be the means to find out what really happened."

"So why do all of you want to find out so bad?"

"We owe Harry. It's the last thing we can do for him."

"What do you mean, you owe him?"

"Harry helped people. And he died before anybody could really help him." Lee looked at me like she was seeing through me to something way down in the middle of me that I didn't even know I had. "Those women you saw— surely you saw them— with the little babies. They were unwed, teenage mothers, on welfare, trying to get GEDs or some kind of a job. Harry was their social worker."

"So what about the rest of you?"

Lee leaned toward me. "You don't get it. You're not listening. They weren't friends, they were clients. How many doctors have patients at their funerals? How many social workers have the deadbeats and down-and-outers they work with show up at their funerals? Harry really tried to help them, beyond what the state gave and what the state said he could give. He was one of those people who'd do that for other people, too."

"So was Jessica Hudson some sort of a mistake?"

"I didn't say he always made wise choices. I figure you're different from Harry. You'd show a little discretion in who you associated with. With whom you had an affair."

So that one did hurt. I sipped my drink. Lee started again. "Harry is like you and me. He's less like Greg. He's not at all like Jessica Hudson. Stacy used to be more like us. We don't have families. Instead we have those we choose to be close to us. We don't have the obligations of blood to take care of us. So we have to take care of one another."

"I'm not sure I'm up to all this good will. I'm getting awfully confused."

"Well try it this way. I'm going to find out what happened to Harry. And I need your help. My friend will meet you at eleven. That will give you some time to get dinner. Don't just keep drinking. Where should he meet you?"

"I hang out at a place called Nothing to Lose."

Lee thought for a moment. "An older bar, alright, a sleazy bar, on the edge of town, off Tram Road. Am I right?" I nodded. "Now, the only question is whether I pay you something or not."

I remembered the worn shape of the house, and the promise of yet another person paying me for what the police were going to make me do. "Can you afford to pay me?"

"Say goodbye to Balanchine, and go wait for my friend. One way or another, you're going to help."

On my way to Nothing To Lose, the thunder and lightning started rumbling toward me, and my mind went to work on me. I might be doing something illegal. I tried to remember my legal studies. But I'd been skirting around criminal activity and intent so long that I didn't know where the line was.

With a crack of thunder, I began to feel close to Harry. I knew what his fate was.

Cops don't catch the smart crooks, just the stupid ones. When Texas first passed its concealed weapons law, like the cops, I opposed it. I thought it would allow for us all to be shooting each other in the streets. But once I took the course and passed the test, I changed my mind. During the first two years of the law, Texas caught a number of felons who registered for the privilege to legally carry a gun. Now they are in prison. They were the stupid crooks. The first thing that my classmates and I learned in packing-a-piece class is that if we fucked up and committed a crime, with all the records about us that we had to submit to the state and the national government, we would be caught. On the other hand, we were told that if we had a license to pack in Texas, as soon as a cop stopped us, we had to show our license—at least in Texas. That way, a cop knew that we were gun nuts and not some other kind of crazies. The card showed him how to treat us. The law turned out good for the cops. So mostly cops only catch the dumb criminals. To have a license and get away with a crime, you had to be smart. Whoever killed Harry Krammer was probably pretty smart. I hoped whoever it was wasn't smarter than me.

SIX

My mind was cluttered but my time was my own, and I had plenty of time to get to Nothing To Lose. So I drove around thinking. By four-thirty, I had an idea. I found myself pulling up to Amber's day care. Amber had been serving out her suspension from school so probably had had only the younger kids to play with all day. But now with school ending, some of the older kids were starting to show up. I watched the children playing on the swings, teeter-totters, jungle gyms. I spotted Amber.

I stepped out of my truck, and Amber saw me. She ran to the hurricane fence and poked her fingers through it.

I slowly stepped into the street and crossed it. Amber was not yet old enough to be embarrassed by adults. She was young enough to have no self-consciousness. "How you was, Roger?" Amber asked and giggled. She was imitating some of the Cajun kids she played with. Some of her chums gathered next to her and asked who I was. I had picked her up several times from this day care center.

"I've been pretty good, Amber. But I wanted you to know that I miss you." She just smiled.

A teenage playground attendant came up behind Amber, gently placed her hands on Amber's shoulders and whispered for her not to talk to strangers. "It's okay, he used to date my mother," Amber said.

"Amber," I said. "Go join your friends. And whatever your mother says, we're still pals. You need something or you really want something, you call me, okay?"

"Sure, Roger," Amber said, and the teenager who was teaching Amber to distrust all strangers led her away.

I went to see Amber's mother. What can I say? I couldn't control myself.

Rachel worked at a reconstructed railroad depot along with a lot of other lawyers. I got nervous inside of Beaumont lawyers' offices. Ever since this semiretarded kid with some past prison time got mad at a law firm for not representing him and then walked into the office and shot and killed a matronly lawyer, Beaumont lawyers got concealed weapons licenses and kept themselves well armed at work, at home, and in the car. The kid got the death penalty.

I got to her office just as they were about to lock up. Some of her suited colleagues stared at me. When Rachel stepped into the reception area and saw me, she dropped her head. "Roger, what are you doing here?"

"I went to see Amber."

Rachel pulled her head up. The receptionist snapped her head up, ready to reach into her desk for her pistol if I proved to be another crazy. "She'll just get confused if you keep showing up."

"Confused about what? That I want to see her?"

"Confused about whether we're together or not."

"I'm a little short on that explanation myself. I need some more whys or wherefores. You owe me something."

Rachel stepped up to me, grabbed my arm, pulled me into her office, and shut the door. Her office smelled and glowed with polished wood and leather. "I'm sorry, Roger. I'm truly sorry. It is my fault. It has nothing to do with you. It's just me."

A pretty worn-out line. "What's you?"

"I just can't trust myself to . . . to trust you as I should."

"Why? Why? Why? Why give up a good thing?"

She paced in front of me. She was in her businesswoman's suit, but my mind made me see the body that was behind it. "Roger, I just realized that I can't love you. We got too close. It was my mistake."

"Could you talk to me? Just talk."

"About what?"

"I'm a little confused. That guy who was murdered. That Harry Krammer guy. Did you hear about him?" Rachel closed her eyes and gulped. I stepped toward her to hug her. She pulled away from me. "I took photos of him."

"No just stop. Just stop. Just stop right there."

"I was working for the husband of the woman he was running around with. Now the husband and the wife are suspects. They want me to help them."

"Oh, God. Poor Roger."

"So I'm asking you, what should I do? I'm asking you to maybe have dinner with me."

Rachel stiffened. "See there. That's just it. That's just it. I sympathize with you. I want to help you. But I have a child to raise. I'm going to adopt another child. And I don't want your world in theirs."

This from a personal injury lawyer. "Heard any good lawyer jokes lately?"

Rachel chuckled, then shook her head. "Leave me alone, Roger. Give me some time. Give us some time. Don't call me until you really need to. And then call first, no surprises."

"So just like that. Poof. And you're through with me. No regrets. No second guesses. Not even a twinge. Don't you even miss me?"

"I do what I have to, Roger. So should you."

"I am doing what I have to."

"Go to your bar, but leave me alone. Please."

SEVEN

Ridley and Edmore must have gotten caught in the rain. They smelled like wet leather. Zia was annoying them by talking about dirty pictures. Leroy was still talking to Shirley, even holding her hand.

I was in my corner of the horseshoe bar, with my back against the wall, where I could see whoever Lee had sent come in the door. Lynette was soon by my side and asking what I wanted to drink. I thought about getting a hazy feeling as soon as possible, but decided to stay sharp, so I ordered a beer. Zia was at my side. "Hey, you like fuck movies straight from the Internet?"

"Go back to Edmore and Ridley," I said.

"New DVDs, straight from the Internet. Cost you thirty dollars a month for best of 'Barely Legal Teens' on the Internet. Thirty dollars and from me you get two months' worth. And no download."

"Zia, are you a Muslim?" I asked.

"No, I became Unitarian. But now I'm thinking about joining the pagans. You interested? I can get you free DVD for Unitarians, but pagan DVD for five-ninety-five."

"Zia, bother somebody else," Lynette told him and set my beer in front of me. When Zia scurried back to Ridley and Edmore, Lynette said, "Roger, you look a little nervous."

I said, "I'm scared, too," when Bruce walked in, damn near jangling as he walked because of all the jewelry hanging from his face.

Dressed in a green tank top and wet biker chaps, Bruce sat a chair away from me. I took a sip of from my beer before sliding over into the empty chair. "Bud," Bruce said and slapped me on the back.

"Bruce, you done a lot of different things," I said.

"Hell, yeah." His tongue stud made *yeah* come out like *yeth*.

49

"Ever sell any real low-grade, extra-cut Houston grade-B cocaine, oh say, to a social worker?" I didn't care how Bruce made ends meet, and I was no crusader against a person's drug or vice of choice. I wanted to lead Bruce into some answer, but my mind was churning on high power, making me tired.

Bruce simply turned to look indignantly at me. "I've never been involved with drugs in my life." He turned to his beer. He rubbed his shaved head and stared at his beer. "The idea, you'd even say anything. Shit, that hurts. What gives you the idea I'd do something like that?" He rubbed his head while a little blink of thought lit his bald head. "You haven't said anything to the cops, have you?"

"Just before Harry Krammer got killed, I took photos of him and a cheating wife."

Bruce shook his head and hunched his well-built shoulders. "You're going to have to slow down."

I looked at the eagles, the banners, the American flag, and the misspelled names of past girlfriends on his bulging biceps. "If I were going to get some really bottom-of-the-line cocaine, say from somebody in a place like this, who would I go to?"

Bruce crossed his arms to scratch at both of his biceps and rolled the stacked muscles on his shoulders. The horseshoe in his eyebrow caught a little of the light and reflected it at me. "You. You're trying to trick me." He relaxed a little as his simple chain of reasoning gave him some confidence. "'Cause you don't ever want drugs. Hell, you can't risk getting caught with drugs because of your profession. So I ain't telling you shit. Hell, I ought to whip your old ass just for suggesting I'd sell drugs." He made a motion as though to thump me in the chest, but lost his script or actually got afraid of my old ass, so he folded his arms and scratched at his biceps. "You haven't told the cops, have you?"

"Somebody might have. Somebody like me, who has some influence with them, could lead them away from you—if I had somewhere to lead them."

Thunder clapped outside and the blink of thought in Bruce's shaved head stopped. "You shouldn't do business where you drink." He grabbed his bottle and walked around to the other side of the bar to join Ridley and Edmore. Biker solidarity. They all gave me a lazy nod.

After another loud clap of thunder momentarily knocked out the lights, I looked around at the startled faces. As the neon beer signs sputtered back on, Shirley pushed herself against Leroy's chest, and he circled his arms around her. Edmore, Ridley, and Bruce were grinning sheepishly. "Damn, you nearly jumped in my lap," Edmore said to Bruce. Lynette had pushed her butt up on the cooler and was just pulling her hands from her mouth. Zia was still talking. We were like old Neanderthals, gathered in our cave, shivering with fear at the sights and sounds of a rainstorm, some dim memory of the last hundred or so we had seen reassuring us, but still not convinced that we were safe.

Then the rain started. As I was prone to do, with my second cool beer in hand, I stepped outside under the awning of the patio and listened to the wind and rain in the trees. I opened my mouth and the wind blew some of the rain into my mouth. The wind and spray on my face made me alert, yet calmed me to face what was coming. I was the tribal prophet, the seer; I had trusted my memory of the last hundred rainstorms and ventured out to listen and watch the storm. I was leading the way toward monotheism. This scary but consistent display couldn't be the voice of many gods, but the one true, confused, pissed-off Pentecostal God, talking to me in tongues.

Amber liked to watch the rain, too. Rachel lived next to the fifteenth hole on a golf course. During this past July, when the heat just got so oppressive that the humidity exploded in rain, Amber and I went out to Rachel's screened-in back porch and watched the afternoon showers. With the rain's spray on our faces, we felt cooled, exhilarated, and peaceful.

When I went back inside, Bruce had left. Lynette bought me a beer, and I leaned across the bar. "If I wanted some cocaine, nasty stuff, who could I see in here?"

Lynette pulled back from me. "Roger, don't make me go there."

"Go there for me, please."

"There's meth heads want some coke to go with that nasty meth stuff. If they come in here, they talk to Bruce."

"Thank you, you angel."

"But Roger, we all know he's a fuckup. He's just doing that because he thinks it makes him cool. He thinks maybe it'll get him laid with one of those young chicks."

"I know," I said.

The door to Nothing To Lose blew open, and with the spray a tall, well-built middle-aged black man stepped in. He had an umbrella over his head and was most conscious about protecting his white straw, rolled-and-curled-brim, gambler-style hat from the rain. He tried to shove the door shut with his foot, but the wind pushed against him. Finally he had to drop his umbrella, place his hat gently on the rail next to the door, then put his shoulder to the door to get it closed. He turned around to survey the room and then picked up his hat and positioned it on his head at a slight angle.

He looked at each one of us: Zia, Leroy, Shirley, Ridley, and Edmore. His eyes settled on me, and so did his smile. As he crossed the room, I took note of his dress. He had on black pointy-toed boots. They looked like women's boots, not at all western. He had on pressed blue slacks, a pink shirt, and a black leather vest. He had a gaudy ring on every finger of his left hand except his thumb. Above the fingers, on his wrist, was a broad leather strap, the old-fashioned kind from the seventies, that held a watch. On his right wrist was a gold chain bracelet. He sat next to me and ordered a double scotch in a tall glass filled to the top with ice and then water. After ordering, he stuck out his hand. "I'm D. Wayne Deshotel. That's *D* period, then Wayne. Not *D U A N E*. And not *D E* then Wayne."

I shook his hand. "I'm your new partner. We're gonna find who murdered Harry Krammer," he said.

Lynette set his drink in front of him. Anticipating my drinking speed, she set another beer in front of me. "I don't normally have a partner."

"You do now."

"I promised the Hudsons that I'd find Harry's murderer."

"Lee Tomlinson *told* you that you was helping her." He sipped on his drink. "I'm glad to see there's some fellow African Americans in this place. Pulling up I got the idea that this was a real cracker bar. You got to be conscious of such things when you're a black man in Beaumont."

"Look, Mr. Deshotel..."

"We all better be on a first name basis. We got to trust each other. Call me D. Wayne."

"I don't know what Lee told you. I never agreed to anything. I think

I'd be compromising my job if I worked for you and the other clients."

"Your other clients smell bad. They paid you anything, yet?" I shook my head. D. Wayne pulled a rolled wad of bills out of his pocket. He let me see that the first two were hundreds. "I normally pay in cash."

I caught myself staring. D. Wayne said, "That Lee is a fine-looking woman. Don't you think? I mean she ain't just let herself go, like a lot of middle-aged women do. Like most of these white trash women and poor black women around here."

"She is stunning."

"Yeah, she is stunning. I dated white women, black women, Mexican women, and I can tell you not one was like Lee. I aim to keep her. That's why you and me partners."

"I'm going to need a little more background, D.Wayne."

D. Wayne removed his hat and set it crown down on the bar. His hair was cut short so you couldn't tell how bald he was. "Lee liked that Harry guy. They had some kind of thing. Now I know she had the liaison, let's say, because I don't want to say *pussy bumping*, with that Stacy, but that's in the past. She don't do that no more. What I can't forgive, I just forget, as concerns Lee. So when Harry gets hisself murdered, Lee is upset. I ask her what's wrong. When she tells me, I tell her I'll use my influences and natural talent to help. Then you show up at the funeral. So Lee decides that you and me is partners."

D. Wayne saw that I was shying away from him. "Now you may be asking yourself what a nice white lady like Lee and I got in common. It's *showmanship*. She used to be a dancer, a performer. I'm something of a performer myself. I dance in my own way. As you can see I got showmanship."

I knew it was a dangerous question, but I asked him what he did.

"I help people," he said. "Bright in here." He put on his hat. I looked at his drink. It was already empty. He gave the slightest nod to Lynnette, and she set another tall scotch in front of him. I saw what might have attracted Lee to him, but I couldn't figure out why she would stay with him. "That answer ain't good enough for you, huh?"

I shook my head.

"I come from Double Bayou, out toward Anahauc. You ever heard of Double Bayou?"

I shook my head.

"A man named Tuttle comes to this area from Alabama way back in the 1830s. He brings his slaves, and they become his cowboys. He trusts them so much, he lets them drive cattle to New Orleans and trusts them to bring the money back. But the whole time he has two families. One white and one black. Builds both a nice house. Leaves both sets of children money. Separate but equal. When he died, the family didn't keep separate. Look here, at my nose." He turned his profile to me. "In Double Bayou we all mixed race. So we know how to get along. That's what my momma, most blessed woman ever lived, taught me. That's what I do. Help people get along. I'm sorta exporting the Double Bayou spirit to Beaumont."

"And if people don't want to get along?"

"Sometimes, I have to encourage them."

"How did you and Lee meet?"

He stood up. "I wasn't always the handsome black gentleman you see now. I used to drag around a belly." He stopped and looked at me. "Even bigger than yours. So I switched from beer and bourbon to this straight up scotches. I started aerobics. I never knew a woman could move like that. Just the way Lee would move.... Well, I shouldn't tell you 'bout my sexual fantasies till we know each other little better."

"What qualifies you to look for Harry's killer?"

He looked at me as though he were getting angry. "Same thing qualifies you. You got pictures. I know people. I got information."

"Look, I'm sorry for any misunderstanding, and no insults, but I'd rather just do this on my own."

D. Wayne looked straight ahead. "You gonna be one of those people don't want to get along? Somebody I got to explain things to, things about their health?"

A few people in the bar were staring at us. I couldn't count on anyone to back me up but Lynette, and she didn't look like a match for D. Wayne. "Okay, okay," I said. "But can I talk to Lee?"

"Soon enough." Wayne smiled and patted my back. "Now partner, what is it you know?" I tried to explain to D. Wayne, but it sounded a lot like nothing.

✦

When I got home, I went out to my screened back porch to let the storm's cool spray hit me and tell me what to do. The pines groaned with the power of the wind and slashes of rain. The lightning and thunder applauded the damage that wind and rain can do. The lesser, gutless, artificial Chinese tallow trees whipped every which way as though just begging for some kind of mercy. And so was I.

The spray through my screen sobered me up, so I fought it with sips from my own whiskey. The rolling thunder was not so much dramatic as consistent—droning, demanding some action from me. I listened to the plunks of rain on the blades of my heat pump, then heard the whir as it churned to cool my A-frame house. Swirling rain, churning blades, bending and bowing tallows, the false pride of new pine, my own roof straining under the downpour, the spray in my face, the dry feel at the back of my throat despite the whiskey I had drunk. That night the rain told me to hide.

The next morning had been made almost cool and brisk by the norther the night before. The soles of my jogging shoes slapped the wet pavement and sank into the wet grass on the canal. A Jefferson County sheriff's department car pulled up to me just as I was getting near to my house. It stopped, and Emily Nguyen stepped out. "For a man in your business, you sure are easy to find."

I cautiously walked up to her. "At least let me take a shower and get dressed this time."

Emily leaned against the car and crossed her arms. "I just wanted to chat."

"Nice weather, today. Think it'll stay cool. Is summer finally over? Nah, can't be. It's still too early."

"Roger, what makes you think that you can do better than the police?"

"I can't do better. And that's such a disgrace to me. So I'm gonna make myself scarce."

"You mind giving me a number where you can be reached?"

"So you wouldn't want to tell me anything, would you?" I asked.

"No. I mean, I have nothing to tell you."

"Emily, come on, just a little?"

Emily crossed her arms. "You really going to hide?"

"I am hiding. You just happen to have found me."

"We've been talking to known and suspected lowlife, bottom-of-the-food-chain drug dealers. Arthur found sand in Harry's apartment.

Harry tracked in Beaumont mud or clay. But the sand is from a river-bottom area. We're thinking somebody selling drugs north of here."

"Sounds like you don't need me."

Emily frowned.

"Emily, you're a couple of semesters away from an MBA. Why are you so concerned about being a deputy sheriff?"

"Being concerned with what I am at the time is how I'm getting an MBA. You said yourself I work harder than any three white men."

"So are you going to tell me which discount, low-count drug dealer you suspect?"

Emily stared down at the ground. "I don't think that I better do that."

"Emily, you ever heard of D. Wayne Deshotel?"

"Law enforcement's job is to catch the dumb criminals. We can't do much about the smart ones." Emily, a bright woman, knew, like me, the would-be practicing lawyer, that the justice system didn't so much keep justice as keep apparent stability. Emily went on, "D. Wayne is so smart we don't know if he even is a criminal."

"But odds are . . ."

"Odds are you better stay away from him."

"Like I said, I'm running away."

I gave Emily my cell phone number. She nodded her head, stepped into her car, and pulled away.

EIGHT

It wasn't failing to find the answer that scared me. It was the answer that scared me. True, real, hard answers are always tough to live with, and always messy. As Emily had said, repeating my point, dumb criminals and crimes are easy, smart ones aren't.

First, I went to the Lamar University library late in the day. I used their computers and books to look up as much information as I could about Hardin, Tyler, and Newton Counties. Poor, predominately white, isolated, economically unlucky. When the Civil War started, there were very few slave owners. The populace couldn't afford food, let alone slaves. Half joined the Confederate army; the other half hid out from the southern draft in the Big Thicket. They trapped, fished, and made moonshine. The timber industry came, cut down the fifty- to sixty-inch-diameter old growth, and went. The railroads passed through but created no major hubs.

Today, a high school diploma was higher education. Teen pregnancies were among the highest in the state. Sex was mostly unsafe. Cigarettes sold well. When people figured out how to make methamphetamine in homemade labs, and meth replaced crack as the poor man's drug of choice, mobile homes and houses all over the area started blowing up. With isolation, back roads, and moonshine in their background, the counties' numerous poor found another industry, but they sampled their own product. Somewhere in the sandy river bottoms of those counties was Harry Krammer's killer.

When the announcements came on that the library was closing, I went into the men's room, sat on the tank of a toilet in one of the stalls, rested my feet on the lid, and waited for the lights to turn off and the doors to lock. I pulled my flashlight out of one pocket and my flask out of the other. D. Wayne, the police, Lee, or Cody might be calling or coming by my house. I wanted to be lost. Spending the night wasn't so bad either. I devised a plan where I could spend every night in the library.

But then I thought some real distance might be the answer. I decided to drive to Houston and then Austin and see if I wanted to keep driving, or go back.

When my wife and my marriage left me, I didn't become a lawyer as I had thought, but I became a private detective specializing in the divorce business. I worked for Buck Cronin, the meanest, toughest lawyer in Austin, Texas, a booming city with celebrity status, and about to boom even more with dotcoms, and thus with divorces. What God could bring together, Buck Cronin and I could put asunder. Buck and I shared our talents. His tactics and strategy involved the courtroom or hearing. Mine involved finding photos or testimony.

But then Buck turned me on to a job for a personal injury suit in Beaumont. Beaumont, the only unionized town in Texas, full of refineries, was a paradise to personal injury lawyers because of the sympathetic, unionized, refinery-worker juries. So the personal injury lawyers slithered through the dark, smelly legal undergrowth of Beaumont, making themselves large sums of money. I photographed and got testimony about dials, emissions, asbestos tests, ledger sheets, e-mailed memos, and shredded documents. Then the devil whispered in my ear, and I returned to the divorce business. I missed humans. Separating people seemed cleaner than personal injury. So I began to learn even more about the Pine Curtain. Buck Cronin knew how I got here and knew a better me, so I thought that he could tell me what to do. When I ran from Hurricane Rita, I spent my twenty hours evacuation time wending through back roads to Buck Cronin's retirement home in Austin.

✦

East of Houston, I-10 was a tunnel through the thick air, clogged with humidity, pollution, cloudy skies, and rain. On this trip, as I drove through the swaths of rain, I looked for whatever prettiness I could find in the flat, deforested distance.

And as I drove, tilting my head to see showers and thick air, punching the tuning button of my radio to cruise through the myriad of Houston stations with their droning disc jockeys and talk personalities, I felt very much outside of the Pine Curtain community. Those natives blessed with looks and intelligence may have tried to leave the Golden Triangle, but some deficiency that made them unfit for the rest of society always brought them back. They went to college, the military, or beauty school, but flunked out, got their certificate, or did their time to return to what they knew— low-level dreams in an unsophisticated place. They married what they knew— big hair, lots of jewelry, cheap perfume, and apparent easy money. Both men and women. Maybe the pollution in the air, coupled with the coupling of refinery workers' sons and daughters, produced the pretty and semibright inhabitants of the Golden Triangle. They made good salespeople, sort of a good-old-boy and -girl network. I felt on the outside from everybody. I had come here of my own free will from the outside world.

But I did have something in common with both the natives and the newcomers, everybody except the lawyers. I got stuck because my ambition took me no farther, or further. It simply gave out. That's what united us—the semibrights and me. We had dreams. We knew there was better. But *better* seemed to require more talent and effort than we had to give. Then too, because we knew how we were, we figured we just weren't fated for a better life. We just weren't very lucky. Even if we had any luck, we'd probably just screw up because of the way we were.

So I was glad to be headed to Austin and San Marcos, where I went to college, where some people had a little more ambition and a few more dreams. There were still some leftover hippies and liberals there. Quite a few of the disenfranchised and reconciled unambitious people like me were happy to be stuck in a part of Texas with clear, clean water and a laid-back attitude. I was going home.

I had to stop in Houston to see my parents. My parents went to churches now more than they ever had—the funerals of friends and the weddings of grandchildren and the great-grandchildren of friends. They were polite, not religious. They had never bothered taking me to a church of any kind, and I always appreciated them for that. For I grew up without that great religious burden that so many Texas youngsters have to ultimately put behind them or surrender to. Still, my parents were Baptisty.

My mother and father were great believers in their security and were faithful to it. They had the luck or foresight to be really compatible and so were spared the wants and drudgeries that break up most marriages. They had also been spared real illness and tragedy, and so most of what they had to face up to were inconveniences and problems that they could always overcome. They had money so that they could buy themselves comfort, ease, and security.

And so in their spry retirement, they lived in a gated community with the houses, lawns, and recreational facilities sculpted to the needs of seniors. Luckily, as I pulled into their guarded, safe lives, the gate was open. So I, the interloper, drove to the tennis courts, where I knew at least my father would be.

As I pulled into the parking lot next to the courts, I saw my father returning lobbed balls. He took hurried baby steps and sort of shuffled when he ran to the ball, but he had a powerful return. He was obviously winning. His opponent moved a little like him and was making my father run with lobs, but my father was putting some tight, accurate returns past his opponent. Sometimes his feet splashed some water that was still on the courts from the showers that fell earlier. No matter to my father; he used tennis for penance as I used jogging.

Under a tent between the two courts was my mother. Dressed in a white tennis outfit, just like my father, with a white baseball cap shielding her eyes from rain and sun, my mother sat in a lawn chair and sipped ice tea. Another lady, dressed much like she was, probably my father's opponent's wife, sat next to her and sipped from a wine glass. In front of them, on a small table, was a pitcher of iced tea and a pitcher of martinis. This is what I had come from. I wondered where I had lost it, and if I missed it.

As I walked onto the tennis court, my mother was up and almost running to me. "Roger, why don't you call and let us know when you're coming?"

"I didn't know I was coming until kind of late."

"That doesn't sound good," my father said. He had baby-stepped his way to me. "More problems with your work?"

My mother shushed my father. "Vern, he just walks up and already you're annoying him. Let him get a drink of something before you start annoying him."

My father, smiling, actually glad to see me, motioned toward the tray with iced tea and martinis. "I take it that you'll be having a martini instead of tea."

When we reached the small table surrounded by lawn chairs, my parents introduced me to their friends: Gerald and Harriet Sower. I had disrupted the tennis game and no doubt saved Gerald Sower from a loss. "Your mother can't last through a whole set anymore," my father said.

"I can, too," Faye Jackson said to her husband. "But it's this osteoporosis. I shouldn't push myself. You forget just how old we are."

My father poured me a drink, and as he handed it to me, the Sowers pushed their chairs to the edge of the shade from the tent to allow a bit of privacy for this family visit.

Gin, to me, always tasted like carrot juice. But I liked the cool feel of it on the back of my throat. "So I take it you forgot our number. I'll write it down for you before you leave," my father said. My mother giggled.

"So have you made out a will like I asked you?" my mother asked me.

"No."

"Now you know that, if you don't make one, the state will get all you own."

"Who am I going to leave it to?"

"A charity, one of your liberal politicians. I don't know. But that way you get a choice."

"Mom, I just don't have enough money to worry about."

My father sipped his martini. "Still following that vow of poverty that you took?" He looked from me over to Gerald Sower. "Can you go a few more games, Gerald?"

Gerald waved my father away. "I'm ten years younger than you. And I get more than enough exercise. You should pick on two seventy-five-year-olds." My father looked at my mother, "Faye?"

"My osteoporosis."

My father shook his head and looked at me. "That's the problem with marrying an old woman."

"I wasn't old when you married me," my mother said. Then she looked back at me. "You need a will." I forced myself to sip the martini and not gulp it down and run away to Austin. "So you can spend the night, we have that extra bedroom."

"No, I'm on my way to Austin."

"Where will you stay?" my mother said.

"I don't know," I said.

Ever cautious, my father said, "You better call ahead. Austin is always full."

"I may stay in San Marcos."

"It's even worse."

I sipped and looked over the rooftops at another swath of rain. "Dad, maybe you ought to slow down on the tennis."

"That's what I told him. Then his doctor told him. He pays no attention to his age."

"Why should I? My heart's in great shape."

"You're eighty-five years old. You could fall and break a hip or a leg," my mother said.

My father directed her attention toward me. "Roger, you still jog?" I didn't answer. I wasn't going to get into the middle of it. So my father turned to my mother. "Some things help you no matter what."

My mother shook her head and reached for her purse. "Before I forget, let me write a check."

"I don't need any money."

"Sure you do," my mother said. "Look where you live."

"Again, see, where did you get this aversion to money, to just a little security," my father said rather than asked.

"You know, you are really old yourself, too," my mother said as she wrote me a check for two hundred dollars.

My father turned in time to see the two Sowers toddling off the court, Harriet holding on to Gerald's elbow. My father shouted after them, and when they turned to see him, he waved goodbye with his racket. Then he swiped the air a couple of times with his racket and said to me, "You know, you are a lawyer. You could be doing something besides taking those photos that you do."

"You ever heard any lawyer jokes?"

My mother handed me the check and then demanded that I come look at her condominium. I said that I had to be going. She commanded by not saying a word but walking off the courts. My father and I grabbed the lawn chairs. And as we three old people hobbled to my parents' immaculate condominium, my parents wanted to know what I was doing to improve my life, to make it more secure. They had money enough to help make my life secure. But except for my mother's checks, I refused the big gifts. I had this thing about money.

As we get older, fewer years seem to separate us from our parents. With what I had become, I wondered if I could have earned a life like theirs. I wondered if I wanted a life like theirs. I didn't have that many years to find out.

NINE

I drove into the monstrosity of a city that Austin had become with no clear notion of what I wanted to do.

Out of nostalgia or my sense of being a Texan, I drove down Congress Avenue for a view of the Capitol. I got stuck in the left lane trying to turn left against the damn-near-touching bumpers and drivers' rage next to my fender. The rush hour traffic was not going to let me turn. There was no left turning lane in what used to be a wide avenue. Several cars going opposite ran the yellow and then even the red light, and I got caught in midintersection with a red light in front of me and honking cars on either side and behind. I put my truck into reverse and backed up just enough to keep from jamming into the front end of a honking BMW. Then after turning to shoot a finger at the driver of the BMW, I heard a thump on the hood of my Toyota truck. I straightened to see a kid with a blue Mohawk and with metal studs poked into all the loose flesh or cartilage on his face pounding on my hood and screaming about pedestrian rights. "You fucking redneck," he screamed. I wanted to get out of the truck and take a tire tool to him. I guess he was right. In this new Austin, I was a redneck.

Austin had jerked itself out from under me again. So I got on with my initial mission, to find some more support, to find Buck Cronin.

Buck Cronin was maybe fifteen years older than me. He had become a barometer of sorts for me, warning me of the indignities and infirmities of age and vices waiting ahead, the antithesis of my parents. He had remained married to a knockout, but with the kids gone, though she didn't divorce him, Buck's wife just left him. Then he lost his health. His emphysema demanded a constant supply of oxygen. A stroke left him with a shake in his left hand and foot. So with his absent wife's hearty approval, Buck checked himself into a nursing facility.

I waited on the veranda of the large restored building under an outdoor fan churning up enough breeze to cool me off. Buck clumped out, his walker leading his one good foot, while he dragged his bad one. His oxygen tank was strapped around his waist and a tube leading from it forked into each of his nostrils. But he was dressed in sharply pressed khakis and a plaid shirt, wore a straw beach-style hat, and managed, somehow, to smile.

As he got closer, he kept nodding, whether he wanted to or not. He slumped into a wicker chair, and I sat next to him. Turning to me, with some effort, he slurred, "God, I wish I had a cigarette and a shot of scotch."

"I wish I had brought you one of each."

"Together, at one time, they'd probably kill me. My wife and I would both be grateful."

I couldn't help myself, so I patted his knee, and he looked down at my hand. We were both embarrassed, and I quickly removed my hand, and I got even more embarrassed when a couple of tears formed in my eye, and I had to rub at my eye with the back of my hand. "Goddamn it, Buck. This wasn't supposed to happen. You aren't supposed to be . . . well, like this."

"*This* is probably where we are all headed. I won't be one of those old prissy women and warn about your vices, but I'll tell you to be prepared for their results." He looked at me with this great look of appreciation in his eyes.

"Penance," I said.

"Ain't nothing free. But just to feel that rough liquid sliding down my throat. I'd be ready to die."

"Not sex?"

"Not sex, love, or honor, but a drink of scotch, or a cigarette."

"Is it all right in here?" I looked out at the grounds and back over my shoulder at the home.

"Sometimes, if I was more dexterous, I'd like to flop it out and wave what was left of it at the old ladies. Just for kicks. But other than the just-smelled-a-turd looks when I talk to any of them, this place is okay. As far as what it is and what I've become, we're a pretty good match."

I patted his knee again. This time, we didn't get embarrassed, and I didn't lose a tear. "How's your life?" Buck asked.

"I lost the latest woman. I drink too much, and I'm still in the divorce business."

"So nothing's changed."

"Well, I'm stuck in this really particularly bad case."

"Tell me about it. I have to live vicariously now."

Buck listened while I told him about D. Wayne and Lee and Harry and the Hudsons, Beaumont rising up around me as we talked. When I finished the story, I told Buck that I was thinking of staying in Austin to dodge the whole ugly incident, but I added that Austin now seemed sour—and too expensive.

My father once asked me what I had against people with money or money itself. A self-styled radical in my college days at Southwest Texas State, I forced myself to see that the disparities in power and health matched the disparities in money. I edited and wrote a radical newspaper, had my car firebombed, protested, and got myself arrested. Then I got married, lived with my father-in-law to see what the lack of money had done to him and his family, and then, after my divorce, I went to work for Mike Cronin and learned to live with inequities and photos of cheating spouses.

"Go back. Go back, and deal with it," Buck said.

"Why? The money's not going to make or break me. So why? To help whom? Cody and Jessica Hudson are starting to spook me. And I'm a little scared of D. Wayne and Lee Tomlinson."

"For Harry's sake."

"He's dead."

"Exactly. So he should have some justice. He can't get it himself, so we should find it for him. That's what the law says we're supposed to do. It's what we are supposed to do as lawyers, instead of what we did do as lawyers. Go back and fix it for the one who can't fix it for himself. Get the truth, even if nothing comes of the truth.

"Hell, as you probably noticed, everybody who had anything on the ball around here got well-off. Everybody in the damn city has become proud of getting rich or well-off, even me. Like it was some big accomplishment to get lucky, work hard, know about money, or marry well. With their money, they're proud of living in a cool place with good music. But I'll bet back in Beaumont, people aren't nearly so proud of money or where they live."

"Back in Beaumont, the money is connected to Jesus, and nobody likes living there."

"Least it's not money for the sake of money, or for the sake of a comfortable life. In the end, it's about what you've done. It sounds like you've got a chance to do something."

I nodded and then Buck began to nod, or to feel a tremor work its way into his head. "Buck, why don't you come back with me? Why don't you find a nice place like this in Beaumont, and you could help me with my cases and my life. I could tell you about what happens down at Nothing To Lose."

"That would be fun. If it was possible. But I'm here. I mean to die here."

⟡

I found myself in the warehouse district, wandering aimlessly, noting the cleaned-up, gentrified, yuppiefied, dotcom-financed trendy bistros, bars, and health food restaurants. I found myself drinking strong beer in a microbrewery and talking to a coed who seemed to be growing studs out of her lips and nose. The more I drank, the more her jewelry began to look like moles or warts. But her youthful zest and hope cheered me up. After a while the coed sprouting facial jewelry asked me what I was doing. I tried to tell her and got lost in my own story. She asked me how old I was. I told her. She asked, "Do you ever wake up and forget just how old you are?"

"Never," I said.

As I left the bar, my cell phone rang. It was Rachel. "Well, honey, I've been thinking . . ."

"No you haven't," Rachel said. "If you had, you would have called."

"You don't take my calls."

"Still, you should have tried." I was starting to see why I was a problem to Rachel. I was a different species.

"I'm in Austin, on some business. Say when I get back . . ."

"I'm calling for Amber." In the pause, I heard the shuffle of Amber's feet as she ran to the phone. "She got into trouble again today. She wants to talk to you. In fact, she demanded to talk to you. Roger, think about what you tell her."

Before I could say anything, I heard Amber's breath on the phone. "What's the problem, Sis?"

"I hit that mean boy again," Amber said. I could tell she was holding back tears.

"You know you shouldn't be hitting boys. No wait, you shouldn't be hitting anybody. If you keep on, eventually somebody will hit you. And if enough people hit you, you get kind of crazy."

"Like you," Amber giggled through her tears.

"Like me, that's why I don't see you as much. So don't hit people."

"But I had to. I couldn't help it."

"Did you get suspended again?"

"It was after class. I learned not to hit him in school."

"Well, that's some progress. Now just work on not hitting him after school, and you'll be in good shape."

"But he called me names."

"Sticks and stones . . ." I couldn't believe where I was going with this. "What did he say?"

"He called me a homeless person. He said my mother wasn't my real mother. He said I was really a nigger, not a Mexican."

I wanted to blurt out that she should kick the little shit ass's ass, but I gritted my teeth while I tried to force my mind's natural smartass inclinations down another track. "Amber, honey, you've talked to your mother, right? She's explained things to you."

"She tried."

"So just don't hit people. They'll come to understand."

"Roger, am I nigger, or a redneck, or a Mexican?"

When Rachel pulled Amber out of a series of foster homes, she had lived with a black family, an Asian family, and a white family—all of them keeping this mixed-race girl for the government subsidies. "It doesn't matter," I said. Amber's mother, we knew, was a scared, sickly white girl from behind the Pine Curtain. She wasn't even sure who the daddy was. Among the suspects were a black boy, a Mexican boy, and your garden-variety budding white redneck. DNA tests and accusations wouldn't have done anybody any good. Since Rachel was Hispanic, she had been telling Amber that she was a *Latina*. But Rachel's explanations didn't have much conviction, so Amber doubted. "You're the same as all the other kids, you need the same things, but you have a few peculiarities that don't really matter. They don't make you any different."

I listened to her breathing into the phone. "But I want to know."

"Amber, honey, some things we just can't ever be sure about. We just can't ever know. Just like this. It makes you mad, doesn't it?"

"Yes," Amber said.

"What's he telling you?" I heard Rachel say in the background. "Nothing," was Amber's response.

"You're mad, and you feel like hitting someone, right?"

"Yes," she said, and my mind made me see her wipe away the start of a tear of indignation from her eye.

"But you don't want to hit me, right?"

"No, Roger, I never want to hit you."

"So when you get mad in that way that you're now mad, just think of me. And think that whoever made you mad is me."

"I hope it works," she said.

After a moment Rachel was back on the phone. "Be careful what you tell her. Bye, Roger," she said all in one breath, no time for me. My mind let in an uninvited thought. Amber's biological mother could have been at Harry Krammer's funeral. Harry Krammer might have helped rescue Amber from her real mother and her foster homes. He might have put some little government sponsored Band-Aid on the gaping social wound.

After spending the night in a cheap fifties-era motel out South Congress, I jogged early the next morning, shortly before the sun rose. I jogged along the Lady Bird Lake trails, east toward the rising sun. I tried to shut out my mind and absorb all I could of what was left of the Austin I had left. Money, image, tourism, promotion were tearing up Texas.

I got hit by a wave of nostalgia for Beaumont, not Austin, and by eight o'clock Austin was in my rearview mirror.

Except for that short spurt at Spindletop and the oil that ultimately made Houston rich instead of Beaumont, we had never gotten rich. We had never valued our tough soil; in fact we polluted the whole area first with timber production and then oil production. I cussed the statues and paintings of cowboys, bluebonnets, old homesteads, noble Indians that were just decorations, with nothing at all left of the dirt-down low poverty and hardships of all of the subjects. In Beaumont, we knew about dirt-down low poverty and hardship.

I felt my own familiar and comforting corruption, sin, and decomposition as I entered the thick, smelly air on the eastern side of Baytown. Then sin, corruption, and decomposition got thicker as I saw the Anahuac cutoff. Just down the road was the Double Bayou, the harmonious, loving home of D. Wayne Deshotel. I decided to stop and ask some questions about D. Wayne, a little investigation of my own.

TEN

D. Wayne's mother, Ruthie, looked like a standing mop. Her limbs and trunk were straight and stick-like, and her hair twisted gray rope coils. I thought she might break if she moved too quickly, but she held her shoulders back as she kept a steady forward pace.

There really was not any Double Bayou, just a sign announcing it and a decrepit convenience store with an ancient gas pump that hadn't pumped anything in years and an overhead awning with sections peeled off by wind or time. The store was a leftover from rural, impoverished East Texas. I had pulled into the convenience store to ask directions and to perhaps slide into some questions about D. Wayne. Inside, the store had the usual long shelves for the tacky gadgets and food that you find in old convenience stores, but it had no order. There were some loaves of bread piled on one shelf, while other loaves of bread were piled on another shelf. And so it was with canned goods, motor oil, candy, and junk food. At least the beer and the sodas were stacked reasonably behind the one modern addition—the glass-doored refrigeration units.

As I wandered through the aisles, a very old man with a crutch under each arm hobbled out from somewhere toward the side of the store. He really didn't use the crutches, though he did limp. He just held the crutches out to either side, as though to catch himself if he fell to one side or the other. "Help you?" he asked.

"Yes, you could," I said. "Do you know of D. Wayne Deshotel?"

He giggled, and I saw that most of his teeth were missing. "Do I know D. Wayne Deshotel? I all but raised the boy. Why you asking?"

"I'm thinking of going into a business transaction with him. I was in the area, and I thought that I might just check into his background."

The owner or manager or whatever the old man was stopped laughing.

"I don't know that's a good question or bad question to be asking. Ain't no need to check on D. Wayne, he's a good boy. Man, I mean. Ain't nothing wrong with him. He say it, it happens."

"So what exactly are his business interests?" I asked.

"Why don't you ask his momma?" As he said that, the woman who looked like an upturned mop stepped into the store from the room off to the side. "You give me a ride to my house, I tell you all about D. Wayne, my bestest child."

"Miss Ruthie stay up the road in that new Taj Mahal D. Wayne built for her." The old man smiled at Ruthie as he said that, and she smiled back.

"I walk down in the mornings to get my exercise and to help Mr. Peveto with his morning chores," Ruthie Deshotel said. "But now I need a ride back."

"Your own feet got you here, they ought to take you back," Mr. Peveto said, then looked at me. "You going to buy something?"

Looking around, I went to the glass doors and grabbed a soda. "Mrs. Deshotel, would you like something to drink?"

"I would love a Co-Cola," she said.

When I put the two sodas on the counter, Mr. Peveto stepped up to the computerized cash register and pushed a few buttons. The cash drawer opened, but no amount lit up. "It broke two years ago. Selling Ding Dongs and Twinkies ain't enough to get it fixed," Mr. Peveto said.

He took my five and, and as clerks did in the old days, figured out the amount of change in his head. I took my change and held the door open for Mrs. Deshotel.

"You be careful of that gentleman," Mr Peveto said to Mrs. Deshotel. "You don't know him or his intentions." They exchanged smiles, and I realized that I was in between the appreciative, adoring, yet teasing words and gazes of two elderly lovers.

After I helped D. Wayne's mother into the cab of my truck and pulled out of the parking lot, she asked, "You ain't no cop, are you?"

"No. I'm a business associate."

"That don't say just a whole lot."

"I'm with the Beaumont Chamber of Commerce."

"Right," Mrs. Deshotel said as she struggled to pull off the tab of her Coke. Holding the can with two hands, she daintily took a sip. "I sure don't want to spill none on your nice new truck."

When I pulled out onto the road, she started talking in between sips of Coke. "You go ahead and do your deal with D. Wayne. He's my smartest child. He's smarter than his brother that's a Houston preacher. Smarter than his sister that's a Houston lawyer. He's of course smarter than his other brother that's done some little bit of time."

"He is a trustworthy man?"

"Wait, you wait and look." She pointed out the window with a long skinny finger. "That there is a historical site. You can't see much of it now, but there's a concrete slab and some high hurricane fence all around it. There was some of the best blues played in this state right there. Nobody in this little ol' town could afford a proper dance floor, so my parents and their people poured the concrete and put the fence around and would lock themselves inside for some grand dances. Now only me and Mr. Peveto remember."

I was going too fast to note the concrete slab or the high wire. "Now you slow down, slow down, slow down, slow down." When I slowed to a crawl, she said, "Now turn right, right here, now." I quickly turned off onto a gravel road. Ruthie Deshotel laughed at my turn. "I told you to slow down. Most people don't know how to look for little country roads."

"You walk from here to that store."

"Every morning."

"You must enjoy Mr. Peveto's company."

"We been enjoying companying up since D. Wayne's daddy got shot by a bad old ex-Kluxer deputy sheriff over in Hardin County."

Then she extended her finger again. "See there?" I looked at her Taj Mahal. It was a typical modern house with the faux Victorian style. "D. Wayne built that house for me. If you notice, we come up a little rise. In a way I can look over all of Double Bayou. D. Wayne look out for Double Bayou. He built a community hall with a concrete basketball court right down the road here. Kids love him."

"An honorable gentleman?"

"The honorablist."

She invited me to come inside to look at her house, but I felt as though I had no more to learn. If I did stay, I'd start to feel bad about mistrusting D. Wayne. I excused myself and drove on to Beaumont.

As I reached the outskirts of Beaumont, I felt like a nooner, and I didn't want to be at Nothing To Lose. I had been to Austin: liberal, yuppie, and the alternative capital of Texas. As well as the capital of regular Texas. All over central Texas were bumper stickers that read "Keep Austin Weird." Most of the rough cowboy West Texas manners and the redneck East Texas parochialism had been scratched off the residents of Austin. Though the yuppie scum and dotcom-ers made my liver ache, they accounted for some nice places to have a drink. I wanted to drink someplace clean.

I drove downtown to Crockett Street and went into the bar at the Spindletop restaurant. Several of the very rich lawyers got together and resurrected the glory of Beaumont's downtown, which, until the Texas Rangers closed it down in 1961, was several blocks of whorehouses, gambling parlors, and saloons. Beaumont and Port Arthur were the most wide-open towns between Galveston and New Orleans. Sailors and oil refinery workers could find all the comforts of sin, then get right on back to the miseries of their profession, religion, or families.

But the Baptists won, sin lost, and with only legal businesses to support it, downtown Beaumont turned into a mixture of law offices, uniform rental stores, and crack houses. Downtown Port Arthur was even worse; it looked like downtown Beirut. But now all had changed because of lawsuits by the state against the tobacco companies and lawsuits for individuals against all sorts of maladies and deformities caused by accident, ignorance, indifference, or greed, mostly in the refining industry. The rich lawyers, out of civic pride, resurrected the glory of sinful Beaumont. I was hoping for illicit gambling and whorehouses, but mostly, in the "entertainment district," there was dancing, music, food, lots of liquor, and patrol cops who were lenient with drunk pedestrians. The MADD mothers stayed away, or at least they didn't complain. In the early evenings, you could catch the breeze that usually blew up from the Neches and through the shallow canyon created by the three- and four-story buildings.

While I was sipping a beer, looking at the authentic, reconstructed bricks and brass, watching the few patrons with their scrubbed manners, looking almost as well-off in their social rung as the patrons of the

Austin bars and restaurants, Rachel walked in with a couple of her lawyer friends. In Beaumont, Rachel and her crowd were as close to Austin class as I was going to get. My brain scolded me for blowing my life with her, told me that I should have begged, pleaded, cried; should have saved the goddamn jokes and comments. I walked to her table to beg.

Rachel tried to duck me. She scrunched her shoulders and lowered her head. As I stood in front of the table, in front of the lawyers in suits, and me in my jeans, jogging shoes, and T-shirt, she had to acknowledge me. One of the lawyers whom I had met somewhere along the road with Rachel, perhaps somebody she had dated, scooted over for me to join them. I refused, told Rachel I was at the bar, and asked if she'd like to join me when she finished.

Forty-five minutes later, Rachel had her legs braced, her short skirt rising up to midthigh, her arms crossed, ready to argue for my conviction. "You were right," I said. "I've just been to Austin. And you were right."

"Of course I was right. But that's no excuse . . ." My attitude and her reaction grew funny to her before she could finish her sentence, and I was reminded of why I wanted her back. She chuckled, "What was I right about?"

"My life. It's too scrambled, too unsafe. There's no direction there. Hell, I'm in my fifties, and I'm still hiding in dark corners and spying on people. It's unbecoming. Worse, it's an insult to you and Amber. I don't want to do it anymore."

"You have so many other talents."

"I'm a lawyer. I'm educated. I could clean up."

The knot that was usually in Rachel shoulders relaxed, and so, as her shoulders drooped, she dropped herself onto a barstool next to me. She ordered a cosmopolitan, lest I was in any doubt about her cleaned up, Austin style. "So how's Amber doing?"

She looked up at me and sipped her drink, and some warm thick air flowed between us and made me, at least, feel close to her. But the warm thick air turned suffocating when I said that I was going to find something else to do after this one last case.

"Why one last one? Why any at all?"

"It won't take long."

"So don't do it."

"I've got to. I made promises."

The air thickened. The knot between her shoulders grew tighter and pulled her into her rigid but poised pose. "Why don't you call me when you have quit?"

"Maybe a dinner or lunch before then?"

"Maybe."

"Maybe I can see Amber?"

"Let's take one step at a time."

She said that she had to get back to her office, so she left me with the ersatz Austinites in Beaumont's one so-far successful attempt at being sophisticated, at being something other than Beaumont. And like a few hours before, when I was leaving Austin, I missed the old Beaumont.

✦

Because I was downtown, I drove to the St. Elizabeth's Wellness Center and asked for Lee Tomlinson. One of those bright youngsters radiating health, a girl in her early twenties who had toned golden muscles all over—without ever having left air-conditioning, all-ergonomic machines, and tanning booths—gave me a tour through the facility. I had said that I felt like joining, all along feeling that it was antiseptic, too clean. Workout facilities and weight rooms were supposed to have graffiti on the walls and broken glass in the parking lot.

The tanned young lady left me at a pool. In it, Lee was giving elderly ladies water aerobics lessons. A thought occurred to me that I had better clean up and do more than hungover jogging; otherwise, not too many more years and I'd be in Lee's water aerobics class.

Lee waved to me, and I waited and smiled at the persistent, cheerful ladies thrashing against the water. Good Lord, the ladies were my age. Good Lord, Lee was my age.

After ten minutes, the ladies applauded themselves as Lee offered them further encouragement. As they waited in turn by a ladder to climb out of the pool, or tried to haul themselves far enough out of the water to roll over the tile lip, Lee, in one bound, hoisted herself out of the pool. Her hair was wet only on the ends, so she shook her head and sent a spray out away from her head.

Without makeup, her face showed some wear and tear and worries. Her one-piece suit hoisted her breasts that wanted to go in the other direction, and her legs had a few veins and splotches. But when her toes pointed out and she came toward me in that dancer's gait, I saw muscles bulge in her thighs and calves. When she walked, Lee flowed with a natural grace, like, well, like a dancer, not just a titty flopper.

She stuck out her hand. "D. Wayne said he thought you disappeared on us."

"I was a little stressed. D. Wayne can be a bit, well, intimidating. I ran away."

She held my hand and led me to a bench along the side of the pool. She motioned and we sat. "I know what you are going to ask," Lee said. "You are going to ask why me and D. Wayne."

"Isn't D. Wayne . . . well, just a little shady for you?" I took a chance, "I mean he seems more in the titty flopper category, not at all a dancer.'"

"And isn't that thrilling? Isn't he wonderful? Before him, I thought that what I might do with my life was over. I *had been* a dancer. Hell, look at me, I've been in recitals and toured with *A Chorus Line*, learned to twirl my tits in some really lowlife titty bars in Houston and Oklahoma City, and look at what I'm doing now."

One of the water aerobics ladies interrupted and waved by flexing her fingers and saying. "Oh, honey, this makes me feel so much better. Thank you so much."

Lee smiled at her, then smiled at me. "See there. See, you never know."

"But you were explaining D. Wayne."

"So with D. Wayne, I still have a life, and it's all a surprise. If you look really close and listen to him, you'll see that D. Wayne's not just a titty flopper but a dancer, too."

I wondered if her apparent happiness was that easy to find. I wondered why I couldn't find it in someone like Lynette. "I guess I envy you, then."

"Don't you have anyone?"

"I did. Up until Harry's death. Now she's sort of haunting me."

"Her bad luck. Her obtuseness."

I suddenly wished for someone like Lee. "I wish that what I can find, I could find attractive."

Lee shook her head. "Watch D.Wayne close. He has more confidence than you. He doesn't think anything is beyond him. He is one of the freest people I've ever met."

"But is he dangerous?"

"You bet," Lee said, and her hand was on my leg.

"What about you and Harry?"

"Your job is to find his killer," she said, sounding a bit irritated.

"The more I know of him, the better I can do my job."

"You're a lot like Harry. You've got some charm because you don't know you have it. Like Harry, you could have done something really great if you had ever known what it is you wanted to do. All the energy in the world but no direction. Unless someone gives it to you. For you, it's your job. One case to the next, one intrigue to the next. For poor Harry it was women, I fear. He realized his true strength, his true potential in living out his misguided dedication to them. He had other talents, but he never knew it."

"That woman-chasing and -wanting part doesn't sound like me." I was growing irritated.

"Doesn't the rest, dear? Like Harry, you're ambitious. You just don't know what your ambitions are." She again rested her palm on my thigh. I looked through the plexiglass at the exercisers, walkers, weight lifters, and cross-trainers, all busy and ambitious, all going someplace though standing still.

"Didn't Harry make some dangerous choices in women?"

"He made choices. But if he had just known himself more fully, he might have made better choices."

"What about you and your choice?"

"Don't be mean, dear. D. Wayne is true blue if he likes you and trusts you. Just be sure that he likes you."

Lee left me to join her friends, coworkers, and students in their total wellness. I wanted to go home, change clothes, and go breathe some smoke at Nothing To Lose.

ELEVEN 11

Shirley and Leroy must have worked on their relationship. When I walked into Nothing To Lose, Shirley was nibbling on Leroy's ear. Her nibbling fit: she was tall and horse faced. Leroy evidently accepted what he had in slow-witted, horse-faced, too-tall Shirley. No ambitions for what he could never achieve or deserve in Leroy. I envied him.

When I sat down in my usual place, Lynette tilted her head toward them. Shirley had love in her eyes. Leroy had this look of resignation in his as though he had found somebody he could make himself settle for.

Big Billy, in his overalls—the only pants that would fit him—and straw farmer's hat, was back at Nothing To Lose. He must have gotten barred from one of the other bars. Billy would go to a bar, stay quiet, then start mouthing off about something, and one of the other patrons would want to whip his ass. Sometimes women threatened to whip his ass. He was on his third or fourth round of regular stops, and his suspension from Nothing To Lose was up. He was bothering the teachers.

The teachers were actually a group of professors from Lamar University. Because of the world they lived in, they had maintained the drinking habits they had learned as undergraduate and graduate students. In fact, their schedules were close to mine. Because they didn't think the patrons of Nothing To Lose would understand what they actually did for a living, they called themselves teachers and not professors. One of the men was about to profess to Billy, so Lynette called to Billy and told him to come sit his ass at the bar. Most of us at Nothing To Lose liked the professors but commented that they didn't live in the real world, that they couldn't do anything practical or useful. One of us envied their unreal world and wished that he could have found himself in it. They had escaped with thought rather than with money and empty, misplaced hope. If not for

Victoria, if not for my divorce, if not for . . .

I couldn't be one of the teachers, and I wasn't sure if I was a part of the bar people. Beaumont is an incestuous, cliquish town. As much as everyone bitches about "Boremont," no one ever seems to leave. The young look forward to going off to college, but always return. So their whole lives, residents of the Golden Triangle know only the Golden Triangle. It's as though the world beyond the Pine Curtain is much too large to be trusted.

Since I was never really a part of this area, I started to think that I needed to expand my horizons, to get to some other bars, make new and maybe better friends. Then I heard Lynette talking to Leroy and Shirley: "My third husband got tired of me after five or six years. Now look at me, and imagine me ten years younger. Would you get tired of me? But that two-timing bastard did. He starts getting into these Internet swinging clubs. And posting my photo to bring women over to our mobile home, and then we'd have a ménage à trois. Well, I finally got smart. I told that bastard I wasn't eating no more pussy and left his sorry pervert ass."

Besides better friends, I came back from the Hill Country wanting better work. Before I could even start, though, I knew that at least I had to find out what happened to Harry. As I thought that, D. Wayne came in the door and spotted me from across the room. Behind him a huge black man with a shaved head that looked like an inverted bucket came in. I mean the man's neck was bigger than his head. He tilted kind of sideways when he walked; no doubt trying to squeeze his wide shoulders into tight spaces, and for a man that big, any place indoors was a tight space.

The last of the sunlight coming in through the window reflected off D.'s rings and his huge companion's head as they crossed the room to me. D. Wayne must have changed his hat for the cool front. He now wore a black felt hat in the same style as the straw one. I was guessing that he probably had them made for him.

When he got close to me, D. Wayne stuck out his ring-heavy hand, and I shook it. He sat by me, and bucket head stood behind him. I nodded a hello, and the large man nodded a hello to me. "This big nigger is my tax man," D. Wayne said. When my look showed that I didn't understand, he explained. "You owe me and don't pay. You make a promise and don't keep it. My taxes are due. He collects my taxes." The large tax man nodded.

"So you figure I owe some taxes?"

D. Wayne smiled. "You just missed some work. We got things to do to catch up. You know I explained the arrangement to you."

I didn't want to add that I never agreed to the arrangement, so I just said, "I needed a vacation, just some time to get away."

"You just used up your vacation, and your sick leave. You got no more. We need to get back to work."

"What do you have in mind?"

D. Wayne smiled to me and then to the large man. "I thought with your vacation, you might have figured something out and might have something to tell me."

I tried to make my mind cover the case. "The police found sand instead of dirt in Harry's house. So they think it was someone up north of here. The cops are still looking for somebody with a name or a trace of that really cheap-cut cocaine." Lynette showed up to take D. Wayne's and the tax man's orders. Bucket head got a beer, and D. Wayne his usual large glass of scotch and water.

"I got a name. See, I ain't been sitting on my ass vacationing." D. Wayne sipped his drink. I just stared at my beer. "But I want some confirmation on this name, and I want some more information."

"What would the name be?"

D. Wayne leaned back and folded his arms. "I thought maybe you could confirm it."

I felt my face split into a shit-eating grin.

"Excuse me," I said. "I've got to go to the men's room." I wanted my mind to stop worrying and start thinking. I had to cross somebody, to hold back some information from somebody, but I didn't know who was the most dangerous to me. Now, with the large tax man smiling behind my back, I knew who presented the most immediate danger.

I felt both their sets of eyes on my back as I walked into the men's room. I stepped up to the urinal beside Big Billy. He immediately started annoying me, trying to get into some sort of conversation about the teachers.

"Leave 'em alone, Billy," I said. "They didn't ask you over."

I heard the door swish open, and a voice, "You, fat man. You're finished.

Shake it and get out of here." Billy looked around, shook, and left. In midstream, I turned to see D. Wayne's big pal. Unlike a teenager's, my stream immediately stopped. "Relax, man," bucket head smiled.

Then D. Wayne stepped in. "Finish your business, then we'll finish ours."

I turned my attention back to the urinal, my mind relaxed, and my stream started. Then my kidney exploded. My knees buckled. But before I hit the ground, another explosion went off in my right temple, and then my right eye went blind.

Before I hit the ground, I pissed along the side of the wall and on my pants. As I curled on the tiles I pissed on myself and in a little puddle beside me. I felt like I was pissing blood.

Almost as bad as my blind eye and the explosions in my kidney and temple were the smell and feel of the floor. People had pissed on the buckled, pried-loose, cracked linoleum for years. Without repair, the boards beneath the linoleum and the linoleum itself were rotten and mildewed. So I also felt nauseous. I stopped pissing and rolled over. The linoleum was under the side of my head, and I tried to point my nose away from it. My right eye got its sight back, and I saw D. Wayne and the tax collector standing over me.

D. Wayne motioned to the tax man. "This here nigger likes eating pussy more than any nigger I ever knew. Hell, he probably likes eating pussy more than any white man does. You know how you white boys are about eating pussy. But you know what he likes more than eating pussy?"

I could only shake my head. D. Wayne looked at the big, pussy-eating nigger, who said, "I like beating up punk white boys. Makes me feel like I'm getting even for all the wrong done my race." He reached down, grabbed a hold of my shirt with his two hands, and jerked me up like I was a rag doll.

D. Wayne said, "You like fucking niggers? That it? 'Cause I told you the deal. You ain't got a choice. You my partner, man. So you not only like fucking niggers, you like fucking partners?" The pussy-eating nigger dropped me, and my knees damn near buckled, but I was able to stiffen them and stand up. I felt the wet thighs of my jeans.

My instincts told me to talk; my mind took over and told me to shut the fuck up. No telling how much trouble I could get myself into. "Now, this big nigger ain't gonna whip your ass no more if you play straight with me. But . . ." D. Wayne held up a finger in front of my face. "If you ever talk to my momma again. You ever ask questions about me. He gonna give up pussy eating for whipping your ass." The big nigger just nodded.

D. Wayne held up another finger. "Two. I ain't got shit. All I got is what you got from Lee. And that includes a name. That name is Bruce. You know Bruce?"

I was done protecting Bruce. He knew the game was dangerous when he got involved. He should have stuck with the tattoos and the piercings. "He comes in here. Hell, he'll probably be in tonight, later."

D. Wayne nodded. "Now you doing better. What else you got to tell your partner?"

I didn't dare lie. My mind told me I couldn't outfight him, but I could probably outbullshit at least the big guy. I told him what I knew before I left for the Hill Country, what had scared me into trying to resurrect my past life. "You can understand a middleaged white man looking forward to his golden years, can't you? Well, with you making me a partner, with Lee telling me there's turds floating in Harry's flooded life, with the Hudsons giving me pause and making me think that maybe my newfound partner is as true-bluest as I can get; I decided that golden is connected to leaving."

The big guy nodded to D. Wayne, "I can see that."

"But a truer-blue partner than you told me that I was looking at things wrong. I think that you're looking at it wrong, too."

D. Wayne pulled back from me. The tax collector pulled back his fist. "Wait, wait, wait. You've made me piss my pants and go blind in one eye, so you made your point with the beating part." The big nigger's eyes didn't look like he wanted to hit me. "What we all forgot was that this shit storm ain't about justice, or Lee, or you and Lee getting along all right, or me, or the Hudsons. It's about the fact that Harry got fucked more than he deserved. The only one so far has kept that in mind is that nice lady you been lucky enough to get."

"You a lawyer, huh?" The big nigger said.

"Okay, you're being sweet enough," D. Wayne said. "You whispering in my ear. But you got any more?"

"I think my partner and I, with the help of your colleague here, ought to have a conversation with Bruce."

"See, ain't that easy?" D. Wayne said.

The big nigger smiled and dusted me off. "You ought to pull out your shirttail, hide that piss spot on your pants. Maybe go outside and let it dry out a little."

"You got a name?" I asked.

"Buttermilk," he said. I looked at him and then at D. Wayne to see if I ought to ask why.

"Go ahead," D. Wayne said. "We all partners now. Ask your other partner why he called Buttermilk."

Buttermilk smiled, "'Cause buttermilk taste a little like pussy. Got that name in high school, just before I got kicked out for beating the shit out of a white boy for teasing me about eating pussy."

✦

When Bruce was writhing on the floor with piss on his pants, I stepped back and let D. Wayne and Buttermilk conduct the interrogation. Bruce kept saying, "I don't know what the fuck you guys are talking about." Then Buttermilk stepped on Bruce's chest and gently stood. Bruce couldn't get any air in or out.

The piss on my pants having dried, I thought that I'd better intervene. So I squatted, again smelling the cracked, split, mildewed, piss-stained linoleum. "Bruce, look, you fucked up. Or maybe you didn't fuck up. Say things just conspired to fuck you over. Like me, you got to accept the inevitable. The inevitable is that unless you tell us something that guy standing on your chest starts jumping. I'd like to help. But if I do, then he starts jumping on my chest."

Buttermilk chuckled but stepped off of Bruce's chest. "Now like I told you before. This whole ugly incident has a positive side. Neither of these guys are cops. So you are in the clear."

Bruce tried sucking some air in but only wheezed. Some of his facial piercings seemed like they'd pop right out of his skin. From trying to breathe, from the blood rushing to his head, Bruce seemed to be swelling. "Now just answer a few questions."

Before he said anything to Bruce, D. Wayne looked at me, "That was impressive. I think we got a good partnership here."

"What, you two are partners?" Bruce asked. Buttermilk kicked him with his toe, and Bruce curled up.

"Bruce, can you stand up?" I asked. Bruce tried to stand but shook as he got his legs under him. "Go back to sitting, Bruce."

Big Billy walked in. As big as he was, he must have had a small bladder or a big prostate. Buttermilk smiled at him, Billy smiled back, looked down at Bruce, looked at the urinal, then backed out.

"Maybe we ought to go sit in my car," D. Wayne said. Buttermilk grabbed Bruce by the front of his shirt, just as he had grabbed me, and hoisted him to a standing position.

"Can you walk?" I asked Bruce.

"It don't matter. He can be drug out," D. Wayne said, and led the way out of the bathroom. I stepped to one side to let Buttermilk drag Bruce through the door. Once we were back in the bar, Buttermilk stood Bruce up and guided him toward the front door. With most of the eyes watching us, I ducked because I feared I'd be the one barred instead of Billy.

Once outside, Bruce twisted and broke free of Buttermilk. Maybe his muscle building made him try to hit Buttermilk. Maybe his faulty reasoning told him that he had to strike back. Maybe instinct took over. But he was soon lying semiconscious on the ground, writhing in the gravel-and-mud parking lot. Buttermilk picked him up. While D. Wayne held open the back door of his Lincoln, Buttermilk threw him in. "Goddamn, you ignorant pussy-eating nigger," D. said to Buttermilk. "I told you not to knock 'em cold. That's a leather interior. They get it all muddy and then puke or piss in there, you know how hard it is to clean it out? In fact, he piss or puke, you gonna be cleaning it out."

D. Wayne and Buttermilk got in the front seat, and I got in the back seat next to Bruce. As D. Wayne cranked the motor, I looked out to the edge of the parking lot, out by the trees, and saw Big Billy pissing.

Nothing To Lose had just one tall street lamp to cover the entire parking lot. Beneath it was a perfect halo, almost like a spotlight in a theater. D. Wayne, used to such lights, probably scouting the place before he ever pulled up the first time, parked at the periphery of the halo. He could see, but not be seen.

The night was cool. So D. Wayne hit the driver's control and the windows rolled down. We stared as Big Billy walked past us back on his way to the bar to refill his bladder. The cool air revived Bruce, and he looked dejectedly at me. I heard a buzz and then slapped at the mosquitoes. So did Buttermilk and D. Wayne. We were all swatting instead of talking. D. Wayne rolled up the windows and turned on the air.

Bruce looked dejected. "I can't rat on nobody. I couldn't do that and make any business."

"So don't rat," I said before Buttermilk could punch him. "Just answer a question. I want some cheap cocaine. I'm thinking of adding it to my meth." Buttermilk and D. Wayne looked at me like I was either cool or crazy. "Now could you get me some?"

Bruce looked at all of us. I started again. "We're not cops. You know that. We ain't going to tell cops shit. Cops can't whip our asses like that big gentleman in the front seat just whipped your ass and mine. So the cops can't make us talk. And we . . ." I hesitated. "We got nothing to hide, like you do, so the cops can't threaten us with anything. So could you have a conversation with me about where I might get some bad coke to go with my meth?"

"Yeah, I could."

"Good, good," D. Wayne said. "See how simple it is." Then he faced Buttermilk. "You know if most people would just see reason, I wouldn't need your ugly ass."

"People ain't reasonable," Buttermilk mumbled.

"Okay," I said and scowled at my new partners. "Did you ever sell any of your real cheap-ass cocaine to Harry Krammer?"

Bruce looked around, and then panicked. "Hey, I know where you're going. I didn't kill him. I had nothing to do with killing him."

"We're not the cops, Bruce. Remember? I ain't asked you about a killing. I'll cut to the chase here. I know that you didn't kill him because you were here same as me the night he was killed."

Bruce calmed himself a little as he tried to push his skewered reasoning into working. Buttermilk interrupted Bruce's reasoning and my interrogation. "With all the people with pissed-on pants, it's beginning to smell acidy in here."

I didn't have to say anything. "Would you shut the fuck up, you ignorant nigger?" D. Wayne said. "Maybe the three of us together could whip your ass."

Bruce smiled.

"Bruce, I know you didn't kill him. Just play *hypothetical* with me."

Bruce's face scrunched up like he didn't know what hypothetical meant. "Now what I'm asking is if I wanted some better cocaine than what you got, who would I see?"

"There's a lot of people."

"Who do you get yours from? Whose do you cut?"

He said the word before he even knew that he had said it: "Jewel."

D. Wayne leaned toward Bruce. "What? What did he say. Some sort of jewels?" He looked at Buttermilk as though to tell him to start beating on Bruce again.

"We need some more explanation about this Jewel, Bruce," I quickly said.

"Jewel McQueen."

"You mean Jules?" Buttermilk asked.

"No, Jewel," Bruce said and spelled it out.

"He's got to be a white man. Who else but some backwoods hillbilly would name a child that?" D. Wayne said. "So we know, whoever he is, he ain't smart."

"And how would I get ahold of Jewel McQueen?" I asked.

Bruce's mind got jumbled or he just gave up. "All I know is he comes by this bait shop and store up between Buna and Silsbee. I just call up there and leave a message when I want him."

"Where does he live?"

"I don't know."

"But he probably lives up north of here, along a river bottom. He could get sand on his shoes."

"He doesn't live here is all I know. I don't know if he has sandy fucking shoes or not." Bruce looked around him.

"So did you ever connect Harry with Jewel McQueen?"

"They met."

"Did you ever sell anything to Harry?"

"No. Well, once or twice. I knew him but hardly not at all. I just called the store, got a call from Jewel, and gave him Harry's number."

"What's Jewel look like?"

"Scrawny little fucker. And he's a guy, not a girl." Bruce laughed. "Like you said, what kind of mother would name her son Jewel?"

"Any more questions?" I asked D. Wayne.

D. Wayne nodded at Buttermilk. Buttermilk reached over from

the front seat and shook Bruce's hand. "Sorry, man. No hard feelings," Buttermilk said.

"See there, man. All you got to do is answer the questions," said D. He looked at Bruce, then he looked at me.

"Go put some ice on your head and clean yourself up," I told Bruce. Bruce looked at me, then opened the door and stepped out.

"Same advice to you, partner," D. Wayne said. "Tomorrow, we got a business meeting at the Pig Stand on Calder. Nine in the a of m. Get some sleep."

I stepped out of the car. My partner and his tax man swirled up dust as they drove past me. I wanted to have a really long discussion with Lee. But I had piss-dried pants and an ache in my kidney and head. I wanted one more drink before I went home. And to think, not more than twelve hours before, I was actually missing this goddamn place and these goddamn people.

I didn't go back into Nothing To Lose because I didn't want to explain anything to anyone, so I drove home and sucked on my bottle of Jack Daniels. Luckily, I wasn't pissing blood. Buttermilk knew how to place a punch. So did D. Wayne— and so did Lee Tomlinson.

TWELVE 12

I once drove to Big Bend just to see what that part of Texas was like. For a while I thought that I was on another planet. And once I got accustomed to the area, its deadliness, and its isolation, I knew that I was on another planet. The Chihuahuan desert, with its dry heat, flora, and fauna, can kill you. The East Texas swamps, with their humidity, heat, flora, and fauna, are less likely to kill you but will make you so miserable that you'd wish you were dead. Maybe the environment accounts for our self-destructive acts. I was about to act self-destructively based on my trip to Big Bend.

I was on a hike by myself, and I stepped off the path to piss. I heard the high mountain brush rustle and saw a baby bear cub running toward me. He thought I was his momma. Behind him was his momma. Momma sniffed, reared on her hind legs, and growled.

Big Bend National Park was boasting that it had imported so many Mexican black bears they were starting to be a danger to the tourists. So the park had posters warning tourists not to feed, taunt, or pet the bears. I read one warning that you should never run from a Mexican black bear. They are far faster than humans. Instead of running, you should play like you're a bear.

So, still pissing, I raised my hands and growled back. The cub stopped and ran back to its mother. Momma dropped to four legs, kept one eye on me, and sniffed her cub. When she saw that the cub was okay, she stepped toward me and reared once more. Now I couldn't piss, but I growled back. Momma again dropped to her four paws, turned her ass to me, then ran away with her cub following her.

Just as I had after my confrontation with that bear, I had piss on my pants during my interrogation in the men's room of Nothing To Lose. So the next day I was hoping a bear act might at least keep momma bear D. Wayne and his cub Buttermilk sniffing me instead of running me down and mauling me.

I met them at the Pig Stand on Calder. It was one of the originals. They used to be all over Texas, but now only depressed parts of towns or towns with no rapid growth still had the kitschy-looking predecessors of McDonalds. Without my morning jog to shake me into recognition, repentance, and then acceptance of the night before, my head hurt worse than usual. Of course, besides the usual alcohol, I had been kidney punched and gone blind the night before.

It was hot again, back to Beaumont weather, so I wore my shorts and a T-shirt.

The greetings were cordial, and D. Wayne said, "Glad you got dressed." We sat in a turquoise vinyl booth (the color left over from the last redecoration in the sixties) with some tears spitting out stuffing through a duct-tape repair job. An ancient waitress with stains down the front of her white uniform tried to concentrate hard enough to get our orders right. D. Wayne was by far the most impressive looking of all of us. His black hat was cocked to one side. His white shirt and khakis were starched, and his black boots had a mirror shine. Buttermilk had on nylon workout pants and a T-shirt. After a while sniffing around, D. Wayne cussed the smoke drifting over from the smoking tables. When our breakfasts arrived, Buttermilk just lapped his. As I peered into my coffee and tentatively bit into my breakfast taco, D. Wayne gave orders: "Now, I figure we go drive up toward Silsbee and look for this place where Jewel hangs out or calls from. Then, we have another talk with Bruce to see if he can't remember no more."

I sucked in some air. "Listen, since I don't have a choice in working with you, since I have the experience, I'm giving the orders."

D. Wayne stopped talking. "You don't seem to be too good at what you do."

"So you give the orders and watch me fuck off. You can make me work with you, but you can't make me work well. Now this is what we're going to do."

D. Wayne squinted. Buttermilk looked up from his breakfast as though he was going to have to disrupt it to start punching on me again.

"You and the pussy-eating nigger go up to Silsbee and look around."

"Hey, I told you my name was Buttermilk."

"You and Buttermilk, the pussy-eating nigger, are going to have trouble getting any information because the places you'll be stopping aren't used to dignified black gentlemen asking questions. So you get what you can, and I'll follow up."

Buttermilk dabbed at his oozing egg yoke with a piece of bacon. "D., you gonna let him be telling me what I am and what I ain't gonna do?"

"Shut up. The man is right. The crackers up there ain't gonna want to talk to us two niggers. It's best they don't think we with Roger. Then if he follow up, see, the crackers think there's all kinds of crooks and cops and white and black boys looking for this Jewel. Then maybe they get scared and tell Roger something—after . . . after we impress them a little."

I shrugged. "I ain't a cherry at this."

"I might be busting your cherry you keep calling me nigger. It don't sound right coming out of a old white man's mouth," Buttermilk said.

"You got any objections to just pussy eater?"

Buttermilk smiled, "No, you can call me that."

"So you two have cell phones. So you call me and let me know what's going on."

"If we can get reception up there in hickville, behind the Pine Curtain. Cell phones don't always get reception in them pines," Buttermilk said. "That Sprint man don't like going up there."

"Then we'll use a pay phone," D. Wayne said. "And so what are you going to do?"

"I may just sit here all day and drink coffee. But first, I'm going to jog to clear my head, and then I'm going to go talk to Jessica Hudson."

D. Wayne motioned toward himself. "Why don't you talk to the rednecks and me and Buttermilk talk to the lady?"

"We're a team, remember? Besides, if she sees you and pussy-eating Buttermilk coming toward her, she's liable just to haul ass. Now ask yourself if that ain't right."

D. Wayne nodded in agreement. "So Buttermilk and I are going to go amongst the crackers," D. Wayne said. "I almost wish Buttermilk wouldn't have hit you so hard. I kind of like you now. So it'd be a shame to have to whip your ass again."

I didn't jog, and I didn't go see Jessica Hudson. Instead I drove to the St. Elizabeth's Wellness Center, asked for Lee Tomlinson, and found myself going through the "employees only" door to a waiting room. At the Wellness Center, wearing cargo shorts with the Velcro pocket snaps, I fit right in. Everyone wore shorts, even the fashionable, cheerful young folks who greeted you at the desk.

Lee flowed out of an office door in a red suit. I could see her ex-dancer's body gently outlined behind the red jacket and slacks, and I dropped my head to see her two feet facing outward. She stopped in front of me, pointed her toes out, and said, "Don't start with me, Roger. Don't. I'm sorry."

A red tailored suit. Lee made concessions to conservative style, yet even her concessions were outlandish. "I spent the night pissing blood," I said.

"Well, you just disappeared." She crossed her arms. "And quite frankly, I was a little worried, too. I thought you had run out on us."

"Well, quite frankly, I almost did."

"Roger!" Lee suddenly sucked in some air. "We shouldn't be talking out here." She twirled around. I assumed that she wanted me to follow her into her office. I followed her into her cubicle surrounded by glass walls. I closed the door behind me. Assuming even further, I sat as she did.

"I'm still not sure I want to go through with this."

"D. Wayne may not give you a choice."

"I can just run away, back to Austin."

"You trust me enough not to tell D. Wayne?" She rolled her eyes toward the ceiling and then back at me. She held her wrist out in front of her to check her watch.

"Seems like you and D. Wayne have this figured out so well that you don't need me. Now the only reason I came back was because of Harry. I thought I owed Jessica Hudson something, but now I think I owe him something."

Lee leaned back in her shoulder-high office chair. "You and Harry. If either one of you could ever have just figured out what it is you wanted, you'd both have been hell on wheels."

"You're talking in past tense. I'm still alive."

"You're also older than Harry and set in your ways. I figure you're past tense."

I began to bristle at her. I wondered what gave her her strange powers of manipulating men. D. Wayne and I were both doing her will, as did Harry, when he was alive. Maybe she got that ability when she was a stripper and had men's attention and fantasies. Then I started having a few of my own fantasies about her. I think that she noticed.

"Isn't it enough that we are paying you? If you have no cause or commitment, at least the money ought to interest you."

"It's not worth getting beat up over."

"See, together you and D. Wayne are a perfect team. You're sneaky. He's threatening. You've got your camera. He's got Buttermilk."

"What do you and he talk about?"

"He's a philosopher of sorts. I've got him taking continuing education courses out at Lamar. He's made two As in freshman English. He'll surprise you." She smiled at me, and I wasn't sure it was a smile to show that she was pleased with him or a smile just daring me to fuck with her or D. Wayne.

"Could you just keep me from getting beat up? If I fuck up, why don't you just scold me or cancel the check. Don't send Buttermilk to see me."

Lee chuckled. "Roger, I'm sorry about that remark about your being old. You're probably no older than me. I think we'd be a good match."

I blinked my eyes against the sudden image my brain conjured up. Buttermilk was beating me again as D. Wayne looked on—because I was flirting with his woman.

"Lee, I can't match you in much of anything. And I sure don't want to piss off D. Wayne."

"He hasn't pissed on his territory. I'm with him because I want to be. He knows it." Lee dropped her eyes to think. "At my age, with my life, like you and your life, I can go back to just being alone. Who isn't alone when it really comes down to it? D. Wayne knows this. You know it, too. So D. Wayne knows better than to push me anywhere or any way."

"Sorry," I said. "You kind of scared me."

Lee smiled. "Oh, that's nice to know. Thank you."

"Excuse me, I've got to go do your job."

Lee grinned as I pushed myself out of my chair.

I heard "Come back, anytime," when I closed the door.

Finally, I drove to Caldwell Elementary school and found myself wading through waist-high children to the reception desk. I shouted at taller people about where Jessica Hudson might be. In bits and pieces, I learned that Jessica's class was outside for recess, and she was running copies off in the teachers' lounge. When I stepped in, her eyes widened, a deer caught in headlights. She quickly swivelled her head to look at her colleagues. She mumbled, "No, no, no, not here."

"Could I have a word with you?"

She looked at me with such exasperation I thought she'd wilt. "Not in here. Not in here. Not in here." She led me out of the workroom, down a hall, to her classroom. I found myself watching her well-formed butt working like pistons behind her tight, white jeans. She was an attractive woman, probably a cheerleader, a sorority princess, daddy's favorite daughter, the prize catch all through high school and then into college. Only now was she discovering that even though good looks and youth could be extended and preserved well after college, good luck could not. Her looks, her money, her marriage to a good man just couldn't protect her from plain human calamity. Somewhere in her mind she probably thought that bad things just shouldn't happen to cute, well-to-do, well-married people.

When she entered her room, she twirled around to face me. "Don't ever come here again. This is off base. You can't come in here." Her room had the usual kids' drawings: pictures with presidents, and trite or cute directions, commands, or sayings. But it was also filled with smiley, feel-good, commercially produced motivational photos, drawings, and sayings to help with self-esteem. We had stopped scolding them and barking orders at our children, and now we were begging them to be presentable and sociably acceptable. We conned them with all the self-esteem crap filtered down from Oprah. God forbid that someone like Jessica or a child ever really questioned herself, ever really had to deal with self-doubt. What if you were just stupid, clumsy, lazy, or limited in some way? Like Harry or me, as Lee had said.

"I've got a couple of questions."

"You could call. You could talk to my husband."

I was getting heated up in the Caldwell Elementary School air-conditioning. Everyone involved seemed hurt, worried, or dead; she now seemed indignant and exasperated. She should have felt worse, so I asked, right out, no cushioning easy questions, "What do you know about the cocaine found in Harry's house?"

She gasped and flushed red. "Why, nothing, nothing. I don't know anything." I shifted my eyes from her to the DARE Chicken, a police-sponsored program to con kids into staying off drugs by giving them lectures and twice a year crowding the kids into an auditorium and letting a guy in a chicken suit lead them in screaming cheers. Of course, the program didn't work, but neither the police nor the school board would admit it.

I reached up and scratched at my nose and then rubbed my teeth. She wrinkled her brows as if to ask what I was doing. I was mocking her. "Are you sure that the cocaine wasn't yours?"

"Why, why, why? I teach children. I don't do that. That's impossible." She stamped her foot as though she were an angry cheerleader. She dealt with children and with an engineer husband who saw the world through an intricately designed tunnel. She had no need for complex ideas or coherent answers.

"Have the police asked you the same question?"

She looked at me like I was as dead as Harry and beginning to ripen and stink. "Why of course not. They wouldn't dare." After all, the police were a service organization. They were supposed to support her. They should be polite. To Jessica Hudson, you dealt with the police, with trouble, with a murder, the same as you would with a rude clerk at Dillard's. The customer, the taxpayer, the rich guy is always right.

"They will," I said. "Don't lie to them."

"You better leave."

"Just one more question."

"No more questions, please."

"Do you know Jewel McQueen?" Jessica's eyes darted up as though she were trying to see if sweat were running down her forehead. She rubbed at her teeth with her forefinger. "Jessica, do you know Jewel McQueen?"

Her eyes leveled off on me. "Man or woman? Strange name."

"Are you sure?"

"I'd remember a name like that. Now why can't you do your job and leave me alone? I don't know what you think. But let me remind you that my husband and I are paying you."

"Right now you're paying to find Jewel. That's what I'm doing, same as the police. Same as them, I'm going to have to ask difficult questions."

"Your questions are absurd and insulting."

I nodded to thank her. She looked down at my legs. "We try to encourage the kids to wear slacks," she said.

"I never really grew up in regard to dress. Kids usually forgive me." I left her room just as a tide of children swirled back through the halls. My stomach felt a little queasy.

THIRTEEN 13

My partners got into only three fights with the rednecks behind the Pine Curtain. I had figured as much. They were like the canaries in the mineshaft, better them than me. Somebody in some broke-down store selling beer, tackle, Ding Dongs, reheated frozen pizza, deep-fried everything, and VCR tapes would no doubt say something. D. Wayne and Buttermilk, of course, wouldn't back down, so somebody would threaten or call the cops or actually throw a punch.

D. Wayne described the fights over the cell phone. I decided that I'd go see the fighters who offered the most resistance, the ones most adamant about not talking about Jewel. I got directions from D. Wayne and told him that I'd get on it in the morning. I told him that he knew where to find me if he wanted me later in the evening.

I got a call from Rachel. She wanted to meet me the next day, for lunch. She had some big news for me. Then I got a call from Cody Hudson demanding to see me as soon as possible. I agreed to a later lunch with him at Kampus Korner, a student and refinery workers' restaurant and bookstore next to Lamar University and Exxon's refinery.

I got to Nothing To Lose just as the sun was setting. As I stepped up to the front door, the door flew open, knocking me back, and a man came running out. As he passed, he whirled around and pointed at Lynette, who was now standing in the open doorway while I held the door open for her. She said, "Get your ass out of here before I call the cops."

His arm out, forefinger extended, the man yelled, "Whoremongers, perverts, drunks, the Lord shall punish you all. In the name of the Lord, I condemn you."

"And I condemn your ass outa here," Lynette said.

"Whoremongers, perverts, drunks . . ." the man started again, but

Lynette threw a pitcher of water on him, soaking him and stopping his speech.

"Now get your ass outa here!" she said.

The man backed away, across the parking lot, then he unlocked the chain holding his bicycle to a tree and pedaled off. As Lynette and I watched him dwindle down the road, she said, "He met Zia."

Inside, with a beer in front of me, I listened to Zia's version of the story. He had done nothing, just offered the man some dirty pictures, and he went into this tirade. After Zia calmed a little, he said to me, "You know, no more money in dirty books or movies. Now it's all Internet. I need to get a website."

I let him exhaust his sales pitch, and finally he left me to bother someone else. Lynette then leaned across from me to annoy me with her questions. She remembered the previous night. She asked me what I had done to Bruce and who my two new friends were. I stumbled through an answer but could really give nothing. "If they're going to be regulars, they're gonna have to spend less time in the bathroom," Lynette said. "Billy was about to bust his bladder." I nodded. I was tired. I hadn't jogged. I decided to head home early.

Three beers later, I walked to my truck, parked under the yellow halo of the one streetlight in the parking lot. As I stepped into the halo and opened the truck door, someone grabbed me. I twisted and his hands slipped until he only had a grip on my shirttail. When I heard the rip I yelled, "Okay asshole, that's a new shirt you owe me."

Before I could get a good glimpse of his face, he rammed me with his head and butted me into my truck. My feet slipped on the gravel and I fell to my knees. I was still trying to get my feet back under me when Bruce closed one hand around my throat, his other hand cocked above him. At that moment, with shorts on, I was more worried about my skinned knees than Bruce's fist cocked above me. "I got to do this, Roger."

"Wait," I yelled. "Got to do what?" The halo became a spotlight, and Bruce and I had to act out some drama that was in his mind but not mine.

"What kind of respect would I have if I let you fuck me like that and not do anything?"

I could have twisted out of his grasp, struggled, run, but instead, because we did drink at the same bar, because he did have a point, I tried to argue. "Okay, I see your point. Why don't I just tell everyone you whipped my ass?"

"Just one punch. One punch is all I want. I don't really want to whip your ass. Just once. Sit still and take it."

I raised my hands and slowly raised myself. My knees groaned with pain. I looked down at them. "Isn't it enough that you skinned my knees?" I asked.

Bruce was proud of his muscles and figured that they gave him the same sort of power as Buttermilk. Of course, he wouldn't have dared to take Buttermilk on. So I resigned myself to take the punch, to be a part of his drama, performed under the lights of Nothing To Lose's parking lot. My brain agreed. At least I was standing now.

But when Bruce pulled back his arm, and the punch was just starting, my instincts overruled my brain. Fuck that, I said to myself, then reached up and grabbed the gold loop in Bruce's eyebrow. I yanked.

Bruce's hand hit the side window of my truck and cracked it. Then he started dancing in front of me, shaking his right hand and pressing his left hand against his eyebrow. I kept my eyes on Bruce and, with my thumb and forefinger, felt the gold loop in my hand. I felt some stiff hairs and a lump of what was no doubt eyebrow meat.

I stood up and couldn't think of what else to do but hold out Bruce's eyebrow loop. "Here, I don't want to drop it and lose it."

Bruce tried to punch me. But he kept his hand over his left eye, and his aching right fist missed me. Instinct again took over. I gave him a forearm shiver. I bent my wrist back and planted the heel of my palm at the point where his nose met his forehead. Cops used that punch quite a bit. He jerked back and put both hands over his nose, and I saw not only the bloody lump of jagged eyebrow but a spray of blood across his chin and on to the top of his white, body-hugging T-shirt. We both had ruined shirts now. "We're even on the shirts," I said.

Besides the lisp created from his tongue stud, Bruce now talked in a high nasal voice. "What is with you? Why you want to fuck me?" My forearm shiver was too low and had hit him in the bridge of the nose instead of the forehead. I feared that I had broken his nose.

Tired, disgusted, resigned to being a fuckup, Bruce stepped out of the spotlight, to the edge of the halo where the light met the dark, and just plopped his ass down on the gravel and started shaking his head.

"I'm sorry, Bruce."

"Fuck you," he said.

"Well, if you hadn't tried to hit me."

"Why can't you cooperate?" Bruce asked. I could barely understand him.

"I tried."

I lowered the tailgate to my truck and helped Bruce up; then we both sat on my tailgate in the light where I could see his bloody, pulpy face. "You need to get out of the drug business. You ain't cut out for it."

"I ain't cut out for nothing," Bruce said, no doubt forgetting his muscles, tattoos, shaved head, various piercings, and Harley, and sinking into the self-doubt that sent him into his muscles, tattoos, shaved head, piercings, and Harleys—and drug dealing.

I felt so sorry for him that I wanted to circle my arm around his shoulder, like a pal. I also felt guilty, like I had broken some brotherhood of the bar. At Nothing To Lose and a dozen others like it in Beaumont, and hundreds others like it in East Texas, we were a fraternity of losers, hard luckers, fuckups, social outcasts. We had started up the ladder of success, lost our holds, and slid back down. "Look, I'm sorry about D. Wayne and Buttermilk. I had no choice. I had to let that happen. All I could hope for was that it would be quick." Bruce started nodding, making the blood flow more quickly.

"I didn't give you the whole story," he said.

He shouldn't talk to me anymore about his involvement in the drug business if he wanted to remain safe, but he couldn't help it. So I took advantage of his need. "The more you tell me, the more I can cover your ass," I lied.

"I maybe seen Jewel McQueen twice my whole life. All I did was to call this place, and some old man would pass along a message. I'd get a phone call back. Jewel would always call from a different place. My call waiting always had different numbers."

"You remember any numbers?"

"Not now."

"You got a computer?" Bruce looked at me real funny, then nodded his head, making blood drip onto his chest. But Bruce no longer noticed his own blood. "You e-mail me the numbers. Just the numbers, nothing else. Then I delete your message." Bruce looked at me like he wasn't sure. I put my arm around him. "Look, you're a bust at drug dealing. But maybe you're good at my line of work. You send me another e-mail with the price you'd usually get for an eight ball of coke. I'll pay you that amount for information—in cash—when I get my money." I patted his shoulder opposite me. "What do you say?" Bruce nodded. "Now since I'm paying you, and you got another expertise, one that ain't nearly as dangerous as selling drugs, one that's legal, well sort of, you need to tell me some more." I waited.

"Like I said," Bruce said after a moment, "I never did see much of Jewel McQueen. But from what I hear, he ain't no problem. You just be careful of his brother Sunshine if you go after Jewel."

"Who is Sunshine?"

"He's an ex-con. Went up for murder. Twice. They say he ain't right in the head. They say he's real protective of Jewel."

"Who is *they*?"

"The other people I get drugs from."

"I don't need to know who they are right now. But I may. Who are your customers?"

Bruce started shaking his head.

"Tell me about one. Harry Krammer."

Bruce started nodding his head. "My nose hurts. I think you scarred me for life."

"Tilt your head back and let me take a look." Bruce tilted his head. Both his nose and eyebrow looked like they had stopped spurting and were just dripping blood. I gently touched his eyebrow and his nose, and Bruce whimpered. I feared I had scarred him for life. "You're fine," I said. "About Harry?"

Bruce looked at his bloody hands. "My nose okay?"

"Fine."

"Harry and I both worked with kids. My day-care center kept getting a kid with bruises. His mother got her welfare and child care from Harry. I just knew him. That's all."

"Then one day, out of the blue, and I don't know where he even gets this idea, he asks me where he can get some coke. I mean, in his position he shouldn't be doing illegal drugs. . . . Then he wants a slightly better grade. So I give his name to Jewel. I just start delivering. Then, I think, he starts getting stuff direct from Jewel. Jewel drives in and delivers it."

"You think Jewel killed him for not paying his tab?"

"I don't know. Maybe somebody like Sunshine did. But Jewel, the few times I seen him, just looked scared."

I didn't want to ask any more, but I did. "Do you think he could have shot Harry for any other reason?"

He shrugged and a few drops of blood splattered on his shirt. "I'm bleeding again."

"Don't worry; answer the question."

"Are the cops going to find me and start asking me these questions?"

"The cops don't have people like D. Wayne and Buttermilk—or me, for that matter, asking the questions. So I'm not going to lead them to you."

"To tell the truth, I don't think Harry ever was interested in any kinda drugs until that woman come into his life, that Jessica."

"Did you know her?"

"She works with kids, too. I sold her stuff before I sold anything to Harry."

Before I could lead Bruce onward, Lynette stepped into the porchlight at the front door of the bar. She turned our way. "Who is that? What y'all doing?" she yelled.

"It's me, Roger," I yelled back. "And Bruce."

She walked toward us and stepped into our pool of light. Bruce raised his head and smiled.

"Oh my God, what happened to you?"

"He fell," I said.

"Good God." Like the bar's mother hen, she reached out very gently and tilted Bruce's head back. "My God, my, my, my. Wait here." She ran back into the bar and came out with one bar towel filled with ice and another dry one. "Put that ice on your face and keep it there."

She stepped away and squared herself. Her eyes stayed on me instead of on bleeding Bruce. Maybe a part of her job, the unwritten part, or maybe just a part of her that made her a good bartender, was her role as confidant, bouncer, nurse, counselor, and high priestess. On the edge of our halo, she got better looking to me. "Roger, you get him to a hospital, now."

We both helped Bruce into the cab of my truck. When I said, "Try not to get any blood on the seats," Lynette slapped at me.

She said, "Serve you right to have your whole cab filled with blood for your 'discussions' with him the last two nights. I know what happens in my bar. Now get his ass to the hospital. It's the least you can do after you beat him all to shit."

She circled to the driver's side as I started the car and said, "I'm thinking of barring you, not Big Billy." Then she smiled. I pulled out into the darkness, drove to St. Elizabeth's Hospital, and stepped with Bruce into the bright searchlight of the emergency room.

FOURTEEN 14

As my feet sank into the carpet of long, wet weeds instead of slapping gravel as they had two days before, my mind cooperated with my body. As old as I was, that still happened when I jogged. Sometimes. I pondered my plight in rhythm with my footfalls.

Jessica and Cody Hudson were upset because all their cushioning cash couldn't soften their fall into bad times. The same cash that had bought upper-middle class and truly rich Beaumonters youth, good looks, and health had sucked their souls right out from their stomachs, where their souls and the souls of those like them resided. Or maybe, instead of souls, they had simple faiths: the right memberships (church, club, or civic groups), family values, the sanctity of business, the MBA, the right private schools, the manners of the upper-middle class.

The folks like me down at Nothing To Lose believed ourselves to be graduates of the school of life. But our school of life was like a remedial class. We had just a little basic training, no real education. Deep down, we knew that we were just too ignorant, too uncultivated, or too parochial to deal with all that life could throw at us. So we didn't duck life, as our social and financial betters did, but we were very wary of it. We knew, eventually, life would just beat us down.

And here I was, slapping soft mud and weeds, wishing that I could find some of Jessica and Cody's comfort, but unable to get my sorry ass out of Nothing To Lose. Thinking too much, my mind took too much of my concentration and rhythm from my feet, and I stumbled. On the way down, a thought made me wince; eventually I might even have to give up jogging. Instead of rolling, as I knew I should do, I skidded–on my hands and knees. When I came to a stop on my already skinned, muddy knees and palms and began sinking into the ooze, I felt the night's long stay with Bruce, the booze, and the early morning sourness in my stomach. I stayed hunched over to puke.

With an empty stomach, I struggled to my feet and continued, pushing myself to jog farther down my trail. Emily Nguyen was waiting for me at the end of the canal and Tram Road. She had pulled her car off the road and leaned against it, her arms crossed. "You look awful," she said. "Maybe you ought to take a day off of jogging."

"I needed to take the night before off."

"I heard you had some trouble."

"A little."

"Want to talk about it?"

I crossed my arms. "So if I show you mine, then you'll show me yours?"

"If yours is big enough."

I said nothing, so we had to stare at each other. "Look, Emily, let me say a name. You tell me if you have it."

"Let's hear the name."

"Jewel."

"I've got it."

"How did you get it?"

"How did you get it?" she retorted. "Wait, don't answer that. I don't want to know so I don't have to explain."

"He's a nice boy, from what I hear."

"Roger, don't play cowboy on me. Let the police do it."

"You get to be the cowboy, right?"

"Please, let me know what you are up to." I stared down at my wet, muddy, expensive jogging shoes. "You're not going to, are you?" When I didn't answer, Emily said, "What's become of our relationship?"

"You're not leaving me for another photographer, are you?"

Emily shook her head. "I hear you're playing with some dangerous people."

"I thought you were dangerous."

"I'm not like that."

"You're a good woman, Emily."

"I'm nothing of the sort."

"Then you're my favorite kind of a woman."

"Why do I bother with you?" Emily uncrossed her arms and sidestepped, barely ducking, into her patrol car. "You will call, right?"

"I will call, right. Especially after all we've been through together."

"Be careful, Roger. Get some sleep or stop drinking or stop jogging. You look sickly." Then she churned up enough mud to splatter my shins with mud and gravel.

When I walked up to my house, my landlady, Dottie Phillips, was waiting for me. She got out of her car and waved some checks at me. "I don't have yours. Where is your rent?"

"Oh Jesus," I said.

"Don't say that. Don't take the Lord's name in vain. Where is your rent?"

"I forgot."

"For two months?"

I asked Dottie to step inside with me while I wrote a check to her. As we entered, my frustration overcame the usual calm that jogging forced on me. Lately, my calm lasted less and less time. "Why is it that everybody wants to disrupt my jogging routine?" I found myself asking myself. "This is supposed to be my cooldown."

"You should get a treadmill or start swimming. Jogging is hard on your joints," Dottie said as she sucked on her cigarette. She didn't even bother to put it out when she stepped into my house, which was, I guess, technically her house. But still, I was living there.

I started turning over slips of paper, picking up shoes, shoving the accumulated mail off the dining room table, trying to find my checkbook. "You know, I can get you a maid."

"I don't need a maid," I said.

"That's a debate," Dottie said.

I finally found my checkbook and started writing in the amount for two months' rent. Dottie found a chair, pushed off some of my clutter, including a CD I had been looking for, and sat down. When I finished, I handed the check to her. She looked at it as if to see if it was made of rubber.

"You can throw it down and see if it bounces," I said.

"Don't be funny," she said.

I was hoping that her business was done and that I could be done with her. But she looked up at me with aging doe eyes and said, "Roger, I switched churches."

The look in her eyes told me that this was serious. I imagined, for a moment, that she had become a follower of some Muslim sect. "I've been going to the Baptist Church instead of the Assembly of God," she said.

My brain, tiny and used up, rattled around inside my skull as I tried to make sense of what she said. She hung her head and made her confession. "I think that I would have better luck finding a man in the Baptist Church. And I have. A gentleman has met me for lunch now twice. Not just Luby's, but nice places." I found myself wondering why I was the one she chose to receive such earth- and heaven-shattering news. "I didn't mean to. I don't mind the Baptist Church, and it's not all that different, and I've started dabbing on some more make up."

"Dottie, in the long-term scheme of things, I don't think it's going to make much difference."

"Do you think God will care?"

"Why do you ask me?"

"You always seemed smart to me. You know things. So you must know about religion."

I sucked in air. What I sucked in was hot air that made me angry for having my cooldown disrupted. "I don't think God will care." I said, and then kept on going. "Your choice isn't exactly earth shattering. God is thinking about a lot."

"I knew you were smart," she said.

But I couldn't stop. "No one really wants their religion bad enough anymore. It's all so easy. Used to you had to give up something, sacrifice a child before God would have you. Hell, look what God did to his own son. Now ain't he a bastard for that?"

Dottie's mouth dropped open. "Jesus, oh no, I mean 'shoot.' Look what you've done to me. Don't say that. Don't even think that. Don't say those things."

She rose up from her chair, looked at me, and backed toward the door.

I backed up a little, too. "Maybe what I mean is that God is busy, and he just wants us to figure out what we can on our own."

"But we have to take Jesus as our Savior."

"Take what you want, Dottie. I can't give you any answers. I can't say and don't know and don't care."

She gasped, backed toward the door, and when she opened her mouth, I thought that she was going to evict me. "You better start thinking about your soul," was all she said.

I hung my head and nodded. "I know. My soul is in terrible shape."

Dottie inched back toward me. "Would you like me to console you? To pray for you?"

"No, Dottie. No Dottie, please," I said.

"Maybe you could go to church with me. Maybe you could meet a nice lady. The Lord will help you if you ask him to, and church is the right place to ask."

"And to pick up some ass?"

"I wouldn't put it like that. But you meet nice people in church."

"Thank you Dottie, thank you. I've got to get to work, but you think about this for me."

Dottie Phillips smiled for me and at me and then left me to wrestle with my soul. What I wrestled with was that I didn't want to deal with Harry Krammer or Lee or D. Wayne. Lock your problems up with you in your own setting, and don't let other people's problems into your house.

✦

Rachel actually smiled at me during lunch at Brad's Place. She tried to hide the smile, but the edge of her mouth twittered, and then there it was, a smile, as though she actually did recall something good about me. With a tiny shred of lettuce at the corner of her grin, she said, "I see that you tried to dress for the occasion."

"What do you think?" I held my arms back to show her that I was studying my appearance. I had put on my best shorts, a pair of expensive sandals from Dillard's that some coed sales clerk told me were cool, and a Hawaiian shirt.

The smile spread all across her face as she said with delight, finally, rather than disdain, "You're improving."

"Buy some slacks," she added. "You'll need them." Then she pulled her briefcase onto the black marble top of the former junior high lab table and beamed. "I've got your life fixed."

Brad's Place was Beaumont's answer to fine dining. Brad had gone to culinary school and worked as a chef in New York. But the same weird luck, homing instinct, or fate that pulled so many natives back brought Brad back to Southeast Texas. With some money in his pocket and a few unsquashed dreams, Brad bought an old building in Old Town that had once been a grocery store, then a jewelry store, then the studio of an eccentric jewelry maker, then a would-be crack house. Brad patched up the windows, used junior high lab tables, and displayed iron sculptures from local artists. He saved by not printing menus. You walked in the door, stood in line, and read what Brad had prepared for lunch or dinner from a blackboard. The food was good, but just as eccentric as the design. Brad mixed his accumulated experience and knowledge of food and cooking with his memory of Beaumonters' tastes. The result was enormous portions of mostly spicy food. Rachel and I split a salad. I could tell that just my half would coax me toward a nap, and I still had a lunch with Cody Hudson to go.

Rachel peered into her briefcase and pulled out several papers. She laid them beside her plate of salad. She patted them. "This is your new job. This is your ticket back to respectability."

"Who's going to start respecting me?"

"Let's start with me." Rachel actually reached across the table as though she wanted me to take her hand. I did, just as I did in the old days. She paused, looked down at my hand on top of hers, then lifted her eyes to mine. The smile sank and a confused look spread across her face. She had involuntarily reached for me, an old habit, so subtle that neither of us ever really noted it. When we had gone out, she would reach for me, and I would momentarily grab her hand, let it go, then we'd continue our conversation.

Now, I let go of her hand. I had held it too long for then, and I was not supposed to touch it now.

"Let's go slowly," Rachel said.

"Let's say to hell with all this worry. I'll come over tonight."

Rachel hung her head. She pulled her hand into her lap. "Roger, slow down." She ordered, not asked. The delight left her voice.

We both breathed in. "These are depositions. We're loaded down with them. We need help. You're a lawyer."

I thought about my camera and Nothing To Lose. I'm not sure if it was the possibility of a respectable job, or the necessity of associating with proper lawyers, that caught me off balance. "I don't know. I'm not sure."

"What's not to be sure about?" I saw her lips move, but my mind was grinding against my skull, trying to absorb this new development, so I really didn't hear her. "Look, Roger, do you want to spend the rest of your life prowling around at night?" I tried concentrating on hearing her speak, but now the clatter and chatter of Brad's Place interfered. The stereo, tuned to an NPR symphony, was overbearing, and the distance across the top of the black marble junior high lab table made me lean toward Rachel to try to hear her.

All I could do was mumble, "I don't know. I mean this is a big step."

"What do you mean? You're perfect for this. We send you out for depositions. We send you to talk to some witnesses, make some phone calls, just a little help with the activity. You could be our own inhouse private investigator. And you wouldn't be taking your photos anymore. Roger, I've talked to the partners on this. I stuck out my neck."

"Geez, you've got to give me some time. I mean, my job's not exactly pretty . . . or enjoyable . . . or lucrative . . ."

"Or respectable, or safe," Rachel broke in. "I thought that you'd be doing backflips out of joy."

"I am, inside."

"I can see that." Now her disdain was back.

"Just give me a few days," I said.

Rachel grabbed exhibit A, the depositions, and pushed them into her briefcase. "Fine, fine," she said. "If you want to make things like the way they were, then a good start is a new job. While you decide, you keep away from Amber."

"Just this one case, just this one," I said, but Rachel didn't hear me. She stared down at the half-eaten salad and stabbed at some lettuce. She ate. I tried to think of something to say, but my mind got tangled. So we both listened to the symphony.

When we finished eating, Rachel simply turned away from me and left. She did that instead of making a scene. I started thinking back through our relationship. She'd get angry or frustrated at something, and instead of losing her temper and doing something that might embarrass her, she'd turn her back to it. She'd go into the other room, take a timeout, order her thoughts. I remembered her turning away from me quite often. I remembered that she had also paid for the meal.

Rachel had taken me by surprise. No, I had let Rachel take me by surprise. I had let my mind churn its way to the conclusion that I wanted: getting back together, not getting a new job. I'm not sure why I didn't jump up, kiss Rachel, and ask when I was supposed to start. I'm an old dog who knows that new tricks just tax your mind and grind your ass into the dirt. So I guess that I gave Rachel the impression that I'd just as soon piss on her new job. The wail of violins accompanied me out of Brad's Place.

I stared down at another salad, this time Greek, while Cody jabbered at me about my responsibilities and duties and nibbled on his gyro. Somewhere back in the seventies or eighties, entrepreneurs eyed college campuses and decided said campuses needed a Kampus Korner. These were bars, restaurants, bookstores, or coffee shops. Lamar University's KK was a bookstore and a Greek/Mexican restaurant. It was across the street from Lamar, and Lamar was across Martin Luther King Jr. Parkway from the age-old ExxonMobil refinery. So our KK filled with students, faculty, engineers, refinery workers, and the smell of petroleum and fried food. Cody Hudson worked at the Exxon refinery, so KK was convenient for him.

This was a late lunch, so the crowd had cleared out. A kid with several plastic baskets filled with crumpled paper and four empty beer bottles in front of him studied his English literature textbook. Several cooks, spattered with grease and wearing hairnets, circulated between the tables cleaning up.

Cody Hudson had eyed my Hawaiian shirt and said, "Nice costume." So I was really pissed when he said, "Your job was to work with my wife, not to harass her."

I always felt the hair on the back of my neck stand when someone began telling me about my job. In my line, where I basically hire myself out to the morality or lack thereof of my client, I get told about my job quite often. Chunks of feta cheese and breadcrumbs were floating in the combined water and vinegar of my salad. I poked at a tomato with my fork and chewed while I looked at Cody. All that lettuce was twisting into knots in my stomach.

"You're supposed to find this person. This suspect."

I swallowed my tomato chunk and rubbed my palm over my stomach. "How do you know what person? How do you know my progress?"

Cody's eyebrows rose. He stuffed his gyro into his mouth to chew instead of talk. He tried to think as he swallowed. "Jessica told me," Cody said and swallowed. "Jessica said . . . she said."

I wanted to watch him squirm as he tried to outguess me, but the lettuce was twisting, and I felt like I needed to take a sip of some cooled grease that KK used to fry the burritos and fries, just to put an upper and lower stopper on my spoiled salads. So I said, "Jessica didn't really tell me anything. She didn't really know much."

Cody tried to think. "And that is just the problem, the way you approached her, where you approached her. It was as though she were the criminal."

I held out my hands. "Did I imply that? Sorry." Cody turned his gaze back to his gyro. The look on his face showed that he was battling his stomach, too. "But let me ask you. Have you ever heard of a Jewel McQueen?"

Like his wife, Cody had to think, not as to whether he knew Jewel or not, but as to what he should tell me. "I think I've heard the name. But I'm not sure where."

"Think, Cody."

Cody pushed back from me and his sandwich. "Why don't you let me think about it a little at my leisure? If I remember anything, I can call you."

"You mean you could ask Jessica." I wanted to stick my fork into my forehead. Sometimes, my urge to be mean trampled my tactics. Somebody did need to tell me my job. I was glad D. Wayne and Buttermilk weren't here. If they were, I'd probably be getting another ass whipping and puking my lettuce up on them.

"What are you implying here? Let me remind you that I hired you."

I leaned on my elbows across the table and started backtracking. "I'm sorry. I didn't mean to imply anything. I'm just being snotty. I get that way. A character flaw."

"I'm the client here. I'm paying the tab."

"You're not my only client here." I damn near bit my tongue. I would have deserved it for being an asshole and tipping off Cody to my suspicions. Like my father said, I have this thing about moneyed people. My thing was that moneyed people were always letting me know that their money made me the shit hook to catch their floating turds. Cody, like most people comfortable with cash, was way too quick to tell me that his money gave me my orders. And maybe even worse, Rachel wanted me to go to work for a bunch of lawyers who drove Mercedes, BMWs, Humvees, and Cadillac SUVs. I'd be taking orders from their cars, their mistresses, their boats, their tax write-offs.

"Who, whoa, whoa, whoa," Cody said. "You mean, I'm not your only client for this particular case?"

I dropped my head as though to take my ass chewing from my social better. "That's not what I meant. I mean I can be a prick. I get like that."

"If you're working for someone else on this besides me, well, well, that's a violation of ethics. You can't do that." The last part came out like a question.

"I was hung over the day we discussed ethics in private-eye class."

"I'm beginning to wonder if I should shift my money to a more established investigating firm."

I heard a plop. Both Cody and I looked at the kid who was studying. His beer and lunch had gotten to him. Drowsy and a little drunk, he couldn't squeeze his mind or squint his eyes any longer on the book in front of him. He had just dropped his face onto his open book to catch a nap. So much for English literature. Eventually, after he flunked out or got through with a low C average, I'd probably see that kid down at Nothing To Lose. "Let me ask you a question," I said to Cody.

"I don't know if I want to let you ask me any more questions," Cody said, and I respected him a little for his response to the Southern cliché, "Let me ask you a thing or two." I couldn't hide my smile.

"Just why do you care if I find out who killed Harry Krammer? I mean what does it matter to you?"

"I want the police to stop talking to me and my wife. I want all that to let up."

"Come on, Cody. Nobody is going to prosecute you. They need evidence. What have they got? You're a prominent citizen. They don't want to take you and the rich attorney you would hire to court and let some fresh-out-of-law-school assistant county prosecuting attorney blow the case."

"Still, I just want the questions to stop. I want it all to stop."

"And so what, I find a scapegoat? Some poor schmuck to pin the crime on?"

"I'd prefer it be the guilty party. I want justice, too."

I relaxed. "Yeah, an actual guilty suspect would be nice. But short of that, would just anybody do?"

"You're right. You are a prick. But I've invested too much in you already. Go find something out." Cody crossed his arms. "Somebody did this. You find them. Or help the police find him. Just fix it." I was the shit hook.

"Cody, I'm leaving here to track down a suspect. Now you see if you can remember Jewel McQueen, and you ask your wife if she can't remember his name, too." With gobs of lettuce flipping around in my stomach, my mind as rancid as my gut, the student snoring on his book, Cody rubbing his stomach, the sleepy cooks cleaning up my mess, the lazy flies bumping into the screens, I left KK for the parking lot, thinking that I'd throw up on my shoes and the hot asphalt. I planned to drive to the Neches 96. But first I stopped off at Nothing To Lose. It was on the way. Three beers settled and cooled my stomach.

FIFTEEN

It wasn't just that Lumberton had abolished drinking, immorality, and sin from within its city limits that bothered me. It was that the Baptist populace tried so hard to be cute yet sophisticated. Lumberton started to boom when the first waves of white flighters left Beaumont in the early '80s to escape Beaumont desegregation, some twenty years late in coming. Those that didn't go to mid-Jefferson County to smell the refinery fumes escaped Negroes by running to Hardin County and hiding out behind the Pine Curtain. They brought what little money there was to Hardin County and built their guarded communities to protect themselves from the blacks that they ran away from and the white trash they moved in with. As Beaumont schools started to decline without their money, Lumberton grew.

Lumberton was the northernmost stronghold of the good Southeast Texas Baptists, insulating themselves from the realities of the world by cushioning their lives with money and imitating suburbs in big cities. They cleared the choking, thorny vines and brush from under the pines and drained some of the Big Thicket swamp to make way for their pleasant, manicured suburban tracts with their single-gated entrances and cul-de-sacs and loops. In between the white-flight Baptists were the stubborn trailer parks and salvage iron dumps, neither of which could afford to clear the underbrush or even mow the lawns. The new, well-to-do locals then opened cute shops: Bible, flower, knickknack, and pet stores (and other tax write-off businesses for good women). For sophistication, they imported the lower line of franchises: Burger King, McDonald's, a Walmart Supercenter.

Because of the influx of the barely sophisticated, the barely rich, the barely educated, the lily white, Lumberton made a bottleneck of the two north-south running highways on either side of the town: 96 and 69. So as I waited in my Americanized Toyota, jammed in their traffic, I shook with something like an alcoholic tremor.

Silsbee had less money and thus more Pentecostals from behind the Pine Curtain than Lumberton did. Kountze, the county seat, had even less money, but more folks who lived their entire lives in the undergrowth beneath the pines, trying to choke out a living. Silsbee had a good chunk of Village Creek—a pleasant, clean stretch of water—and some bars.

The Neches 96 hunkered under some pines just off of 96, off the frontage road, along a curving Silsbee city road. It had a gravel and dirt parking lot. I had done some research. Its number matched one of the numbers Bruce had given me. I suddenly regretted pulling Bruce's eye jewelry out and perhaps permanently ruining his eyebrow. I felt that I owed him.

I had heard about the Neches 96 from my barstool at Nothing To Lose. Nothing To Lose formed the southern edge of a bar run from the 96, on down the city road to the Tin Roof Bar, over to Jackie's, and then on to Laverne's on 69 in between Lumberton and Kountze, then the Starlight and the Armadillo west of Kountze, toward Honey Island. I never heard of any bars in the actual towns. Silsbee and Kountze, maybe in imitation of Lumberton, pushed the bars to the outskirts of town. Keep the city pure and the drinking confined to the periphery, they must have figured.

As I got out of my pickup, I sized up the Neches 96. Three long, high, blacked-out windows ran along a long wooden building covered with mildew, a typical East Texas bar. I opened the door and immediately shivered from the air-conditioning. I squinted to adjust my eyes to the dark.

To my right was a stage with a long poster of the Dallas Cowboys. On the back wall was a poster of the Houston Texans. The small dance floor was surrounded by folding chairs and card tables, very few of them matching. I turned toward the bar and the whirring of two slot machines.

The Texas legislature outlawed all gambling but the lottery and lotto, and since we chased out all the Indians back in the 1850s, we had no Native Americans to open casinos. What we had were the boats in Louisiana. Here inside our state we could practice with nonpaying computerized slot machines. But sometimes, in the office or backroom, the bar owners might keep a tally of the practicing gamblers' winnings. Sometimes, there were arguments about the record keeping of the winnings. I had heard rumors of fights over these winnings and over illegal cockfights at the Neches 96.

Since Texas didn't want to tax rich people by creating an income tax, the legislature taxed sin. The proceeds from gambling, cigarettes, and alcohol funded schools. So teachers were underpaid and worked in decrepit buildings. The latest scheme was to tax lap dances at strip bars. "Tits for Tots," a headline in the *Austin Chronicle*, an alternative newspaper, said. So the Neches 96, in a way, contributed to the education/indoctrination of our most precious commodity, our airheaded students, like the guy passing out over his literature book back at Kampus Korner.

I felt eyes on me as I walked toward the bar. Even with the wail of a country song, I heard the wooden floor creak under my weight as I made my way across the room. Each creak screamed that I was an outsider. The Neches 96 was far bigger than I imagined. When I sat on a barstool, a waitress with a dead black tooth stopped her conversation with a short man in cowboy boots and crumpled cowboy hat sucking on a cigarette. I ordered a beer. The guy in the cowboy boots and hat stared at my Hawaiian shirt. The black-toothed waitress told me her name, Charlene, and fetched my beer. She pulled it out of a gurgling cooler, which was all that was behind the bar.

A throwback to the old days before liquor-by-the-drink, the Neches 96 had no liquor license. It sold only beer and setups for the liquor you could bring in. I'd noticed a liquor store just down the road, also on the edge of town. Liquor licenses were expensive; after all, they were helping to pay for our future by undereducating Texas school children. I nodded at Charlene and looked to my right, down the length of the bar. It ended at a door. The door, I guessed, led to an office.

From beside me, I heard Charlene and the cowboy's conversation. The cowboy had a seventeen-year-old flunking high school, but she wanted to go to college. He had no money. Charlene knew about Pell grants. I smiled at them until Charlene turned her attention toward me. I thought that I'd interrupt and try to explain: "Excuse me, but I had a couple of associates drop by the other day. They probably got just a little out of hand before they got the information they wanted."

Charlene smiled, "What did they look like?"

"Two black guys. One wore a straw hat. The other is a very large man."

"Niggers," the cowboy mumbled into his beer.

Before I could say anything, the door to the office opened and a round man with a Dutch-boy hair cut and sideburns left over from the seventies stepped into the space behind the bar. "Them two black fellas sounded like police," he said.

I swiveled around on my barstool to face him. "They aren't police." I held out my hand. "I'm Roger Jackson. I'm helping a poor couple try to find the truth about a mutual friend. My associates were asking about a contact."

The office manager, owner, or whatever he was tilted his head, but his Dutch-boy 'do stayed in the same position. He stepped toward me and shook my hand. "J. C. Deevers," he said. "Your associates were kind of irritating."

From behind me, I heard the cowboy. "Just like niggers. Just like flies, always bothering people and eating shit."

"Come on, now, that's enough," Charlene said to the cowboy. "Keep your opinions to yourself."

J. C. glanced at all of us. "Black or white, they were short on manners."

"And I am here to apologize for them and buy you a beer."

J. C. Deevers locked his elbows and leaned on a shelf behind the bar, right in front of me. "No need to buy me a beer. Those two who came in here scared me because of the way they talked—real rough like, full of bluff mostly. You scare me because you talk like a cop who's too smart for his own good."

Both Charlene and the cowboy stared at me. "Believe me, I'm not smart. If I were, I would be doing something other than cleaning up after my friends."

The cowboy said, "You still sound smart."

I wanted to tell him that he'd better hope that his daughter had cheated her genetic makeup if she planned to get through college. But I didn't shift my gaze from J. C. Deevers. "Look, I just want to have a conversation with a fella who might come in here once in awhile. That's all I want."

"One of the reasons I stay open is I don't give out information on people." The jukebox stopped playing. Without a background score setting the mood, I got a little anxious.

I swiveled to look at Charlene, "Would you give me some information, Charlene?"

"Hey, you were talking to me," J. C. said.

I kept my gaze on Charlene. She shifted her eyes from me to J. C. For a moment, I thought that her confusion made her black tooth sparkle. "It's better that I talk to Jewel McQueen before the police find him." The cowboy looked at me. Charlene stared at me. I felt J. C.'s eyes on the back of my head.

"You sure you ain't no cop?" J. C. asked.

I swiveled back to J. C. "No, but I know that the cops suspect Jewel of something he may or may not have done. I can help him." He just barely nodded toward Charlene, then turned away and started to polish something on the shelf.

I swiveled toward Charlene. "We have bands on Friday and Saturday nights," she said. "Jewel likes to come in on those nights."

"Are those trips for business or pleasure?" I asked.

"A little of both," Charlene said, and J. C. tapped the bar. She looked at him so that he could tell her with his eyes not to talk anymore. I thought that maybe, if I'd had him with me, I'd have unleashed Buttermilk on J. C. and the cowboy.

J. C. said, "You just come by on Saturday night and look around." Then he went back into the office.

I stared at Charlene's blank face. "Thank you, Charlene," I said. To show my appreciation and trust, I had two more beers with Charlene and the cowboy.

"So how was your trip to hard-on county?" Lynnette asked.

"Hard-on!" D. Wayne chuckled. "Gives me a soft-on. Ain't but something like 6 percent black people up there. You know why?"

Lynette looked at me. "Does he always start talking like this? No wonder they kick him out of bars."

D. Wayne banged his forefinger on the bar. "Should be called 'cracker county.' You know what the average annual wage is up there?"

"You shouldn't talk politics in a bar," Lynette said to D. Wayne. I wasn't really listening to either one. I had given up on my bear act for

119

D. Wayne, and when he wasn't threatening me, he wasn't a bad sort. But I was watching Lee Tomlinson flow to some music in her head.

Lee was by herself on the dance floor, the jukebox was blaring out the southern rock that played so consistently you would have thought the songs local anthems, but Lee moved to something inside her, not the music. I once begged Fiona, the weekend waitress, to open up the jukebox for me. I replaced a Lynyrd Skynyrd CD with a Mozart CD. Lynette kicked me out for two days.

"I'm just saying that county is just nothing but poor white trash back for a century. They was trapping and eating bears not fifty years ago. Live off of catfish. Hell, out in Chambers County, my Double Bayou people had twice the money, the education, and the *savoir-faire* of those trailer trash rednecks."

"'Salve wha' what?" Lynette asked.

Before D. Wayne could go on, we heard from across the bar, "You goddamn sand-nigger camel jockey." When we looked, we saw Zia backing away from Leroy. Zia raised his hands and shook them. He looked at Lynette.

"What the hell is going on? Quit making racist remarks like that in this bar. Leroy, I told you about that. This ain't like those sleazy-ass, redneck bars up in hard-on county," Lynette said.

Shirley had her hands over her horsey face. Leroy pointed at Zia, who protested, "I ain't done nothing. Just doing some business. I got to make some money too. Just like everybody." In Zia's raised left hand was a foot-and-a-half long dildo.

Billy was hunkered over a beer a few stools down from them. "That's disgusting," Billy said.

"Zia's been flashing his nasty shit around Shirley," Leroy said.

Shirley lowered her hands. She smiled, looked over at Zia, and giggled. Zia's goods must have intimidated Leroy.

"Decent people shouldn't be parading disgusting shit like that around. I think he oughta stick it up his ass," Billy said.

"Go on, Zia," Lynette said. "Get out of here. I told you not to flash that shit around in public."

"Taxpayer got a right to make a living. This is the US of A," he said.

"Go outside. Cool off. Then come back in," Lynette said.

Leroy sat back down beside Shirley and wrapped his arm around her shoulders. He kissed her gently on the cheek, and she, in turn, gave him a peck on the lips. Big Billy watched Zia slink away and smiled, because he had not been the one to do something disgusting and get kicked out.

Lee, her eyes closed, writhed and twisted to the music playing in her head. She was sexy and more suggestive than any stripper I had ever seen. "That's my baby," D. Wayne said as I watched Lee.

The song ended, and Lee started back toward us, but she was stopped by Zia. D. Wayne pushed himself off his barstool, but I held my hand out and coaxed him back onto his barstool. "She can take care of herself," I said.

"That she can," D. Wayne said.

"You got a woman?" D. Wayne asked.

I sifted Rachel through my mind. Her offer of a new job lodged somewhere in back of my forehead. "I just lost one. Depending on what day of the week it is, she might take me back."

"That's the way with women. You never know where you stand. If you *do* do something, it's the wrong thing, and if you *don't* do something, then it's worse. But Lee ain't like that."

D. Wayne looked down at his beer, then we heard Lee yell, "Get that dismembered part out of my face. I've got bigger and better at home."

Then Lynette screamed, "Zia, you're out of here."

Both D. Wayne and I chuckled and stared at the tops of our beers. "You're a lucky man," I said.

"I ain't losing her." He jerked his head in Lee's direction. "I'm staying true blue."

"I'd say you're doing more than your part."

D. Wayne smiled as he watched Lee. "I don't give a flying fuck about no Harry Krammer except that Lee does. What Lee wants, Lee gets—if I can do it. . . ." D. Wayne stopped to sip his beer. He turned to look at me. "By looking at the suave, gentle, handsome man in front of you, I bet you're thinking I got no problem with women. But I did a few women wrong, ran out a few times, let the wrong head do the thinking, so I been lucky at finding and fucking, but not at keeping. Her, I aim to keep."

A bit of envy surged through my throat. I didn't dare tell D. Wayne that, so I said, "Speaking of fucking, where's Buttermilk?"

"He's got a date," D. Wayne said and circled his tongue around his lips.

When Lee came over she put an arm around each of us. "So you guys are going to take me dancing in Silsbee on Saturday night."

I looked at her and then dropped my gaze to D. Wayne. "No, we're taking Buttermilk dancing in Crackerville."

Lee turned to me, "Roger, is this your decision, too?" I shrugged my shoulders. Lee's eyes held firmly on D. Wayne. He tried to duck her gaze. "I suppose, because I'm a woman, you think I shouldn't be exposed to any danger. What kind of backward, twentieth-century chauvinistic bullshit is that? When I called you two, I told you that I was in this. I told you that the only reason that I wasn't actively running people down was simply that I had a job to keep. If there is anyone who gives the orders here, it's me." She slowed down and breathed in. Then she turned to me. "And since I'm paying you a fee, I'll go where I damn well please." Lee didn't have that much money, but now, like Cody Hudson, she thought money gave me my orders.

The hairs on the back of my neck rose up, but then flattened back down when she swung her arms around my shoulders. "Yes, m'am," I said.

Lee then turned to D. Wayne. "I told you that if we were partners, then we were partners in everything."

D. Wayne lifted his head to meet her steady gaze, and his smile spread across his face. He broke his gaze from her to look in my direction and say, "See why I love her."

The Lamar professors gave me hope because they seemed to have found something comfortable without looking or working for it. D. Wayne and Lee gave me the same kind of hope. And to tell the truth, Rachel had given me some hope. But Jewel McQueen was out there somewhere with an explanation of Harry Krammer's fate. And hope depended on explanation and reason as well as wants, desires, druthers, luck, and envy.

SIXTEEN 16

I stopped at the juncture of Tram Road and the canal and waited for Emily Nguyen. The sun had brightened and dried the area, and I had stayed on the safe side of six or so beers the night before, so the wait was almost pleasant. I didn't know for a fact that Emily was going to come by, but I just figured that there was enough momentum circling Jewel McQueen that it would whirl Emily toward this place and time so that we could compare notes.

When Emily pulled up to me, she stepped out of her car and offered me a Dixie Creme doughnut. Out of politeness and out of the need for a prop, I accepted it and nibbled around the edges of the hardened glaze.

"I can smell you're up to something," Emily said.

"I just got through jogging. I sweat a lot."

"That's not what I smell. I just know that you're up to something. That's what I smell. Your bad intentions just leak out your pores."

"I can smell you getting closer to Jewel."

"Have you found Jewel?"

"I can't tell you that. That's in the private investigator's ethics manual, right there on page two."

"I thought you skipped that day 'cause you got drunk and lost the manual."

"The manual only has three pages. I memorized it."

Emily dropped her head and almost began to laugh. "So you got to give me some hints of what you're up to, so I can show you some of mine."

"Why don't you show me yours and let me see if I like it before I show you mine?"

"It doesn't work that way."

"Emily, if I had a good woman like you to run my life for me, no telling where I'd be."

"You'd probably be a sleazy private investigator because, no matter what me or some other woman did for you, you'd still be surly, bitter, and grouchy." Emily didn't smile as she said that. It was almost as though she felt a little sorry for me. Ever since I turned fifty, people were calling me bitter and grouchy, like I was already an old man. I thought I was getting smarter.

I walked to the fender of her police car, leaned against it, and took a bite out of my doughnut. Emily leaned beside me, bit from her doughnut, and sipped from her coffee. "I didn't think to bring you any coffee. You want a sip of mine?" She offered me her paper cup with the cardboard holder. I grabbed it and took a sip. Hell, she offered, and I needed it. The coffee made my doughnut taste better.

When Emily relaxed, she started talking: "Two days ago, Jewel paid five thousand dollars down on a new pickup from Kinsel Ford. Somebody dropped him off; he walked in and said, 'Show me your trucks.' Stupid SOB. We're gonna catch him because I figure he's really dim."

"Could he have gotten the money from his meth or from this new cocaine he's probably gotten ahold of?" I asked.

I took a bite of my doughnut, looked at the edge of it, and threw it down. "These things'll curdle in your stomach. They're too damn sweet."

Emily kept munching her doughnut, "I like 'em. But if I keep eating, I'm going to be as wide as I am high." She threw her doughnut down beside mine. "Let the ants or birds have 'em."

"They'll be thrilled," I said.

"And fat," she added. She didn't make a move to leave. "Could have been Jewel's drug money." She waited for me to finish her point. When I didn't, she said, "Or he could have gotten the money from somebody for killing Harry Krammer."

"So Harry Krammer's life is worth a down payment on a new Ford pickup."

"From what we can tell, Harry never earned much while he was living. Hell, I don't make much more than Harry. I can't afford a new car. What about you? You've got that new Toyota."

"So all of us genuine, true-blue public servants don't earn shit, and thus have to take orders from dipshits with more money than they deserve."

"Roger, you sound some like some kind of socialist that just let time pass him by while he was getting drunk or stoned. Just like Harry."

"And Emily, I don't doubt for a minute that, with all your studying and ambition, you'll get rich some day."

"Unless I get a social conscience," she said.

"I don't see that happening in your line of work."

"So what about Jewel?"

"Emily, I'm going to try to find Jewel and talk to him. As soon as I do, I'm going to call you and tell you what I know."

"Don't. Don't find him. Forget this whole thing and let us worry about him. You don't have the firepower. Go back with that girlfriend of yours and take that job with the lawyers."

"How did you know about the job offer? How did you know about Rachel?"

"It's a small town, and I have a lot of business in the courthouse."

✦

D. Wayne pulled off of 96 and onto the street that ran beside the Neches 96 club. We followed the curve around, and then D. Wayne pulled off the side of the road. He looked over at Lee and said very tenderly, "Now Lee honey, why don't you wait right here, with the car running, in case we get into some trouble."

"Now D. honey," Lee said, mocking D. Wayne. "I want to go in and see, too."

Buttermilk and I watched from the backseat of D. Wayne's Lincoln. "Now honey, let's think strategically," D. Wayne said.

"Hell, let's go get his ass," Buttermilk said as he opened his door and the interior lights came on.

"Sit your ass back down," D. Wayne said. "We ain't got a plan yet."

"What is it we got to plan about? We go in and ask him some questions," Buttermilk said and pulled his door closed. The lights went off again. D. Wayne turned the lights on from his console, so we could see each other.

"D. Wayne, you or Roger wait in the car," Lee said.

"Hey, I'm the professional here," I said. D. Wayne and Buttermilk both looked at me like they were going to hit me. I looked at Lee and talked to her. "Look, I know more of the whole story. I've actually done this before." I looked around for agreement.

"Yeah, honey, we need professionals," D. Wayne said.

"Professional bullshitters," Buttermilk said.

"Wait, wait, wait," I said. "D. Wayne, where are we?"

"What the hell you talking about where are we? We're at this cracker bar in Hardin County, Texas."

"Exactly," I said. "So you and Buttermilk go in, you're going to be the only two black people in the place, and somebody may say something. Or at least people are gonna be suspicious."

"Fuck 'em," Buttermilk said and pushed his door open.

"No wait, wait, wait," I said.

I shifted my attention to D. Wayne. "Look, you know how he gets." I motioned my head toward Buttermilk. "He ain't gonna take no shit. Somebody'll say the wrong thing, he'll say something back, smack somebody around, and you know you won't just sit still. So everything goes to shit, and we don't even talk to Jewel McQueen."

"So Buttermilk stays here," D. Wayne said.

"Bullshit," said Buttermilk. "You two fuckers can fucking go fuck yourselves."

"Now think, think. I'm a chickenshit by nature. I'm too old to fight anybody. If I did, I'd just get my ass kicked."

"You right about that," Buttermilk said. "You a real pussy."

"And so look, I put on some long pants and some old boots so I'm inconspicuous. Not like D. Wayne in his nice hat and silver-tipped black boots, and you Buttermilk in your muscle shirt."

"Comes to the point of you making fun of my clothes," D. Wayne said and shook his head.

"Tell him to go fuck himself," Buttermilk said.

Lee cleared her throat, glared at Buttermilk, then by the dome light, put her hand out in front of her to rest on D. Wayne's wrist. "Roger's right," she said.

At first the rest of us were stunned, but I was the first to fill in the silence. "Look, we have a good view of the back door here. Lee, you stay in the car just in case. You two just walk up toward the back door to cover my ass. But stay just a little out of sight. If anything happens, I'll run out the back door, then Buttermilk you can whip whoever's ass is chasing my ass."

"It makes sense, D. Wayne," Lee said and again patted his arm. "Let's not forget the objectives here."

D. Wayne nodded, and Buttermilk said, "Fuck."

D. Wayne shut off the engine, and he, Buttermilk, and I got out in unison. Buttermilk walked deliberately, as though a fight was waiting to happen and he would enjoy it. D. Wayne and I both sneaked a look over our shoulders to see Lee. She had turned on the light to check her makeup in the rearview mirror, and then just as quickly turned it off.

I left the two of them to walk around to the front parking lot. I heard music seeping out of the mildewed walls. My feet crunched the gravel in the lot as I made my way around the misparked pickups.

I opened the door into the music, the smoke, and the hum of cussing. To my left, I saw Charlene. She nodded her head, smiled, then swung her head from me to J. C. Deevers. He smiled but turned his back to me and walked away. With his Dutch-boy hairdo, he looked almost like a woman from the back. I hurried to the bar to stop him. Charlene scurried away when I yelled his name. J. C. turned to face me with a grin that asked to be slapped off his face. I found myself wishing that Buttermilk were with me.

"So where's Jewel?" I asked. "That's why I'm here. Remember?"

"Not here yet."

He turned away from me yet again. "Now wait. Hold on. You know why I'm here."

He faced me. "Why don't you find a table, and when he comes in, if he comes in, then I'll direct him over to you. Would that suit you?"

I looked around, saw a vacant card table, and jerked my thumb toward it. We left each other, nodding our heads in the general direction of each other like idiot bobble-head dolls. As I made my way through the thick smoke to the table and sat down, a few of the eyes followed me, and almost as though electricity were in the air, I felt the hair on the back of my neck and arms stand up. Maybe the patrons hadn't fought Buttermilk and D. Wayne because they were annoying, uppity black folks from Beaumont, but because they were trying to protect Jewel. Maybe now someone was waiting for me.

Before I got scared enough to push myself up and leave, Charlene came by the table. "You need a beer, honey?" she asked.

"I need one really quick," I said, hoping a beer might calm my paranoia. While I waited, I scanned the clientele. Lots of tattoos on men and women. A lot of men with braids. A lot of men and women in need of dental work. Everyone smoked. Everyone said *fuck* or *goddamn* in between every other word. Most had difficulty with verb tense, *went* and *gone* in particular.

I wished that I were downtown in Beaumont on Crockett Street with amoral but cleaned-up lawyers who could use proper verb tenses and could afford dentists. Charlene set a beer in front of me. I paid her. After my first few sips, I grew calm. After my second beer, I was almost having a good time and thinking that this had all been a mistake. Jewel simply hadn't shown, no conspiracy, no setup. I wanted to get back to D. Wayne and Buttermilk before they did some damage to the exterior of the place.

Then a man stepped in front of my table and blotted out all else. I could not see around him. He was bigger than Buttermilk. He pulled up a chair directly across from me and sat down. His shoulders must have spanned four feet. His beard was matted. His dingy blond hair was pulled into a braided ponytail. His pale complexion was as bad as his breath, the devil himself maybe, smelling of brimstone, sulphur. He had a gut, but instead of making him look fat, it just made him look bigger. He needed that heft to hold up his enormous shoulders, neck, and head.

He waited to say anything, daring me to open up, but I remained quiet. "I hear you're looking for my brother, Jewel McQueen," he said finally.

I looked over at the bar and saw Charlene looking toward me. Even from that distance and in the darkened bar, I could see the worried look on her face. I followed her head toward J. C. He crossed his arms and smiled that smile. I half wished that Buttermilk had come in so that I could sic him on J. C. I faced the big man with the foul breath. "And you are?"

"I'm Sunshine McQueen. My brother doesn't tend to his business too well, so I'm tending to it. Now why do you want to see him?"

I started to get up, ready to run through the back door and into the protective arms of D. Wayne and Buttermilk. But Sunshine clamped his arm around my forearm. I rose. He dipped a shoulder and twisted my forearm in and down toward the table so that I was sitting back down.

"Don't panic," he said. Several of the others patrons seemed near panic. They looked on but dared not do anything.

"Okay, you've got my attention," I said.

"Yeah, I figured that. Now you answer some questions for me." I nodded my head. "You don't look like a cop. Why you looking for my brother?"

"I'm a private investigator."

"That puts you at a disadvantage.'Cause if I was to beat the shit out of you, it wouldn't be as bad as beating a cop. I probably wouldn't even get any time for it."

"I just want to ask Jewel a couple of questions." I looked down at my arm, and Sunshine's eyes followed mine. I stared at the ragged tattoo on his forearm. It looked liked a hanged black man. Basically it was a fleshed-out stick figure whose elongated neck was bent by a hangman's noose.

"I designed that myself. Three of my Aryan brothers held me down, while a fourth carved that into my arm with a hot bed spring. You like it?"

"It's attractive."

"You ain't gonna run?" I shook my head, and he released his grip.

"I'm not working for the police, but I have several clients, and we just want to find the truth."

"Truth, horseshit," Sunshine bellowed, and patrons tried not to hear him, tried to keep themselves from turning to stare. "Cops? You? Shit! Nobody wants the truth. What people want is some poor, redneck country boy of no consequence to pin a crime on. Say somebody with a criminal activity in his past. Say somebody whose brother's got a record. You fuck up just a little and you become a suspect."

"I'm willing to help. You see, I'm not sure Jewel did anything. I can help him."

"Fuck you," Sunshine bellowed. People did look. J. C. stepped toward us, stopped, thought twice, then turned away to leave me to my fate.

I remembered the bear in Big Bend. "Fuck you too, hillbilly. I don't need you to tell me my job. I just might be the only hope Jewel has, considering the noose closing around him." I prepared to meet my fate, my maker, and I hoped that I would not have my teeth knocked to the back of my throat. I forced myself to keep my eyes open because I wanted to close them so I wouldn't see the blow that was coming.

Sunshine crossed his arms, leaned back in his chair, and smiled. "If you want, I'll give you a free swing. Do your damndest."

"Since you seem to like the ugly facts, the ugly fact is that you can whip my ass all over and up and down this bar. Ain't nothing I can do about it but cry. Ain't nobody in this bar is gonna lift a finger to help me. I'm not gonna take a free swing, and I'm hoping you'll tell me some more of the obvious about Jewel."

Sunshine smiled and moved suddenly toward me, but instead of ramming into me, he leaned onto the table on his elbows and whispered. I scooted into his foul breath to hear him. Then he raised one hand. I quickly scooted well back into my chair. He laughed. Then he leaned on his elbows again. He was the kind of guy who would torture cats. I was like a kitty. But I leaned back into his breath. "Jewel is a fuckup. That stuff he takes makes him worse. He's just plain weak. And stupid. He can't even figure out why he's a walking suspect for every crime committed in three counties. I ought to leave him to his own tangled line, but I'm his brother, and I don't want our momma suffering no more. She seen one boy go to prison. That would be me. She couldn't bear to see another go to prison. That would be Jewel. I aim to see that he's dead before he goes to prison."

"If you could just let me talk to him."

"I'm gonna have to whip your ass, ain't I? You just keep pushing, don't you?"

"So what do you think happened?"

"About fucking what?"

"The murder of Harry Krammer."

"I got no idea. If it matters, Jewel says he didn't do it. But since when does it matter what somebody like Jewel says? The cops have as much as convicted him. Hell, I don't even know if I believe him. But since when does it matter what somebody like me thinks?"

"I've got friends. I could get a lawyer for him."

"Shut the fuck up," Sunshine yelled again. Then he lowered his voice. "I come from a long line of Holy Rollers. Momma's the worst. She can talk in tongues, claims it's Jesus and a whole slew of saints. Me, I just hear voices. I don't know if these voices are God or the devil. But I heed them. It was the people I killed because I was listening to those voices that sent me to Huntsville. I done the crime, but I was the first suspect, just like Jewel is now. I was convicted before I ever stepped into a court. So I know how it works.

"And I know lawyers just itching to have a case like Jewel's. Not because they're noble and want to protect the innocent, but because they could get a hell of a name for getting him off and then make themselves rich."

"And I got this one son of a bitch deputy tailing me and my brother. This Hurtis Lomax just has a hard-on to see me and Jewel in prison. He wants us out of the county and locked up. So every crime that goes on, he comes looking for us. I ain't found a lawyer yet who's willing to side with me over Hurtis Lomax."

Charlene slowly entered into our peripheral vision to interrupt Sunshine's story. "You two want a beer?" She looked back over her shoulder at J. C. He gave a thumb up and motioned her onward. J. C. didn't give a rat's ass about me, but he didn't want my blood and guts spilling on his floor and my bouncing body breaking up the walls and the furniture. So he sent Charlene to try to intercede, or to at least to distract Sunshine.

I looked at my empty bottle. "Yes, I need one," I said.

"Go away," Sunshine said. He didn't even turn his head to look at her. I hoped that she would come back with a beer. I really needed one.

"So you're out of prison now. You can't afford to get in any trouble."

Sunshine pointed his finger at me. "I'm trying to be Joe Citizen. But this is my brother and mother. You know how prison works."

"I've never been there. I can only guess."

"Let me inform you of a thing or two, Mr. Investigator-after-the-truth. In prison you fuck, fight, or five up. I had no money to pay. I wasn't going to fuck. So I fought. And I was a dead man until I joined the Aryan Brotherhood. They don't got trustees in prison no more. So the only order are the gangs. So to keep living, I had to start hating niggers." He held the forearm in front of me. It was indeed a hanged black man. "I got homemade tattoos like that all over my body. I even got a botched one on my dick. Tried to do it myself." Sunshine tilted his head like he was getting choked up or the voices that he listened to had started again.

He started again. "Now I like being Joe Citizen. I don't want to go back to hating niggers. But I will. Because Jewel could never survive prison. He couldn't truly hate a nigger and carve his initials in his dick. I'd kill him before I'd let him go to prison." He paused to let me soak up this information. "My momma figures I'm lost. I've gone to the devil. For her the devil is real. She had me and Jewel thinking he'd prowl around at night outside of our windows. I grew up thinking the shadows could become people and just come right out of the forest and snatch you up. And in the deep woods where I grew up, there was a lot of shadows." I sipped my beer to get my eyes off his face. But when I set my beer down, he moved his face close to mine, so I had to look into his eyes.

"That's when the voices started for me. I was just a kid, and I starting hearing shit in my head. At first I thought it was Jesus, but more likely it was the devil." He scooted closer to me. "In prison they diagnosed me with some kind of mental disorder. Crazy voices, the devil, what's the difference. Doesn't matter what you call it. Then Jewel heard the voices. Momma was proud of him. Praised him to kingdom come. Got him to go to church and babble out the make-pretend words those voices was telling him. I never believed he heard a thing. If he did, same as me, Momma must have had a hand in giving us those voices." His eyes blinked, like he heard a voice. "But I don't mean to bore you with my own problems," he said. "We all got problems." In that apology, I almost found something touching. He had a certain dignity or testosterone-warped, prison-house ethic about staying on the point and not whining.

"Momma couldn't stand to lose Jewel to the devil, to prison, to nigger hating. Better that Jewel was dead than with the devil, killing niggers in prison. Hell, wait, that's wrong. He'd be the first one the niggers killed. Wouldn't survive a day. Better for my momma he dies right here and now, than die in prison."

As he finished his story, Sunshine no longer looked at me. He dropped his head, and at first his eyes clouded over, then his lids drooped so that they half covered his eyes. Charlene interrupted when she gingerly set my beer in front of me.

Sunshine looked at me, looked at my beer, looked around the room. He smiled, then he laughed—or growled. It was some agonizing laugh-like sound that came up out of his stomach. His eyes rested on my bottle of beer, then he grabbed it as though he were snatching at a snake. He drank it down. Then he twirled the empty bottle in his hand and hurled it across the room. The breaking beer bottle sucked the sound out of the place. All eyes were on us. "So don't you fuck with me," he shouted, not to me in particular but to the room. Then he ran.

He was across the dance floor in two or three bounds, then out the back door. My shoulders were knotted, and my mind worked at a crawl. I tried to think, tried to come to some conclusion, but nothing came to me except to follow Sunshine. If I could stay behind him, maybe he would lead me to Jewel. So I ran across the bar, opened the back door, and stepped through the doorframe.

I felt something before I saw it. First there was the swish, and as time slowed for the world around the Neches 96 club to watch, I stuck my hand into the swish. I tried to get my palm up, but before I could, the heft behind the swish hit the tips of my fingers and curled them inward. I didn't so much hear that crack as feel it. A tremor worked its way from the tips of my fingers, through to the first knuckle, and then to the second and on into my hand.

My fingers weren't enough to stop the two-by-four. *Board* my mind registered, and made me twist so that my side rather than my chest caught it. This time, I heard a crack. This crack took my breath away. I sucked in, and the need for air forced me to my knees. On my knees, I missed the second swing of the board.

Behind the two-by-four was Sunshine McQueen. He looked sad, like he didn't want to kill me, like he wasn't going to kill me. I knew from his hesitation, from the weariness in his eyes, that he was not going to kill me. "Go home. Forget Jewel," he yelled, the board cocked behind him like a baseball bat, ready to swing for the fence if he needed to.

"You go home," I said. My ribs gave. My trunk seemed to crumple. But on my way down, I saw Sunshine spin around and swing the board. The board popped when it hit a forearm, and then Buttermilk gasped. Sunshine's head popped back, but he brought it forward and his fists up.

D. Wayne was beside me. The crowd from the Neches 96 club pressed into the frame of the door. The patrons wanted to see, but they didn't want to get sucked into the fury. "You all right?" D. Wayne asked.

"Hell no, I'm not all right," I said. "What the hell else do you want to know?"

"Fuck you, then," D. Wayne said. "I was just asking. I'm gonna help Buttermilk." But he stood at the edge of the spinning, intertwined bodies of Sunshine and Buttermilk. They grappled and pushed and threw uppercuts. D. Wayne picked up the two-by-four, danced around the two dancers—two gyres, one going clockwise, the other counterclockwise, then stopping and shifting direction.

D. Wayne swung. Sunshine groaned and dropped to one knee. Buttermilk pounced, but Sunshine hit the ground flat and rolled out from under him. D. Wayne stepped up and swung the two-by-four again. Sunshine held out one hand, and somehow curled his fingers over the edge of the board and shoved it forward, into D. Wayne, knocking him back and over. D. Wayne was calling him *fucker* even before he hit the ground.

Buttermilk was up and plowed into Sunshine and both tumbled over into the dirt. Dignity, pride, solidarity kicked in, and I got up. To do what, I don't know. Whatever picked me up off my ass got me close enough to see Sunshine twist out from under Buttermilk, jump to his feet, smile at me, then jump on Buttermilk's shoulder. I heard this crack.

Buttermilk rolled to get up, threw a punch from his good shoulder, and knocked Sunshine backward. Sunshine ran forward, butting Buttermilk and pinning him to the wall. D. Wayne was at Sunshine's back, pummeling him with the two-by-four. But with two good arms to Buttermilk's one, Sunshine was throwing fist after fist into Buttermilk's face and throat.

Sunshine turned around and got a punch into D. Wayne's face, knocking him back. I ran toward them, but buckled at my stomach. Still, I ran. I curled, because I couldn't help but curl, gritted my teeth and plowed into Sunshine's knees. I felt some dagger inside of me jab at the underside of the muscles and fat in my side and chest. I felt Sunshine's knee in my chest, and my eyes went starry.

Through the stars I saw Buttermilk stand, his face looking like bleeding hamburger, and send one fist, like a hammer, into the side of Sunshine's head. "Kick his ass. Fuck him," I heard D. Wayne scream. But before Buttermilk could raise his good hand, Sunshine was up throwing a left hook at Buttermilk, catching him just below the ear. Buttermilk stepped back, and I saw his jaw shorter and slanting. He screamed when Sunshine got the next blow, then the next. Buttermilk crumpled.

D. Wayne was about to attack Sunshine with no more than tooth and nail. He was crawling toward him when the headlights caught us all, froze us. Sunshine just ran. The car pulled to a stop. Lee stepped out of

D. Wayne's Continental and ran toward us.

I felt and heard the rustle of people behind me. I turned and saw several khaki-clad deputy sheriffs. They ran past me. One reached and grabbed D. Wayne by the shoulder. D. Wayne spun around, threw a fist, and caught the deputy sheriff in his jaw. Yelling "mother fucker," he bent over the deputy and threw another punch, until Lee ran up behind him, wrapped her arms around him, and begged him to stop.

The crowd slowly oozed out. The stars clouded my vision. For my last bit of consciousness, I looked at busted, mauled Buttermilk.

SEVENTEEN 17

Hardin County should give tours of its jail in Kountze to middle schoolers. That jail might scare them away from crime, or at least crime in Hardin County. When they grew up, the kids might then do their burglaries and drug dealing in Jefferson County, where the jail would be a lot more comfortable.

D. Wayne sat on one of the iron beds in the large drunk tank and looked past me, through the plexiglass, to the night shift jailer. She had just watched him pee in the one toilet in the center of the back wall. In case the drunks didn't have good aim or were throwing up or otherwise leaking or losing vile fluids, the cement floor of the cell sloped toward a drain in the middle of the floor. Jailers could just wash it out with a hose. Down two halls were some more cells, and outside was a razor-wire-enclosed basketball court, but this holding cell was open to see for everybody who made it past the waiting room. Our shame, our sins, our crimes were on display. Middle schoolers would be aghast—or think it was funny.

D. Wayne muttered a curse. Before, he had yelled his curses until he was hoarse. He was not taking the humiliation well. With his cursing and his attempts at defense, the Hardin County jailers at first thought he was drunk. Instead, as I saw, he had this big bad streak of anger. I began to see that his normal personality was a defense against this anger, for when the anger came, he lost his cunning, his foresight, his natural Machiavellian view of his place in the world. Now he was ashamed. He knew that his anger could get him hurt or killed.

I sat with my back against the plexiglass trying to stay as straight as possible so my ribs didn't hurt. In the midst of his tirade, in what I took to be almost a touch of kindness, D. Wayne had helped me into a sitting position, then taken his position on the bed. On the other bed was a passed-out drunk.

I held my right hand on my knee, looked at the still-wet cast, and felt a throb in my middle and forefingers. They were held straight by two taped, pliable aluminum planks. But the planks needed an anchor, and broken fingers needed to stay still, so the Silsbee emergency room doctor had put a cast up past my wrist on my right hand. As he told me, the only thing that you can really do with broken ribs is hurt. Along with our belts and shoelaces, they had taken my Vicodin when they booked us. I spent the first hour wishing that I had some of D. Wayne's anger so that I didn't feel my body throb. Then for the next hour, the throb built into a scream that I finally let out. When I did, the female jailer looked at me with some pity, and the drunk slowly turned over. My second scream made D. Wayne stop his shouting and help me to my sitting position.

Finally a short, thick deputy sheriff walked in and stared at us as he handed some forms to the lady jailer. She read them, checked them, stamped some. As she processed us, the deputy turned to look at D. Wayne and me. D. Wayne kept a straight, angry stare at the man. I could only twist a bit to see him. I couldn't stay twisted for long.

The deputy's head was a crew-cut bucket with bulges where the fat started at his neck and ears. What hair there was on his head looked like it grew in abnormally thick follicles spaced about a half-inch apart. He looked like he had been slapped in the face with the flat side of a shovel. When he walked to the iron bars, like a fat man, like Big Billy, he held his arms out and his palms backward. "You birds are sprung. But before you go, I want to have a word or two with you," he said. He sounded as though he practiced his nasal twang for effect.

He guided us out of our cell to the woman behind the desk who had watched us pee. She gave us our shoelaces and belts back. She gave me my Vicodin. Then the deputy led us down the hall and out a door into the waiting area. Lee was there waiting for us.

Lee hugged D. Wayne. I yelled when she hugged me. They only took cashiers' checks at Hardin County Jail. They didn't trust checks, and cash had a way of disappearing. The bail bondsmen had already made their rounds for the night and so were tucked away in their comfy beds. Lee had to drive back to Beaumont, empty her checking account, and deal with some shady friends of D. Wayne's who were able to get a cashier's check that late at night.

As D. Wayne kissed her and called her honey and said, "Just get my ass out of cracker county," the fat deputy sheriff shifted from one foot to the other. He stared for a moment at D. Wayne kissing this attractive middle-aged white lady whom he had been helping.

"Y'all want some coffee, cokes? We got some of those little orange crackers and pretzels in the vending machine." It was as though his throat was closed, and so he forced air and words out his nose.

"All I want is my ass out of here," D. Wayne said.

"D.," Lee said. "Your mouth got you in here. Poor Roger, I don't know why he's in here. But Hurtis here has been helping me."

"Hurt who?" D. Wayne asked.

"This is Hurtis Lomax," Lee said. She smiled sweetly to him, and both D. Wayne and I saw Lee's flirtations and Hurtis's disappointment that her flirtations were not promises. I thought that I had chased Sunshine McQueen out of my mind, but pieces of his diatribe came fluttering back into my mind. He had said that Hurtis Lomax was always after him.

"Why don't y'all go outside?" Hurtis asked. "Breeze is come up, and the night's turned almost cool. I'm sure you all had enough of the insides of this place. I'll be out directly." His voice hurt my ears.

D. Wayne muttered, "Cocksucker," as Lee pulled him outside. I paused to look around, to remember the place.

When I walked outside, I felt each step, no matter how lightly I tried to place my foot, start a jarring sensation that worked its way up my legs, through my hips— shriveling my nuts—and into my ribs. Holding my casted hand up made my walking uneven, so I dropped my hand to my side, but then my walking hurt even more, so I cradled my right hand with my left. Outside, I stepped into the breeze, felt a little better, and saw the halos of lamplight in the parking lot. D. Wayne and Lee were in the shadow of the building, and Lee was caressing D. Wayne's cheek, saying, "D., D., D., don't get mad. Calm down. Shhh."

"Who the fuck is Barney Fife there with a mouthful of shit so he has to talk through his nose?"

Hurtis came out of through the double glass doors with his arms full of Cokes and goods from the vending machine. "Here, eat something.

Y'all missed dinner."

I took a Coke from Hurtis and just stared at the top of it. Lee stepped up to me, smiled, and opened it for me. In the hospital, with D. Wayne already on his way to jail, Lee sat with me and held my left hand as they wrapped the tape that would become a cast around my right wrist. Just as she now patted D. Wayne's cheek, so she had patted my forehead and whispered, "Calm down, don't get excited. It hurts, but try to breathe normally." When the cast was on my hand but before they came to take me to jail, I thanked Lee and she smiled, dropped her head, then kissed me on the cheek. "I'm sorry that I led you to this," she said.

I had asked about Buttermilk. "They're trying to fix his face," she said. "A concussion or two. He's barely conscious. I think that Sunshine fractured his shoulder."

Lee might have even kissed Hurtis. For, in her days as a dancer, she had learned how to excite, then calm men. She insinuated promises with the way she moved her body. But once the dance was over, her politic charm smoothed the arousal that made them stare openmouthed at grace and art in the form of a stripper. Hurtis and I had benefited from her manner and knowledge. D. Wayne not only benefited but experienced it. I envied him again.

It hurt my ribs to tilt my head back to take a drink, and I thought how in the hell was I going to jog in the morning. I held up my bottle of Vicodin. Lee opened it for me, pulled out a pill, and put it in my mouth. I chased it down my throat with a sip from my drink. "Just what the hell was the need to put us in that shit-hook, unsanitary piece of shit you call a jail?" D. Wayne said. "That place makes some of the jails I been in look like Hiltons."

Lee looked sternly at him, yet again stroked his cheek. Hurtis said, "You had nothing but a citation for public disturbance. You were looking pretty. We were even ready to feel sorry for you with your friend all beat to shit. But then you had to go and hit a cop." He shook his head. After a while his nasal voice rubbed like steel wool on skin.

"Why am I here?" I asked.

Hurtis glanced at me. "Because you were with him, because J. C. Deevers said you started it—though I never believed a damn thing J. C. ever said, and because you got some pictures of a few of the deputies work for this county." He looked sternly at me. "I hope you given that business up." He dropped his head so that he had to raise his eyes to look at me. It was his attempt at looking dangerous. I thought the gesture, along with his voice, only made him look ridiculous.

"Why didn't you arrest Lee, here?" D. Wayne asked.

"That lady drove to your rescue, kept your friend from getting killed, pleaded with us not to haul your two asses in, even after you nailed my buddy, and just paid your bail. You ought to be kissing her feet and thanking us for realizing that she is an angel and the US Cavalry all in one." D. Wayne turned to Lee and kissed her.

Lee pulled back from D. Wayne and opened her pack of pretzels. She dipped two fingers into the bag and came out with a single pretzel. D. Wayne ate a Twinkie in two bites. Hurtis ate potato chips and sucked on his fingers after he shoved the chips into his mouth. Lee stuck one of her pretzels in my mouth, and I chased it with a drink from my Coke. In the background we heard crickets and frogs.

"Do y'all have any idea who you tangled with?" Hurtis asked.

"We tangled with a motherfucker who is gonna pay for all this shit," D. Wayne said.

"You walk lightly, there," Hurtis said. "One reason you two were in jail was to protect you. Keep you away from Sunshine McQueen."

"Have you talked to anybody from Jefferson County or the Beaumont Police Department?" I asked.

Hurtis shoved some chips in his mouth and talked as he chewed. "We ain't the yokels I look like." He looked into his bag for more chips, saw there was none, crumpled his bag, and started to throw it down but stopped. "Give me your empties and trash when you're through."

"Emily Nguyen call here?"

"We got a drug and vice task force with Jefferson County and Beaumont, Mr. Jackson. We know all about this murder of Harry Krammer."

"What do you know?" Lee asked.

"I know that we arrest Jewel McQueen every chance we get. We see him, we arrest him and worry about the charge later. Likely he's violated something. But it ain't because we're redneck hillbilly crackers. We do it to protect him."

"Throwing him in that piece of shit is a funny way of protecting him," D. Wayne said.

"If he's in there, he's not fucking up. He's got it in his DNA to be like his brother, who y'all just met tonight. But Jewel is a fuckup, a punk. So we arrest him here in Hardin County to keep him from doing some real hard crime and getting caught—because he would, because he's a fuckup. He goes to prison he gets killed, or worse he makes it through prison and comes back here and starts fucking up again. So we're protecting the forty some-odd thousand citizens of this county from him and Jewel from himself. Then you three come in here, without authority, without knowing the situation, and meet Sunshine." Hurtis shook his head. I handed him my empty Coke can. He stared down at the trash that he balanced in his large, outspread palms.

"Would you mind if we asked you what you know?" I asked. Lee stepped forward and in the light that caught on her face, we could all see that she implored him with her eyes.

"We know that Jewel is a meth head, a bad one, the type sees little green men in his room. He's probably got him a meth lab somewhere and will burn down a whole fucking national forest when he fucks that up. He deals, too. So we keep him in jail to keep him from dealing and getting a conviction." Hurtis looked at the trash in his hands and just dropped it. It was too much for him to talk and hold the trash too. He pulled his gunbelt up but only got it a little farther under his belly.

He looked at all of us as though sizing us up. "I figure there's this cheap, way-cut-down cocaine from Houston, and Harry Krammer wants to buy some. Or Harry Krammer has some and wants to unload. And Jewel being a fuckup kills him. He can't even wait to spend his money, so he puts money down on a brand new pickup."

"Harry never had money in his life," Lee said.

"Just who exactly are you dating here?" Hurtis asked, growing a little irritated. The short but wide sparse stubs of hair stood out from his head. "What was yours and Harry's relation?"

"Open them doors and unlock the cell because I'm gonna have to hit another deputy sheriff," D. Wayne said. He looked at me. "Roger, you want to go back in?"

Lee pushed at D. Wayne and stepped up to Hurtis. "I know lawyers, too. They're friends, just like Harry was. I'm very faithful to friends, lovers, and people who help me. You're not a lover. Those insinuations don't make you a friend. You're no longer helping me, Mr. Lomax."

"You tell him, honey," D. Wayne said.

Hurtis smiled and switched his gaze between me and D. Wayne. "You two fellas are going to have a court date. But your crime is more than likely going to be dismissed. I'm just going to explain things." He looked at Lee. "Am I helping now?" Lee nodded. "And I'm going to help some more. Sure Jewel did it, case closed. Just born to do it. Oh he didn't mean to, and he won't admit to it. Hell he was probably seeing those little green men do it, but he did it. But he's not the problem." Hurtis paused to raise a finger. "We can't stop Sunshine. We don't have the manpower to get him in here. He's gonna protect his little brother. So now the problem isn't Jewel, but how to do as little damage as possible to local citizenry and law enforcement from the likes of Sunshine."

"I got his ass, now. He wants some more," D. Wayne said.

"You don't got shit. He's just all cross-wired. He talks in tongues. Hears voices. He did time for killing three people. Said the voices told him to do it. He was the collection man for some bad guys. The guys he was trying to collect from beaned him, tied him up, were gonna kill him. All three turned up dead, so he goes to prison. They don't even know how many people he killed in there. So he stays out of sight, off the roads, and we forget he's in our county. And now you two guys resurrect him. Whoever gets Jewel is gonna have to kill Sunshine."

We all studied each other. "Forget about it, go home," Hurtis said. He grunted as he bent over to pick up the trash. With his arms full, he stared at Lee and said, "Y'all go home and stay there, all safe and cozy." He left us in the dark side of the building with a long drive to our cozy homes back in Beaumont.

I had to admit, Hurtis *was* smarter than he looked.

D. Wayne wasn't having any, however. As we got into the car, he said, "Can you see why every black man is bitching about cops? Just the way that redneck, hillbilly cracker sounds just pisses you off. Even white people got to be embarrassed by him."

✦

D. Wayne drove, and Lee sat in the passenger seat. I was barely able to curl myself up to step into the backseat. But once I got there and felt the plush leather interior, I let the Vicodin do its job. My mind went numb and took my body with it. No one spoke until we reached the bottleneck that was formed by righteous Lumberton. "We can't just let the motherfucker fuck up Buttermilk like that," D. Wayne said.

"It could have been us. Hell, it was damn near me," I said.

"D., I don't know," said Lee. "We are out of our league here."

"I got a reputation in this town. What if I back down? What is Buttermilk going to say? I got people who work for me—mostly out of want to or ought to. I don't pay them much. We work on trade. What's it gonna look like, I let one of them sit up in a hospital in hillbillyville while I shit my britches because Sun-fucking-shine McQueen is supposed to be a scary motherfucker? I'm talking pride and livelihood here."

"Maybe I owe it to Harry," Lee said and reached across the seat to take D. Wayne's hand.

I gathered strength. "Think. Didn't we get our asses kicked?"

"Now we know what we're up against," D. Wayne said.

"Roger," Lee said, and turned around in the seat to face me, "if you want out D. and I'll do this together."

"Oh, shit," I said.

They both helped me into my house, and I quickly found a bottle and poured us all a drink of my bourbon. When they finished, Lee waited behind, patted my cheek, and said, "I'm sorry. I didn't mean for it to go like this."

"Why are you with him?" I asked.

"That question seems to fascinate you," she said.

"I don't see it. You're refined. You're an artist. Hell, you're a dancer."

"And ironically, D. Wayne can see that too, and he gives me all the space for my temperament that I need. So I give him all the space he needs for his temperament. Except when it pushes him too far."

"Like now," I said.

"You could help us," she said, and I saw the same pleading look she gave to Hurtis Lomax. "Remember Harry. He deserves the truth."

"You and your men," I said. Lee kissed me on the cheek to join her current and maybe best man.

EIGHTEEN 18

The next morning my ribs and fingers throbbed so much that the ache knocked inside my head. After some grunts, I realized that the knock was outside my head as well. As best as I could, I pushed myself up from my bed. Walking toward the door I cussed my sloppiness, for each step over a shoe, pants, book, or magazine made some part of my side hurt. "Roger, are you in there?" I heard before I ever got to the door.

"Yes," I shouted back as I held my side. The door pushed open, and Dottie Phillips stepped in and held up her key to my house. It suddenly felt strange that Dottie would have the key to my private life. "Dottie, what time is it?" I asked.

"It's time for church. I want to go to the Baptist Church. There are several nice gentlemen there. But I don't want them to think I'm desperate and have no dates, so I thought you might like to be my date."

"Dottie, I can't go to church," I said. I held up my heavy hand to show her my cast.

She tilted her head to match the tilt of my body. "My, it looks as if you do need to go to church. You must have really had a rough night."

"Dottie, I got hit by a two-by-four," I said.

"You drank that much?"

"No, I mean literally. A guy hit me with a two-by-four."

"All the more reason, pray for recovery," she said.

"I can't."

"Please, I just need an escort."

"Dottie, I haven't been to church in years. I wouldn't know how to act. Hell, I'd probably embarrass you in front of those gentlemen you're after." Dottie stopped to ponder. "And what if someone recognized me from bars or my business? Then they'd think that the man you were with was a drinker and a sleazebag. Then where would you be?"

"None of the people you associate with would be in church."

"Come now, Dottie. You can't be sure."

"Okay, okay," Dottie said. "I'll go on my own."

She stepped closer to me. "Is it just your hand?"

"My ribs, too."

"So that's why you're standing so funny. You know, I have this videocassette all about faith. You might watch it. It could make you feel better."

"No, right now a painkiller would help me." My mind glowed a little. "Dottie, on the kitchen counter is a bottle of pills. Could you open it for me, and hand me a pill?"

Dottie tsked. "The life you live." She shook her head and stepped into the kitchen, then came back with a Vicodin between two fingers. She dropped it into my open palm, and I threw it in my mouth and swallowed the pill without water. Dottie tsked again and went back through the door, pulling it closed behind her.

Without my ribs and hand and thus without my jog, I'd spend the day, maybe several days, in sin and sloth.

Though the Vicodin was slowing me down already, I revved myself up with coffee. My mind got hyperactive. I needed the jog, but since I couldn't move, I thought. I didn't want to end up like Buttermilk. I didn't owe anything to Lee or Harry. I stopped for a moment. I started this investigation because I thought that I owed Cody and Jessica. Now I didn't know who I was working for. I was drifting. I was hopeless and helpless. I was too old. I just didn't give a shit. I had no business even trying to be a private investigator. My shape was the shape of most people in the world. We didn't live with a purpose. We didn't know what we were doing half the time, who we worked for, who owed what to whom. We all just drifted, bumping into each other and trying to cause as little damage as possible.

I held my head with my good hand to get it to stop. I was off the case. Sunshine could go on a rampage. Emily Nguyen could get the bad guys. I'd give the Hudsons their money back. I'd beg D. Wayne not to beat the hell out of me. Hell, he couldn't really. He didn't have Buttermilk.

I'd get out of the divorce business. I'd take Rachel's job, become Joe Civilian—straight, cool, shallow. A six-pack and a sitcom, bedtime stories. Then the phone rang. It was Lynette. Somebody had beat the shit out of Bruce.

Both Buttermilk and Bruce were at St. Elizabeth's Hospital. Overnight, on D. Wayne's orders, an ambulance retrieved Buttermilk from behind the Pine Curtain and brought him to hopefully better medical care in Beaumont. I found Buttermilk's room first. Lee was outside the door, sitting in a plastic folding chair with her face in her hands. She pulled her head up to look at me when I walked up.

"God, Lee, have you been up all night?" I asked. Her hair was matted. Her eyes were puffy. She seemed on the verge of tears.

"I didn't sleep too well," she said. "I didn't have any painkillers. And this is pretty painful."

"Want some of mine?"

"The pain or the pills?"

"Looks like you got enough of your own pain."

Before I could ask about D. Wayne, she told me. "He's been out most of the night. He called several times telling me he loved me, saying he'd get the motherfuckers. Suddenly it's all become very personal for him. He's doing the kind of investigation he can do."

"Yeah, *criminal* investigation."

Lee looked at me without any of her charm or grace or flirtatiousness. "I'm tired. Don't make fun of D. Wayne. He's doing what he can."

"How's Buttermilk?

"Get this. A nurse here says that basically he was just beat to shit. Beaumont, huh? You can't clean 'em up. So I ask if she could tell me something besides the obvious. His brain is swelling, just as in a concussion. The hinge that his jaw fits in is shattered. His nose is broken. His collarbone is fractured. Eventually he'll need plastic surgery." Lee pulled her head up to look at me. "Roger, we're going to do something about this. I know what we said last night, but this is existential now. D. Wayne and I have *chosen* to make this important. This, for us, has meaning. I sure hope that you'll help us. I need your help." Her eyes pleading again.

"A friend of mine got beat up early this morning. He was just leaving the bar, and somebody jumps him, cold cocks him, then pummels him.

That's why I'm here."

"That sounds awful coincidental."

"He knew Jewel."

Lee grabbed my good hand. "Then you're with us."

"I ain't with nothing." I jerked my hand away. "Look at Buttermilk. Look at me. Look at what could have happened. None of this is worth it. Your existentialism is just some misguided, bullshit sentimentality. Grow up, be like everybody else. We're all pathetic with no control. Get used to it."

Lee kept her blank look. "Sounds like you've been having that argument with yourself." She looked for a moment like she was both very young and very old. I saw the stripper and the dancer. I saw for a moment why I had decided to become a lawyer so many years ago. The slick ones wanted to make life easy just for them and their kind, but I wanted some for the rest of us. My indignation was tempered by the care and concern in Lee's voice and eyes. Lee slowly let my hand slide from hers. "Maybe we can't do anything. Maybe we're just delusional. I don't even really hold this against Sunshine. But somebody, something is at fault for all this hurt."

"And so you want to find out who it is, if there even is a *who* instead of the way the whole world works. So you're going to point yourself toward a whole lot of shit and heartbreak."

"Guess so," Lee said.

I stepped through the door to take a look at Buttermilk. I walked past the old man in postsurgery, nodded, and he nodded at me. With my good hand, I parted the curtain between the two of them.

Buttermilk had bandages all over his face. Even on his black face, I could see yellow lumps. One eye was still swollen shut. The other one lazily lifted. His busted lips parted, and I saw that he was missing a front tooth. "Hello, motherfucker," he grumbled between clamped teeth. "'Cause of rescuing your sorry ass," he paused, closed his good eye, swallowed, and started again. "'Cause of that, I can't eat no pussy, I got to lip it." He tried to laugh but grunted. "I can't get my tongue out of my mouth." He sucked in some air through his bent nose and grimaced. "I got to sip my food through this hole in my mouth."

"Thank you for rescuing my sorry ass," I said. He nodded, and I could see that talking was too much pain even for Buttermilk. "I'm going to go see another friend of mine. He's beat to shit, too. I'll bring you both some flowers."

"Bring some black pussy," he said. He rolled his head to look at me with watery eyes. "What did that other fucker look like? What was the damage I done to him?"

"I passed out about the same time you did. But you got some good licks in. He got lucky. But I'll guarantee you that he's hurting today." Buttermilk nodded.

I felt someone walk in. D. Wayne was suddenly beside me, "How's my man?" he asked. Buttermilk tried to smile.

I felt like going, but I wanted to say something kind to Buttermilk. I had no idea what to say. "What do you do when you're not working? Other than chasing the ladies, I mean."

Buttermilk smiled, then D. Wayne smiled and said, "Tell him."

"I raise Yorkies," he mumbled through his wired jaws.

"What?" I asked even though I had heard.

"Yorkie puppies, man. I like 'em. People say they're pussy lap dogs, but they're only like that 'cause once they decide on who they want their daddy or momma to be, they're loyal. They'll sit up in momma or daddy's lap and fight a pit bull or sabre tooth tiger it tries to fuck with momma or daddy."

"You gotta admire that," D. Wayne said.

"Do you have one?" I asked, because I had this image of Buttermilk with a Yorkie in his lap. That image pained me.

Buttermilk swallowed hard to talk. "I got a female lives with me. Name's Pinkie."

"Why Pinkie?"

"'Cause 'spite the nasty joke, we're all pink on the inside."

"You gotta admire that," D. Wayne said.

D. Wayne pulled a chair up to Buttermilk's bed, and I backed out of the room, past Buttermilk's postsurgical roommate, and turned to face Lee standing in the door. We found ourselves hugging each other. "Oh Roger, I just hurt," she said.

Bruce was in a four-person room. Bruce was close to the door, the first one scheduled to leave. His face wasn't as dented as Buttermilk's, but

I could see the black eye, the lumps, the broken nose, and the wired jaw. His bald head had cuts and scrapes, like someone had dragged him across the pavement. When he saw me, Bruce tried to smile and jabber.

"Slow down," I said. "Shake your head or nod if I get any right answers." Bruce nodded. "A big guy did this. Punched you right in front of the ear, like he knew what he was doing." Bruce nodded. "That's the mandible. Take out your jaw, and there's just not much you can do." Bruce nodded. "Then he punched your nose."

Bruce couldn't keep silent, even if it hurt. He talked through his wired jaws. "And he kicked me. And said he'd kill me if I talked to the police about Jewel. Who the fuck is he, Roger? What the fuck is going on?"

"I'm thinking that you're just a warning," I said. Bruce's eyes started getting watery. I was wheezing from my ribs, reminding me of my own rearranged body parts. I sat on Bruce's bed.

"Don't go after him on my 'count," Bruce choked on the words behind his wired jaw. "He's too mean."

"I plan to steer clear of him." I held up my hand to show him my paltry broken fingers. "And he busted two of my ribs. With a two-by-four," I added, almost hoping to show that my injuries nearly matched his.

Fear or disgust was making Bruce stare at me with eyes that were just about to cry. "We ain't no match for him." I let my head hang and nodded. Lee, D. Wayne, and no doubt Buttermilk wanted a vendetta. I was like Bruce, whipped.

"Roger, Roger," Bruce said and swiped at my hand with his. He missed and hit my bare thigh sticking out of the leg of my shorts. "I'm a pussy. I'm just a pussy." One tear did roll down his cheek. I wanted to run before he let all of his tears go. "I got whipped by that big nigger. Then I get whipped by the really mean fucker. I even get whipped by you." I swallowed hard. "And you're old. I'm a pussy. I'm growing my hair out, getting rid of all my body jewels and decorations, selling my Harley. Gonna buy a Camry or some nice family car." Bruce was crying now. I stood.

"I'm a pussy, and now I'm never going get no pussy. Look at me." He held his hands up toward his face. "How am I going get any pussy with a busted, fucked-up face like this?"

"One step at a time, Bruce."

He looked at me so that I thought I would cry. "I'll make it up to you, Bruce," I said.

"No need to. I thank you, in a way, for showing me what I am."

"I'm going to help," I said.

<hr />

When I got home, I had a message on my answering machine from Emily Nguyen. "I hope that you're not even thinking about going on with this," was all she said. I got a message from Deputy Hurtis Lomax, "I hope you and your friends aren't even thinking about going after Sunshine."

I felt starved. After a beer to warm up my taste buds, I rummaged through my freezer to find a large sirloin steak. I defrosted it in the microwave, started some water to boil for some rice, and fumbled with a can opener to open a can of corn. When I couldn't get it open, I stabbed at the top with a heavy butcher knife in my good but clumsy left hand. I started some coals in my rusting barbeque pit and made myself a drink.

I'd just flipped the steak over when someone knocked at the door. I opened it to find Lee standing in my doorway. "I'll bet no one's been by to see how you're doing?"

"I live alone."

"Did you call your parents?"

"I don't want to worry them."

"Did you call that girlfriend of yours that you are or are not seeing?"

"She would be upset."

Lee shook her head and glided into my house. She stopped midway across my living room and looked around. "I know a housekeeper who works really cheaply."

Lee let herself plop onto my sofa. All the tautness went out of her body. The poise and the grace wilted into an exhausted middle-aged woman. An unladylike groan she couldn't control rolled out of her mouth. "Does D. Wayne know you're here?" I asked.

"I do what I want. D. Wayne doesn't control me." She closed her eyes then opened them very quickly. "He's as tired as I am. I left him at the hospital." She blew through her lips. "Roger, you need for someone to come by and see you. To see how you're doing. You needed someone to come see you last night."

"Or to talk me into going after Sunshine," I said and was immediately sorry.

"You poor man," Lee said.

I looked back over my shoulder toward my dinner. "I have a really big steak, plenty of rice, and some corn...."

Lee didn't let me finish, "No, I don't want to disturb your dinner."

"You're probably hungry. If you want, you can just watch me eat."

"I am hungry."

"And I'll get you a drink," I said. I went to my one cabinet where I kept my liquor. "Maybe I have some wine." I opened the door with my left hand. "Let's see, scotch, bourbon, gin, rum, vodka."

Lee had gotten up, walked to the refrigerator, and found herself a beer. "This'll be fine," she said.

Lee's beer popped and fizzed as she opened it, and I crossed to the steak. I grabbed the butcher knife that I had used on the can of corn and held it in my left hand. I put a fork in the wedge between my thumb and my palm. I aimed the utensils at the steak. "Let me," Lee said, and took the knife and fork from me. She cut the steak in two. Then she looked at my cast, then at me. She cut my half of the steak into bite-sized pieces. At dinner, she even steadied my hand as I tried to stab a chunk of meat with my left hand.

After dinner, not knowing what to do, I said, "Maybe you'd like to watch some TV. Maybe a baseball game is on. I think the Astros are playing. Do you like the Astros?"

"Maybe I ought to go," she said, even as she was lowering herself back onto my couch.

Two innings into the game, Lee had slipped off her shoes, let her head fall back, and was asleep and snoring on my couch. I looked at her bare feet. They were a physical history of her dancing. Her toes were knotted and twisted. She had scars up both of her ankles. She was fighting her age and winning. I wished that I were her.

I let Lee sleep as long as I dared, then woke her up. She kissed my cheek when she left and told me to call her if I needed anything.

After Lee left, I stepped outside the back door into the dark. There was no breeze. The air seemed to press in on me. I pulled my cell phone out of my pocket and dialed as best I could. When Lee answered her cell phone, she hadn't even gotten to the freeway. "You're right," I said.

"This is existential. Sunshine and Jewel, the Hudsons, and the police are all trying to take our identity away. The only way we can get it back is to do something really stupid."

"So how should we start being stupid?"

"What has D. Wayne found out?"

"That a lot of people would like to kill Jewel."

"How about I go talk to Jessica Hudson? Does that sound stupid enough?"

NINETEEN 19

I waited for Jessica Hudson in the parking lot, right beside her Suburban, on the driver's side door. Even though I was prepared, had girded my loins so to speak, I flinched when the horn sounded as she hit the remote to unlock it. With her arms full of books, she didn't even notice me until she rounded the back end of the tall vehicle. She abruptly stopped. "No, no, I told you not here."

"What kind of gas mileage you get from this thing?" I patted the side of the Suburban with my left hand. "You think it's eating up the ozone? Of course, here in Beaumont we've got a blanket of pollution to take the place of the ozone."

"There's a security guard on duty. I can call him."

"I'm just having a conversation."

She looked down at my legs. "Don't you ever wear grownup clothes?"

"Why are my legs so offensive? Let's start off talking about that." I took off my hat and wiped the sweat away from my forehead. "It's hot. We could sit inside your car in the air-conditioning. Or we could take a drive. My car's down the block."

"I'm not getting into a car with you."

"Hey, I'm working for you, remember? I'm the good guy. That's why I'm here, trying to catch the bad guys."

Jessica hesitated, pasted a smile on her face, and waved to some kids and parents.

"You know, I couldn't even get near this giant parking lot. I pick up this little girl from school, and it's the same thing. A busy thoroughfare made into a giant traffic jam by good parents picking up their kids. What makes normally sane, obedient people disobey all traffic rules when picking up their kids?"

"I don't fucking know, Mr. Jackson. Would you get on with the questioning?"

"I didn't say questions. I said a conversation. I mean look at this, people yelling and screaming. Kids milling around. Crossing guards trying to keep just a little order. Lines of cars honking, yelling, parking in both lanes. All rules gone. Stripped to some basic parental animalism, *protect the young*. They'd be killing each other if they were armed. Hell, half of them probably are armed."

"It's hot."

"Oh, all right, so I remember now, I do have a few questions." I stepped toward her.

"I'm going to scream. Why can't you ask my husband?"

"He wasn't fucking Harry Krammer."

And sure enough, without whatever happy drugs she took to calm her frayed nerves, Jessica Hudson slapped me. I figured that right now she needed some of what Harry bought for her, really bad. "Fuck you. Go away. Where's my husband?"

A security guard was moving toward me. I held up my hand and shouted in his general direction without taking my eyes away from Jessica. "Just a conversation gotten a little intense. That's all."

"Ms. Hudson, who is this?" the security guard asked.

"What's it gonna be? Now or later? You know my mouth and manner never progressed much beyond my choice of clothes. I can be crude. I will get some answers."

"He's a friend." Jessica raised her flat palm to her mouth to push her smile back into place and turned to smile at the security guard. He nodded sternly and backed away.

I took the books from her in my one good hand and led the way to the car door. "Okay, let's get into some air-conditioning." I held her door open, threw the books into the passenger side, and helped her in. She immediately started the engine. I walked around the back of the Suburban, and just as I turned the right corner, Jessica slammed it into reverse and hit the gas. She knocked me into a parked car. My mind gave the okay to my ribs to start shooting pain through my body. I bumped my extended ring finger, and it shot pain on its own under my cast, past my elbow, and into my shoulder.

Jessica would have been gone had she not nearly backed into a BMW.

What was a teacher doing with a BMW? The security guard came running forward. The BMW-driving teacher honked. Jessica shot the finger out her window. I grabbed the passenger door handle, yanked, and pushed me and my throb into the passenger side. "Enough of this fucking around," I said.

The BMW drove by. The security guard came running up. Jessica motioned him away. She slowly backed up, then pulled into the line waiting to get out of the school's packed lot.

"I got two friends waiting in line to get their faces put back together, and if you ain't noticed, my fingers now point the wrong way and my ribs got cracks in them, all because we met the baddest motherfucker any of us had ever seen, and he beat the shit out of most us at the same time, because we were trying to find Jewel McQueen so the cops would stop bothering you and you could get back to buying shit and praying." I held my ribs and breathed in. "So I'm going to need some answers, or I'm going to stop concealing the fact from my friends in the county sheriff's office that Harry Krammer got your coke for you from Jewel fucking McQueen." My head was spinning. My tongue was loose. I wanted a drink. So I went on. "There, there's some ethics. Tell your husband I found my ethics."

I looked over at Jessica. She had tears in her eyes. I yelled, "Stop the fucking crying. It ain't working no more. I need some information."

"I don't have any to give."

"Oh, you can help a little. I'm not going to ask you about getting cocaine or whatever it was from Harry or Jewel. That way you haven't confirmed any of my solid, rock-hard suspicions. They can stay suspicions. And you can thank me for that little courtesy and tell your husband that I gave you that courtesy. But what I want is information about Jewel. So this won't take long."

"All I have is short," Jessica said, and I almost appreciated her for that answer.

"How do I find Jewel? Do you have a phone number, an address?"

"No, Harry knew him."

"Harry didn't have money. How did he get money to Jewel for whatever he was buying from him?"

"I don't know."

"Better to tell me now than let cops find it."

"I gave him some money. Once or twice."

"Did you ever meet Jewel?"

"One time, Harry took me to this party. He said it was going to be great. We were going to swim, barbeque, drink. . . ." She hesitated. I thought she would tell me more about what went on at the party, but she stopped. "It was at this place somewhere on the Neches. It was disgusting. It was some shack, some wood and tarpaper shack. And Jewel and a bunch of scrungy, disgusting rednecks were there. Jewel, when I met him, said it was his place."

"Where was it?"

"On the Neches."

"Could you get me there?"

"No."

"Are you sure that is all?"

"Please don't do this again," she pleaded. "I know deep down you're a good man and don't mean to hurt me."

I opened the door and left her waiting to exit the parking lot.

TWENTY

When I walked into Nothing To Lose, Ridley and Edmore nodded to me in their quiet, dignified way. Both were in their leather and colors. Next to them, sucking up beer through a straw, was Bruce. His mouth never left the straw, but his eyes glanced up at me. True to his word, Bruce hadn't shaved his head that day. He had no jewelry dangling from his face, not unless you count the braces around his teeth and jaw. Where he used to have the ring, which I yanked out, was a red, healing scar that split his eyebrow in two. He looked thinner, like he hadn't worked out.

I nodded at all of them and crossed to the other side of the bar where Lynette had a beer waiting for me. Lynette leaned over from her side on her elbows. "Hear that Leroy and Shirley went on some vacation together?"

"Ain't love grand."

"Go figure," Lynette said. I lifted my beer with my left hand and rested my cast on the bar. "You know, you really look like shit. You should get some sleep or something."

Before I could answer, I felt some hot breath on my neck and turned to see Zia. He had been restocking the condom machine. "Roger, you know I think I would like to be a private investigator like you. How would I do this?"

"I wouldn't advise it, Zia." I raised my cast. "It's got health hazards."

Zia looked at Lynette to check if she would fuss at him for annoying me. Since he flashed the sex toys at Shirley and Leroy, Lynette had put him on a short leash. "The fuck business ain't so good. Nobody likes dirty books or nasty key fobs or fuck movies no more. They get them on the Internet. They buy their rubbers in the drugstores. Everybody sells the condoms now. A man's got to make a living. So I thought I might try some new kind of work. You don't seem to work too hard and you always got money for a beer, never mooching from anybody."

Lynette scowled at him. "What?" Zia said and held his palms up. "I'm being an enterprising American, searching for job opportunities."

"Zia, you can't just start being a private investigator," Lynette said. "And like Roger always says, there's really no such thing anymore. Everybody has gone corporate and high security and high tech, with retirement plans and insurance."

"That's what I want," Zia said and pointed at me.

"Go to school. Take some courses," I said.

"You say a good word for me to your lawyer friends, huh? I could be a snitch. I know lots of things. I'll tell on anybody."

"You watch too much TV."

Zia hung his head and knew better than to push his luck. He drifted away from me toward a quiet beer at the other corner of the bar. I looked across at Bruce. I yelled at him, "How you doing, Bruce?" He looked a little watery eyed and shrugged his shoulders. "My man's doing fine," Ridley said and slapped Bruce's back, making him grimace.

I had some thirty minutes by myself before Lee and D. Wayne came into the bar. D. Wayne had his black gambler's hat cocked at a jaunty angle on his head. He had on his shiny black boots. Lee wore shorts that showed off her still-shapely legs. They sat beside me. "He been here yet?" D. Wayne asked.

"No, I give him another hour."

"Why don't we just jump his ass, soon as he walks in?" D. Wayne asked. Lee got up from her seat and stood between us to hear.

"That won't get any information. D. Wayne, you can't always just beat information out of people."

"It worked with you."

"What if he's got no information to give?" Lee asked sarcastically of D. Wayne. She turned to me. "What if he's got no information to give?" she asked as a real question.

"He may not. But he's going to come looking for me. I really scared his wife."

D. Wayne chuckled. "Yeah, this is working fine. You do all the woman intimidating and leave that big-ass, badass Sunshine to me and Lee."

Lee shook her head. "This is locker room chatter. What's the plan?"

"Why don't you two go sit at a table. Act like you don't even know me. I'll try to get him outside to the picnic table. Then just come on out. Just you, D. Wayne. Lee, don't let on that you're with us."

"What! Do I embarrass you? Don't want them to see that your partner is a woman? Worried about the girl's safety? Don't want to let her play tackle, just touch?"

"Honey, calm down," D. Wayne said. "Roger just don't want to play all our cards right off. Doesn't want to let on who all is on the team."

"Wow, right," I said. "And let's face it. Not counting Buttermilk, D. Wayne is the baddest looking guy on our team."

"Our team keep getting beat to shit, Lee is gonna be the baddest ass on our team," D. Wayne said.

D. Wayne dragged Lee to a table, and they huddled over a drink. Zia kept to himself. Bruce nervously eyed me. Ridley and Edmore left for their other rounds. Halfway through my fourth beer, Cody Hudson walked through the door. He hesitated, spotted me, and moved forward. The idiot didn't even stop to size up the place, to see who might come at him and from where. "Can I buy you a beer?" I asked when he got up to me.

"No, no, well yes, you can. You owe me at least that much."

"Let's not be snotty."

"Your job is to help my wife, not annoy her and scare her." He got right to the point. I motioned to Lynette, and Cody ordered a Bud.

When she set the beer in front of him, he stared at the bottle. "You're fired. I don't want you working for me. Not if you're going to browbeat my wife."

"Why don't we have a more private discussion? Let's go outside and talk about this."

Cody looked at me like I had challenged him to a fight. I held up my cast. "I can't whip you. I can't even hit you," I said.

We left our beers and stepped outside. When I closed the door behind me, I shut us off from the gazes of D. Wayne, Lee, and Lynette. It had just turned dark. Lightning bugs were blinking. "Nice night," I said. "We don't get too many of these in Beaumont."

"Look, enough of this. Do you have anything to tell me? If not, then let's just quit all of this. You tell me what I owe you. I'll write a check, and I'll find someone to help me who won't harass my wife."

"That was necessary because I wasn't getting too many answers from you."

"I'll be in my office. You call me and tell me what I owe you. I'm through with you." Cody turned to walk back through the door. But D. Wayne stepped through the door just as Cody reached for it. Cody stopped and turned to look at me.

"Roger's got a partner," D. Wayne said.

"What is this? Are you trying to intimidate me?" Cody asked. He sized up D. Wayne. "This guy looks well dressed, not like some mean punk," Cody said.

"I'll show you mean, you keep on talking. But thanks for the compliment on the clothes," D. Wayne said.

"There's just a lot of things that need some answers," I said.

"I've told you all I know."

"Your wife at first didn't know Jewel McQueen, then she did. In fact, she's admitted to meeting him. He's a meth head and a would-be cocaine peddler. Is your wife a customer?"

"Why, you son-of-a bitch. She's a teacher. We go to church. I ought to . . ."

D. Wayne interrupted him. "You know I got this bigger nigger friend helps me ask questions. But he's in the hospital. Ask Roger what it's like trying to answer questions with that big nigger around." D. Wayne crossed his arms and leaned against the frame of the door. D. Wayne's eyes caught some light and twinkled. I wondered if his eyes had flashed like that when he and Buttermilk were interrogating me.

"You guys don't look so tough," Cody said and started to raise his hand. "You're both kind of old."

"I'll show your ass *old*," D. Wayne said and stepped closer to Cody.

I held up my hands. "Let's just say we got off to a bad start." I stepped quickly up to Cody, then maneuvered myself between him and D. Wayne. "Cody, I think we can find Jewel."

"Well then, by God, find him," Cody said.

I looked over my shoulder at D. Wayne, then back at Cody. "My associate has many talents. So I'm asking you what I should do when I find Jewel."

"What do you mean?" Cody asked.

D. Wayne was beside me. "Yeah, what do you mean?" I looked at D. Wayne to tell him to shut up.

"Jewel is dangerous in his own right. His brother who guards him is even more dangerous. To talk to him, we might have to hurt Jewel and his brother."

"So do it," Cody said.

"So would you be willing to pay extra to see them hurt?"

"You've spent enough of my money."

"As I have said, my associate has many talents. What if he had to really hurt Jewel? What if Jewel couldn't testify?"

"Jewel is a real easy man to pin a crime on," D. Wayne said. "Say he disappears. Say he's incapacitated. Case closed. No more questions."

I continued. "Your wife doesn't have to bear an investigation. She doesn't have to testify at a trial. No more public embarrassment. Harry is dead and buried." I paused to look at D. Wayne, then at Cody. "And so could Jewel be dead."

It was as though I could smell Cody's sweat. He wrung his hands. He looked at D. Wayne. "You're not a cop?"

"I don't cooperate with cops too much," D. Wayne said.

"See, this isn't a threat or a showdown," I said. "Just a discussion. Just a proposition of mutual interest and benefit."

"So how much would you need if this were to happen?"

Cody swung his head between me and D. Wayne. D. Wayne shrugged. "I'm a modest man."

I felt my throat thicken. "Ten thousand sounds fair."

Cody made perch lips, like he was sucking air, trying to get out an answer but unable to make the words. He gritted his teeth, breathed in. "I have to think," he said.

"Think fast," D. Wayne said.

"Okay, okay. Here's the deal." Cody rubbed his hands through his hair. A lightning bug flickered between his face and mine. "You tell me when it's done."

"You'll probably read about it when it's done," D. Wayne said.

"I owe you nothing else. But when it's done. Well, then, then . . . "

I held out my hand, and Cody shook it. "Now why don't we go in and finish our beers." D. Wayne held the back door open for us.

When Cody left, D. Wayne slapped my back and said, "That's my man. Cool. Smooth. Caressed that motherfucker all to hell." Lee joined us, and I switched to bourbon.

D. Wayne put an arm around Lee. "Roger played him, baby. He's as much as admitted he paid Jewel to do ol' Harry in."

"We don't know that," I said.

Lee twisted away from D. Wayne's arm and grabbed mine. "What do we know?"

"We know that D. Wayne and I could probably be indicted for a conspiracy to commit a murder."

"Stop joking," she said.

"He ain't joking," D. Wayne said.

"That wasn't the plan," Lee said. "You were supposed to see if you could find out more about Jewel. Whether he was selling directly to Jessica, for instance. More important, where he is."

I turned away from Lee to sip my bourbon. "I kind of made things up as I went along."

"You should of seen it, baby. It was gorgeous," D. Wayne said.

"You two are talking in riddles. What happened? What did you make up?"

"The man," D. Wayne said. I looked across the bar at Bruce who seemed to shrivel in front of me. I all but finished my bourbon and relished the bite and the coolness on the back of my throat. "The man got Cody fucking Hudson to offer us money to kill Jewel."

"Cody fucking Hudson offered you guys money?" Lee asked.

"Ten thousand dollars," D. Wayne said. "Where's he get that kind of money?"

"But we still haven't found Jewel," I said.

"You did good, Roger. You were like a musician or an actor the way you played him. Don't nothing make you happy?"

I motioned to Lynette for another drink. I stared at Bruce. I almost felt sorry for Cody. "So how are we going to find Jewel?" Lee said.

"We could call it quits. Let the police find him. Eventually they will, you know."

"You're forgetting, Roger. It's not finding Jewel that we want. It's the answers. We want to talk to him. That's all," Lee said.

"We could make ten thousand dollars if we kill him," D. Wayne said.

"Y'all are both forgetting about Sunshine. We could say we've done our job. We have a pretty good idea of what went on."

"You change your mind more than an old lady," Lee said.

I gulped my bourbon. "So then tomorrow, we'll go back to Kountze and Hardin County Courthouse. Start researching. How are you two at research?"

"Can we just beat the shit out of somebody and find out?" D. Wayne said.

I found the bourbon making me fuzzy-headed and -hearted, so I looked at Lee and asked, "What did Harry see in Jessica Hudson?"

"That's Harry. Like a moth to the flame. She's got a nice body, semi-smart. She's the type of woman men are supposed to want. Cleaned up. She's got her edges rubbed smooth. All he saw in his job were the poor, the undereducated, the desperate. I guess he figured that he'd end up with someone like that. Maybe she was everything he wasn't, but wished he could be."

D. Wayne put an arm around her. "Like you in a way. You're what I wished I was more like."

"But she's got a drug problem and got him killed," I said.

"It's the chances we got to take," D. Wayne said. "My lady, though, is perfect."

Lee looked at D. Wayne like she didn't particularly like his comment. "Poor Harry," Lee said. Then she wondered out loud, "So how is Jessica Hudson any better than Jewel? It's what she is that got Harry killed. Jewel just pulled the trigger."

"She doesn't have a brother like Sunshine," I said.

Lee smiled and wondered some more. "I was a titty dancer. You and D. Wayne have the same sort of business associations. We can fit into our worlds. Harry couldn't quite shoehorn himself into his. He always wanted something a little better. Everything he found that he thought was a little better, like Jessica, turned out to be worse."

"Goddamn, honey," D. Wayne said. "Now you're getting like Roger and making everybody sad." D. Wayne turned his attention to me. "What the hell makes y'all want to do that?"

The two of them sat through two more drinks with me and then began kissing each other. They took their kissing outside and then, I imagine, to one or the others' house. I didn't even know where D. Wayne lived.

After I slowed my drinking down, I yelled across the bar for Bruce to join me. With his jaws welded shut, he tried to say, "So I see you're really buds with that fancy prick."

"He's kind of my partner now, Bruce."

"Takes all kinds," he muttered.

"Bruce, look, maybe I can't pay you, but I may need some help. You want to help me out a little with this case? Maybe some others in the future. It ain't much, but it'll beat selling drugs."

"Will I get the shit beat out of me? You know, I'm getting used to being a pussy."

"I'll try to watch out for you," I said.

When Bruce said, "Sure," I knew just how hard it would be for me to watch out for him, but I would try. I wanted to give him something after twice getting him beat to shit.

Bruce was happy, so he bought me a drink. We tried to have a conversation, but Bruce's jaw muscles wore out.

TWENTY-ONE

We spent the next morning doing graduate-school work, boring library work, primary resource work, in the Hardin County Courthouse in Kountze. D. Wayne complained, "Why don't we get out of this spooky building and go ask somebody something?" But Lee and I pushed ahead. We had started with a phone book and tore out the page with the McQueens. Next we checked plats, registered voters, property owners. We found some land someplace off a dirt county road, just off the Neches, registered to a Ruby McQueen. We found no residence for her. I suggested we call Deputy Hurtis Lomax.

"You guys are just itching to fuck yourselves," he said over the phone. When I explained our determination, he said, "It's not enough that Sunshine is already mad at you? Now you're gonna fuck around with his momma."

Ruby McQueen was in a county-run retirement home in Kountze. Lee and I left D. Wayne to drive around while we spoke to Mrs. McQueen. We figured that D. Wayne's temperament might not be best for questioning an elderly white woman.

The assisted living center had a gravel parking lot in between three glass and brick buildings. Several attendants were outside smoking. The trimmed hedges and rosebushes made the place look well funded, but inside, we could see and smell the lack of funding. The antiseptic tried to cover up other atrocious odors. The bare, dirty floor had a frayed carpet in the TV room. Lee and I waited in the lobby on a shabby lime green sofa while an on-duty attendant went down a hall to fetch Mrs. McQueen.

Ruby McQueen rolled out with her walker. She grunted as she tried to step fast enough to keep up with it. The attendant tried to keep up with her so that she could catch her if she fell. Ruby McQueen wore a purple muumuu, just a sack really, covering her girth. Her gray, curly hair looked as though patches were falling out. She was missing a front tooth on the bottom and one on the top. Curling out of either nostril were tubes going to an oxygen tank fastened to the side of the walker.

The attendant helped Ruby stand and pulled the walker away. Looking at us with a steady gaze, Ruby eyed Lee and me while the attendant unhooked the oxygen tank from the walker and held it with one hand while she guided Ruby toward a chair. Both Lee and I jumped up to help her. She sagged into the seat and grunted while she squirmed to adjust her bulk in it. Then her wheezing started, a low, raspy sound, like we could hear her lungs working. But her eyes sparkled a bit, like Sunshine's, and I could see Sunshine in her face, and my ribs and fingers started to hurt. "I don't get many visitors," she said. "Thank you for coming to see me. Are you relatives?"

"No, we're friends of Jewel's," Lee said.

Ruby leaned forward to peer through her bifocals, trying to zero her glasses and her gaze on us, all the time wheezing. "Some cops come in here saying the same thing. One was this big deputy, the other this little chink girl. You cops?"

"Like I said," Lee said. "We're friends of Jewel's."

Ruby looked at me, and I felt Sunshine's gaze on me again. I rubbed on my cast with my good hand, and Ruby's eyes, bulging behind her thick bifocals, followed me. "That's what the cops said." Her *s*s hissed or wheezed between the holes in her grin.

"We're not police," Lee said. "We're concerned about him. We have a mutual friend with Jewel, and we think that Jewel's in trouble. We can help him."

Ruby pulled back from Lee and studied her. "I tell you same as those cops, Jewel's got Jesus in his heart. Whatever he done, he didn't mean it. He's following the right true path of Jesus Christ our Lord." She stared hard at Lee. "So I don't know if I should be talking to you about Jewel." She shifted in her chair, trying to get comfortable or to settle her weight. "Now my other boy is another story. Sunshine was born with the devil in him. He's as much as said he follows the devil. When he was just a little boy, I felt the devil creeping around my house."

Like Sunshine, she could tell a good story. She had our attention, and she found delight in that attention. She held up a finger, "I've given up one boy to the devil. I should have fought harder for his soul, but when he went to prison, I known he was gone to the devil for good. I'm not about to give up another boy. I may not of fought the devil for the first son, but I sure as hell will fight the cops for the second one." She wagged the finger at us. I could see Sunshine, maybe after he had just shoved a shiv into somebody, making the same gestures as he told some prison legend.

Lee tried again, "But you see, we aren't cops."

I interrupted her. "Your son's soul is exactly why we are here. Sister Lee and I are from the Apostolic Christian Church in Beaumont. We believe in the pure blood of Christ the Lamb. So does your boy Jewel." Ruby McQueen cocked her head like a mocking bird listening to a sound it was trying to imitate.

"Jewel came to our church, and I could see that, though he was troubled, though he had his fight with temptations of his own and with the devil, way down deep inside of him, his heart was pumping the blood of the Lamb."

Lee looked at me like I had lost my mind. "Roger, is this how we're going to do this?"

Ruby McQueen shushed her, so I went on. "Sister Lee and I were especially fond of him. We were part of the church's outreach program. We had brought Jewel in. He was winning. He was fighting the devil. But then these awful things happened, and we don't see him. Then the police talk to us. Sister Lee and I decide that we have to find Jewel first. We want to let him know that the church is behind him. We're praying for him to pray for himself and help himself."

"Glory to God, and to your church," Ruby muttered. She nodded at me. I nodded at her. Lee nodded out of confusion.

"We mean to do more than pray for him. The church has a fund. His many friends have gotten together. We have money for him. We have been searching for an attorney for him. We believe that the police are mistaken. In our hearts, we are betting on Jewel and not the police."

"Praise you. Praise you," Ruby said and stuck out both her hands. I put out my cast to touch her fingers with my two good ones. Acting on what she saw, Lee took Ruby's hand in her own two hands.

I reached for my billfold with my left hand, pulled it out, and saw that I had fifty dollars. I let go of Ruby's hand, clumsily folded up the bills, and handed them to her. "That's from the church, for you, to tide you over."

She took the money, and her eyes lit up. "Bless you, bless you and your church."

With one of her hands in my casted hand, with her other hand in Lee's hands, I asked Ruby, "Where is Jewel?"

She pulled her hand away from mine to wipe at a tear in her eye. "We have this property out by the Neches. It floods all the time, but we got this little cabin. He's there."

"How do we get there?" Lee asked.

"We will find it." I cut Lee off.

As I pushed myself up, I asked Ruby, "How do you afford to stay in this place?"

She was fighting back tears, "My dead husband's social security." She sniffled.

"That hardly seems enough," I said.

"Sunshine sends me money. It's devil's money, I know. But I figure, better I take that devil money to keep Sunshine from spending it on the devil's ways."

"God bless you, Mrs. McQueen," Lee said, and I wondered where that statement came from.

Outside, the sun was shining, and shadows danced on the ground. "What a performance that was. I never dreamed you would do that. Is it ethical?"

"I missed the ethics day in private detective school."

"Apostolic?" Lee asked. "Where do you come up with this shit?"

"I happen to be observant," I said quickly when I looked through the sun-speckled parking lot to my car. Deputy Sheriff Hurtis Lomax was leaning against my Toyota. "Walk softly," I whispered to Lee.

"Where's your African American friend?" Hurtis asked in his nasal voice. He talked to me but kept his eyes on Lee.

"He's investigating other leads," I said.

"Well, how much of a lead was that poor old lady?"

"She didn't say much," I said.

Hurtis looked at Lee. "She say much to you, Ms. Lee?" Lee just shook her head. "You know you look lovely in this sunlight," he said. I wanted to laugh, and I dared not look at Lee or I would have started.

"Now, you two know we're going to catch Jewel, don't you?" Hurtis's nasal pitch was almost like Ruby's wheeze. I wondered if they were somehow related. "The only reason we talked to that poor old lady is because the Jefferson County police did. Now you two are bothering her. I don't see why everybody can't just be patient and let us just nab him when he goes to the convenience store for a Co-Cola and a can of Vienna sausages."

"Hurtis," Lee said almost sweetly, "we have a right to talk to people."

"When you get hurt, you're gonna be my problem. And I just don't like to see pretty and smart ladies hurt."

Hurtis stared at Lee. I thought it time to break his spell. "We couldn't get her to say anything. She's Jesus crazy. Just babbles about the devil and Jesus."

"She's also got emphysema," Hurtis said. "She's been down to some of them scuzzy lawyers in Beaumont to get them to sue the timber processing industries for giving her the emphysema," he said.

"She probably talked to my ladyfriend," I said.

"Lucky you, to have a ladyfriend, I mean," Hurtis said. Then he added, "And she's a recovering meth addict. Got the stuff from Jewel, I'd imagine. To help her with her emphysema."

Lee couldn't help it, "Holy shit, what kind of place is this?"

Hurtis shrugged, "That poor old lady in there on the verge of insanity, death, or both is only fifty-seven years old." Both Lee and I were stunned for a moment. "You two bother to do the math? Sunshine is forty. And he's the second child. When the first one was born, she just upped and left with the daddy. They just disappeared. She came back without that fella—and without the kid, a little girl. So she married Sunshine's worthless daddy. She waits a good while before she has Jewel. That's the kind of place this is." He looked at Lee, who just dropped her head. "Yeah, it ain't pretty, is it? But it's just so goddamn typical, just so goddamn the same. All over and over again."

"Hurtis," Lee said. "That's why we're here. We just want to find out what happened. We'd like to get the truth. We just want to see how this all works out. Please don't stand in the way."

"Well, I'm a country cop, so maybe I'm too simple for truth. Maybe it's too big a concept for me. But I do have a nose for guilt." He tapped his nose. "And Jewel is smelling not just guilty but convicted. That's as close as I'm gonna go to big capital *T* truth." He snorted and pulled some goo out of his lungs and up his throat. Then he grimaced as he swallowed. Showing no embarrassment, not excusing himself, he turned away from us and walked down the road where he had parked. He twanged over his shoulder, "Y'all have a nice day, but have it down in Jefferson County," Hurtis said.

"Maybe smelling guilt makes him talk that way," I whispered to Lee.

"And clogged up his sinuses," Lee said.

TWENTY-TWO

D. Wayne steered the four-wheel-drive pickup with both hands down an unpaved road as we bounced in water-filled potholes and slid in mud. Lee sat on the passenger side and watched ahead to spot holes and steer D. Wayne. I sat in the crew cab and, through the side window, watched the surrounding, suffocating trees and undergrowth.

We had passed a dozen deserted cars and mobile homes, rusting and rotting from the inside out, and one burned-out house. "I suspect they burned themselves up trying to make the meth," D. Wayne said. That morning, the Gulf had sent the clouds inland. As we got deeper into the woods, the overhang of the trees blocked out the sparse light coming from the gray sky. The undergrowth got thicker, denser, and thornier. And I was again reminded of God's millennial wrath. Either the hurricane or its accompanying tornados had ripped trees off midway up their trunks, like a giant Weed Eater had passed through, leaving the tops dangling to the ground, growing, sprouting leaves upside down. In places there were muddy clearings with shallow rootballs ripped up. I noted it all because I felt we might be driving through a tube of vegetation and humidity to our own possible destruction.

Earlier in the day, Lee and D. Wayne had picked me up in the rented pickup. D. Wayne looked at my shorts and jogging shoes and started laughing. "You gonna be cut to shit with briars. Poison ivy is gonna eat your ass up—or eat up your ass. What are you thinking, my man?" So on the way out, we stopped at Academy Sports and bought me some camouflage hunting clothes. "Looks like you're a thirty-eight," D. Wayne said, as I walked toward the changing room with a pair of pants. I told him that I was a tight thirty-six. "Get the big ones and cinch up the belt. Best to be loose," he said. At the checkout line, he said, "Roger, you're paying. I ain't buying no Aryan Nations survivalist costume for your ass."

Earlier still, the night before, on Lee's porch with Balanchine drooling on both D. Wayne and me, several empty, formerly chilled martini glasses on a table between us, D. Wayne had tried to talk Lee out of going. Lee went into her house and came out with a 9 millimeter automatic and threw it into my lap. Then she threw a loaded magazine into my lap. "Load that, Roger," she said. I looked at my cast and then at the gun and the magazine in my lap. "You gonna use Roger for back up, D.?"

Lee then flung a plastic card at D. Wayne. "That's my concealed-weapon license," she said. She looked at me. "Lady alone," she shrugged. "I bought into it." She grabbed the gun and the magazine out of my hand, slammed the magazine in, slid back the top to put one in the chamber and cock the hammer. Then with her thumb she put the hammer back and ejected the magazine. "Want me to do a little target practice? Say at the neighbor's fence?"

"Don't you just love her?" D. Wayne said and smiled at me.

When we came to a dead end, D. Wayne said, "So like we said last night, if you see that bad motherfucking Sunshine, you just shoot at a big part of his body, keep shooting, and start yelling. Hopefully some bullets will slow his ass down, and I'll come running and shoot him in the head. A bad jury and bad lawyer ain't as bad as his bad ass. Think of him as Godzilla and King Kong all morphed and mated in his one ugly self."

D. Wayne had a small sawed-off shotgun that he tucked into his belt. In the pocket of his cargo pants, he had a small 9 millimeter. Lee had a shotgun with a strap slung around one shoulder and a 9 millimeter stuck into her belt. Although I couldn't have pulled a trigger, I had another 9 millimeter. Maybe I could just throw it at someone.

D. Wayne unsheathed a machete. He kissed Lee and looked at me. "Everybody still want this?" We both nodded our heads. "Okay, I'm gonna try to remember or imagine me back in Viet-of-fucking-nam, one of the last to get shipped out, and so that means I'm the boss, the commander."

"Yes, sir," I said. D. Wayne growled and hacked at some undergrowth. The spirit-zapping heat had turned the humidity into steam. The clouds from the Gulf had become black and thick by late afternoon. Soon, rain would start. We started to burrow through the undergrowth and humidity to a point D. Wayne had fixed in his mind from plats all three of us had stared at. He hacked at the bigger vines and thornbushes with his machete while Lee followed him, and I followed her. We hadn't gone ten yards when sweat beaded up on my forehead and then ran down my face to splatter on my shirt. Ahead of me, a dark sweat stain spread across Lee's back. The mosquitos and flies buzzed, taunting me just outside my vision, moving faster than I could shift my eyes.

The briars and thorny vines cut into my bare arms and pulled at my tough canvas pant legs. I felt as though the roiling, tangled, struggling vegetation wanted me to stay, to become like the decaying dead trees that the plants had choked, then used for their mulch as they fought their way upward for the pine trees' air. The mud on my soles sucked at me. Nothing wanted me to get through this tangled mess. So why, I wondered to myself, was I burrowing through it?

My broken fingers hurt as I caught the aluminum splint on branches and tall weeds. Pulling against that incessant tug of mud and vines, I stretched and twisted my torso, so my ribs reminded me that they were yet to be healed. My breathing became labored, and I felt tempted to go ahead and be the decayed life that the undergrowth wanted me to be. Lee turned to look at me, and with her smile urged me on.

The first crack of thunder made us look over our shoulders as though we could see the rolling boom that followed us through the forest. The flash of lightning showed through the woods. The first drops almost cooled us, but then the bigger drops pushed us on in a hurry. Before D. Wayne could chop us through to a clearing, the rain started. I looked through streaks of it to see Lee again turn back to me, this time not smiling, but looking desperate—and lost.

We slid and shuffled forward in the mud that worked its way up to our knees. When one of us fell, the undergrowth caught us before we were face down in mud. But we pushed ourselves up with cuts on our hands and faces. An on–and–off ache flowed between my hand and my side to the time of my heartbeats.

"Don't go fucking off now," D. Wayne gasped as he breathed in and slashed at some more weeds. He was the first to bend over and breathe as we all do when we overexert ourselves, even though we shouldn't because it only slows our breathing. He sucked in the thick, foul swamp smell. He looked at Lee and me and snorted, then smiled. Ahead of him, through another ten or fifteen yards of the undergrowth, was a clearing. With hands on our knees, me wheezing from the pain in my side, we sucked up what tight air we could for our final chops. As we stepped out of the tangle, the rain washed some of the mud off our faces. We turned to look up at the rain, opened our mouths, and swallowed what we could.

We crept through rusted auto parts, old tires, decrepit bicycles, old air conditioners. The decayed material goods that the environment had destroyed were turning into more mulch for the undergrowth. Ahead of us, through the rain, we saw the shack. It had once been the color of wood, but the mildew had turned it gray-green. It was beyond all repair. The undergrowth was starting to grow up the sides of the shack. No paint could ever make it attractive again. "I feel like I'm an amoeba just crawled out of the sludge, and that piece of shit cabin is what I get when I finally get to be human," I whispered.

"Shut the fuck up," D. Wayne said. Obviously he was our leader.

We got to the shack's screen door and huddled under the eaves. D. Wayne blinked against the rain in his eyes. Lee swiped her hair out of her face and over the top of her head. I leaned against the cabin to steady myself. It was soft. The wood had weathered to mush. Rather than holding up the tin roof, the roof was keeping the cabin from folding in on itself. One electrical line ran toward the roof from a pole that I couldn't see. I sidestepped along the soft wall to a screened window and angled my head to see inside. "What you see?" D. Wayne asked.

I saw movement, like someone was lying on the floor. "Somebody's in there."

D. Wayne and I locked our eyes. "If it was Sunshine, he'd probably already be out here by now and killing us," I said. "I'd guess it's Jewel." D. Wayne nodded, and Lee stepped up.

"So somebody got to be the badass to go in, and somebody has to stand guard out here. Where does that leave you, Roger?" D. Wayne almost chuckled.

"Look, I've got the right questions. You're the healthiest, strongest, and best armed. Lee and I go in, and you stay out here and watch for Sunshine."

"Fuck that," D. Wayne said.

Lee lightly slapped him. "D., that's got to be it."

"Shit, shit, shit. Motherfucker. Shit," D. Wayne said, turned, and easily kicked a hole in the door. He reached into the hole, unlocked something and pushed the door open. With his back against the doorframe he surveyed one side of the cabin, then with his back on the other side of the frame, he surveyed the other side of the cabin. "Get it done quick," he said to me and Lee.

Lee went in first with her shotgun in her hands. Then I stepped in. We both squinted in the dark until we saw a light from another room. We stepped into the mildew. That dankness filled our nostrils. The floor was filled with paper wrappers for fast food and some cans. We inched toward a light in the next room. We heard thunder and froze. The light in the room flickered but came back on. Lee stepped forward, and I filled the marks her muddy shoes left on the wooden floor with my footprints.

When she got to the doorway she straightened and held out the shotgun "Don't shoot," I heard. "Least not yet." From what I could see of Lee's back, her shoulders relaxed, and she stepped through the door. Then she stepped to one side. I looked past her to a wet, dirty mattress on the floor surrounded by pizza cartons, McDonald's wrappers, and empty cans of Vienna sausages. Sitting on the bed was a thin, pale figure in a soiled tank top. "Y'all don't shoot." The figure raised his hands. "Y'all real?"

"Who are you?" Lee asked. I stepped alongside her.

"Who you?" the thin figure asked.

"Jewel McQueen," I said rather than asked. "We're here to help you."

Lee looked toward me and started to chuckle. "Do your magic," she whispered to me.

I took a step forward.

"No, no, you don't come near me. Don't come near me yet." He held out his hands, shook them, and pushed his back against the wall. "You got to prove you're real."

"Jewel," I said. "See there. I know your name."

"That don't prove you're real. I could just be imagining you said that." He pointed toward the door, then toward a dirty window. "I been watching the shadows. They take shapes. They come to get me." He pointed toward his head. "But I know they ain't real." At his feet was a cheap hypodermic needle, the kind a diabetic would buy. "How do I know you ain't the shadows?"

"We're real, honey," Lee said. She squatted and reached toward him.

But Jewel held up his hands and batted her away. "How am I to know that?" Lee reached again and did something I could not have brought myself to do. She touched the side of Jewel's face in a long, loving stroke.

His matted hair, cut in what must have once been a mullet, was falling out in chunks. He had bleeding sores on his face and arms, some that he must have incessantly picked at to get at the ache or the demons he saw beneath his skin. His teeth were lined with black, rotting edges. Worst were his eyes. He looked like he had given up on complex human emotions—anxiety, frustration, depression—and had instead let only animal instinct in—hunger, need, confusion, panic. Lee, though, had calmed him.

"We're here to ask you some questions. Maybe see if you want to go with us."

"I still ain't so sure," Jewel said.

Lee sat down beside him and put an arm around him. He quickly scooted away. She smiled at him and left her hand in midair, for him to grab if he wanted. Tears started forming in his eyes. "I wasn't always this fucked up," he said.

"We're here to help you and take you to someplace safe," I said. "If you want," I added.

He slowly reached for Lee to see if she was real, but thunder boomed, and we all jumped. Jewel grabbed his knees and curled up on the corner of his mattress.

"Oh honey, honey," Lee crooned. "What have you done to yourself?"

"Sunshine says I ain't to leave or talk to nobody." He shivered some, even in the dank hot cabin's musk. "But I don't even know you're real."

Lee reached for him again and massaged the side of his face. He closed his eyes to feel her touch, as though her touch might make him human again. He opened his eyes. "Can you really help me?"

"Yes. Just answer some questions, and then we can help you."

His eyes shifted between Lee and me, then words tumbled out. "I ain't done it. I ain't done nothing. Sunshine says not to talk, but I ain't done nothing." He stopped jabbering. "Are you cops? If you ain't shadows, are you cops?"

"No," I said. "We're friends of your mother. We're from the Apostolic Christian Church in Beaumont. We've been praying for you, and now we're here to help." Lee jerked her head toward me to scold me with her eyes. I felt sorry for what I had said. "We've got money and a lawyer, and we'll believe you."

"Oh yeah, oh yeah," Jewel said, held up a hand, pushed up a finger, and waved it in front of my face. "Just what you think I got to say you gonna believe? What would that be?"

"We don't believe that you killed Harry Krammer," Lee said.

Jewel turned to her and started nodding. "Yeah, yeah, that's right, that's right. I didn't kill nobody. But Sunshine says I shouldn't even say that to nobody. He says ain't nobody gonna believe the likes of me. He says I should just hide."

Lee reached out with both arms, and she, by god, wrapped them around that slobbering, filthy, festering fool and hugged him. "He's not right," she purred.

"Where's your new truck?" I asked.

"Sunshine's got it," Jewel said, then snapped to and again raised his finger in front of my face and shook it. "No, no, no. I got that truck, but I ain't killed no Harry Krammer," he said.

"Tell us. Tell us," Lee cooed. "Did you ever talk to Cody Hudson?"

Jewel got excited and pulled away from Lee's arms. "I don't. I don't know him." He looked at all of us. "But this man called me. He called me, you see. He called me. He had a plan. And he gives me money. I bought a truck. But I ain't killed Harry Krammer."

"Was that man Cody Hudson?" I asked.

"He never give me a name. Said he called me from pay phones. I never even seen him. He just left me money."

"Do you know Harry Krammer?"

"We's buds, man. He's helped me. Rehab. The welfare, you know. He knows me. So when he needed some help . . ." He looked at Lee and then me. "You sure you ain't cops? You're Christian people here to help me."

"We're Christian people here to help and not cops."

"I got Harry what he needed."

"Would that be some cheap cocaine?"

Jewel turned to look at Lee, who said, "Go on, honey. Tell him. Tell him."

Looking at Lee, Jewel said, "Yes."

"Did you ever meet Jessica Hudson?"

"I don't know. Don't know," he said looking at Lee.

"She was Harry's girl," Lee said.

"I seen her."

"Did you get cocaine for her?" I asked.

"Don't know. No, don't remember." He looked at me, didn't like my eyes, so turned to look into Lee's soft, tender eyes. "I was going to, you know. Or at least I took the money to kill him, not knowing if I could kill him or not, not like Sunshine would have done. But I never killed him."

Lee wrapped her arms around him again. "I went to kill him, not knowing if I was, but I never killed him, never done it." The studying, the dancing, the stripping, the observing from being a woman in a man's world must have given Lee her ability to be siren or mother, comforter or teaser. She could conjure up sexual fantasies in Hurtis Lomax and now she had all but convinced Jewel that she was his mother. Jewel looked into her eyes and confessed as he talked. "See, I found him dead. He was bleeding all over. So I just run."

"What did you do with your gun?" I asked.

"I just thrown it down and run. Sunshine says I never should have thrown the gun down."

Then a force, which was a lump of human, came flying across the room and crashed into the studs lining the bare wall. I thought that the body was going to crash right on through the rotten siding and bring the whole building falling down on us. D. Wayne grunted, rubbed his head, then raised himself to a sitting position. Lee pulled herself away from Jewel and sat beside him on the mattress. I dropped to my knees to look at D. Wayne. I looked over at Lee and Jewel and saw her slide along the wall away from Jewel. I slowly turned my head to look at the figure filling the entry.

"That's enough and too much already," Sunshine McQueen roared at his younger brother. D. Wayne's shotgun was in Sunshine's hand and pointed at Lee.

D. Wayne stood still and stared at the gun and said without looking at anyone. "I never even seen him. He just came out of the rain and had the barrel of my gun. Goddamn good that whole Vietnam bullshit did me." My fingers and ribs sensed that whatever was going to happen was going to be bad for somebody, and so ached all the more.

"I thought I told you people to cease and desist," Sunshine quietly said in our direction.

Thunder cracked and the rain pelted the tin roof and made the shack vibrate. I listened—and smelled and watched and tasted the copper in my mouth. I tried to make my mind work. I remembered the bear in Big Bend. "Like I thought I told you, we're here to help. And we were. Until you came busting in here."

Sunshine smiled at me. He stepped further into the room and with him came the smell of old sweat and body soil. It was a sickening smell that only humans could create. His eyes darted from one of us to the other, then settled on me. "I know you talked to my momma. I know you told her some horseshit about being from some church. That ain't right." Towering over us, he slowly pulled the sawed-off shotgun in my direction. I pressed my back against a beam in the bare wall. "Nobody told me that you talked to my momma, but I knowed it. The voices told me." His eyes and his mind were on fire.

"You not supposed to be listening to those voices," Jewel yelled at his brother. "Momma told you to stop. The police told you to stop."

Sunshine swung D. Wayne's gun toward his little brother. "You shut the fuck up. You ain't got no say here. You given it up."

"I'll jump for the gun. You get Lee out," D. Wayne whispered at me.

"No," I whispered back.

"You two shut the fuck up, too. Ain't no use jumping nobody. I hear good when the voices talk," Sunshine said, and gently swung the gun toward D. Wayne, then swung it back to Jewel. Then he squared, stepped forward, and squatted in front of me. "My poor momma, and you trying to fool her like that."

"Fuck your momma," D. Wayne said.

Sunshine twirled to put the gun right in front of D. Wayne's face. "Oh, I'm gonna like hating niggers again. I'm gonna start with you."

"No, no, we can help," Lee said in unison with me. Neither of us sure of what we should do or could do.

"Don't shoot nobody, Sunshine," Jewel said. "I seen that Harry all bloody and stinking. I don't want to see that no more."

Sunshine held his gaze on D. Wayne, and D. Wayne wavered. Thunder clapped as Sunshine rose up to a height above us—D. Wayne on his butt, me on my knees, Lee sitting on one edge of the dirty mattress, Jewel on the other. He was judging us, bringing down vengeance or damnation. All we could do was distract him from time to time. "You shoulda thought of that when you took that money and bought that truck, you stupid little shit. Why didn't you think? Why don't you ever think? You ain't gonna make it in prison. You won't last a day. And when the niggers or Mexicans kill you, that's gonna kill Momma. You stupid little shit."

"But I ain't done it," Jewel said.

"We have evidence," Lee said. "We can help him prove that he didn't do it."

"Think, Sunshine," I yelled. "Think."

"Yeah, think, you stupid fuck," D. Wayne echoed me. I flung out my right arm to hit him in the chest with my cast.

"You fuckers," Sunshine bellowed, and the thunder provided harmony. The pelting rain on the tin roof made the background music. Maybe in his confusion and anger, Sunshine had created the storm. "You think that the sheriff of this county and his stooge, that limp dick, motherfucking, piece-of-shit deputy dog Hurtis Lomax is gonna let Jewel beat this charge? That bastard harassed my stepdaddy and momma right out of this county. Then when my momma deserted my sister to come back and take up with my daddy, he harassed my daddy out. He testified against me in a whole bunch of my trials. And now he wants me and Jewel both. You fuckers. You fuckers. You don't know shit." He started growling, maybe talking in tongues, but surely no human tongues. Maybe only he knew the meaning of the guttural, agonized sounds coming out of his chest and belly. Maybe he didn't know what they meant. Maybe they were just sounds, not words, a human imitation of the thunder.

"I know lawyers," I said.

"I can hire lawyers," Lee said.

"You think you got it bad in cracker county. Try being a *nigger* in cracker county," D. Wayne said.

D. Wayne got Sunshine's attention. He stopped his dialog with the swamp gods in his head and crouched to get eye to eye with D. Wayne. "I don't want to go back to prison and learn to hate niggers all over again," he growled at D. Wayne. "But I will. I can. I want to ask you a question, nigger." I could smell the sickening, overripe sweetness of his sweat.

"Come with your question, you cracker ass," D. Wayne said.

"You think that little meth head over there can survive any of your friends in the prison house?"

"That little wimpy fucker, hell no," D. Wayne said.

Sunshine hung his head. "Just like I said." He stood. "Lady, you scoot over just a little."

"What, what, no," Lee said but scooted away from Jewel.

I jumped up, "Don't do anything without thinking," I said.

The gun went off. Jewel's head turned into a spray of blood and lumps of brain and skull. A lot of that mess stained the wall behind him and sprayed across the side of Lee's face. She screamed. Sunshine whirled around, caught me with an elbow, and sent me down to the ground. He crouched and looked eye to eye at D. Wayne.

"I guess I don't hate you yet, nigger," Sunshine said and pushed the shotgun with both hands into D. Wayne's face. Before I could raise up, before D. Wayne could grab the gun, Sunshine was out the door of the room, then out the door of the cabin. I chased him out into the rain. I watched as he hit the woods. Where we had hacked and clawed and burrowed through it. Sunshine melded into it, became a part of the rain, the undergrowth, the mud, and the pines. I yelled after him, "You idiot. You destroyed the case. You destroyed yourself. You fucking idiot." But rain drowned me out.

I ran back into the cabin and saw D. Wayne over Lee, patting her head. "Look at all the blood, honey. Are you hurt?" Part of the blood was his, running down from the cut on the bridge of his nose.

"It's Jewel's blood," Lee said. We all turned to look at Jewel. He had a stupid grin below his disintegrated forehead.

Reason kept me from throwing up. What I realized was that I had just earned Cody's ten thousand dollars for killing Jewel. I was now caught up in the spiraling crimes. "Case closed," I said. "Do we let it rest here?"

"He's too bad for me to be fucking with," D. Wayne said, hung his head, and wrapped an arm around Lee.

"This is awful. This is awful," Lee said and tentatively reached toward Jewel.

"What all do we tell the police?" I asked of all of them, maybe even of dead Jewel.

TWENTY-THREE

A LARUM: PENTECOSTALS
I live in a land of three *P*s: pine, petroleum, and Pentecostals.

Houston, farther west, where the pine swamps and tallow marshes meet the more hospitable blackland prairies, should be the capital of the southeast edge of Texas's Pine Curtain. But Houston, the city where I was raised, from its very founding was just too busy battling itself, too much a sprawling mess of businesses, suburbs, freeways, ethnic battlegrounds—all with no zoning laws—to be the capital of anything but its own wild lust for money and expansion. So quieter, less greedy, dumber Beaumont, the next largest city in the area, is the capital for the southeast Texas edge of the Pine Curtain.

The great southern pine forests make it all the way to East Texas. In southeastern Texas, those pines get tangled up with the briars and near-tropical growth in the Big Thicket. Legend says that up until the middle of the twentieth century a man couldn't ride a horse into the Thicket. He'd have to dismount. Legend says that that same man who dismounted his horse would have to leave his horse and crawl through riotous, clogged swirls of undergrowth and mud. Legend doesn't say what would happen to the horse.

The old-growth pines are long gone, but the symmetrically planted new pines—gifts from the timber industry—have thick vines, wild strawberries and onion plants, poison and other ivies, tallow weed-trees growing in between them and clogging their space and sucking up their oxygen, just as the new pines were once the trash trees for the old-growth trees. The evolution of trash.

At the base of these new pines is mud, mush, or swamp. In the deep swamps and bayous, the pines have to compete with the ingenious cypress trees, which shoot their knees up above the water so that they won't drown. The new pines groan and push themselves above the undergrowth and trash trees before they can relax and actually become trees and sprout and spread healthy green limbs. All that twisting, intertwined, choking growth is without order or symmetry. What guides its growth is an almost unnatural, almost unhealthy, certainly destructive, yearning for life and domination. So all the flora in the area tries to smother all rivals; everything not connected to a plant's far-reaching roots is an enemy. Most of this flora ought to have the dignity to just give up, let go, and die.

The people aren't much better.

People living in Beaumont and behind the Pine Curtain get the desire to get some height or elevation, to get out of their tunnels through the pines, humidity, and pollution. They aren't birds, and their cars can take their bodies so far, but not their memories or souls. They never leave their jobs with the petroleum or pine industries for long. Back home in the familiar dark, smelly tunnels, they know that there is danger, tragedy, perhaps the devil himself out there. They know that they must confront him. They become Pentecostal.

Even the Cajun Catholics turn Pentecostal. Their snake handling and talking in tongues just take on an older, more French, more Papal mysticism. For they too sense evil out there. They don't believe they can avoid it, so they use their own charms and practices to protect themselves from the devil's charms.

But in Beaumont, which aches but fails to be a real city, just as the tallows ache but fail to be real trees, and in the mid-Jefferson County white-flight communities, people turn Baptist. They fear that the Pentecostal view is right and are scared of it. Rather than joining the old-time, rock-of-free-will religion of Roger Williams, they join a mind-set of proscribed safety. Their churches have stripped-down, modernist, post-Stalinist, utilitarian design and crucifixes; no blood-stained wooden crosses for the Baptists, but golden gleaming crosses that are like giant charms from a girl's bracelet. Their houses, similarly, are of a tasteful, nondescript, fashionable design. They live in all-white suburbs, or parts of town with good Baptist or Church of Christ churches guarding the cul-de-sacs of modeled and molded communities. For them and their children, they desire safety and ease—an escape from swamp gas, snake handling, and talking in tongues. For the Baptists in Beaumont and its suburbs, the devil is hiding behind the Pine Curtain and out in the wider world. Their desire is to protect themselves, to hide from the devil, not confront him like the Pentecostals.

The Baptists of Jefferson County provide me with a living. I find the serpent, talk to him, kiss him, and then hide him. On the hard drive of my priceless computer and on the CDs in my safety deposit box are pictures of illicit kisses, embraces, heartfelt looks, and some actual sexual acts committed by the good Baptists of Jefferson, Hardin, and Orange Counties. I have photos of two police chiefs and most of their officers, of one county sheriff, of four city council members, of six deacons and one priest, of countless teenagers, engineers, union members, Junior Leaguers, midlevel managers, teachers, and postal clerks. Some of my photos I give to divorce lawyers. Some, I sell. Some, I use as barter against my own sins.

I don't make much of a living from the Pentecostals behind the Pine Curtain. Pentecostals confront sin. They don't run from it, deny it, or try to escape. They take their own photos. Then beat or kill their own. From living so long in the swamps, they see no reason to involve the authorities or even anyone outside the family.

Only some of the older black folks in the area make a full adjustment to this world. It is as though they remember centuries of poverty, deprivation, soul-breaking work, lynching, and discrimination, and so, reconciling themselves a little to all these past horrors, find some comfort in just plain natural discomfort.

For instance, you know those times when you just can't go to sleep, say somewhere around three in the morning. You wander through your house and hear only the silence of the still world. You listen harder, and sometimes the silence talks back. There are voices in the silent hours. For Pentecostals those are the voices of God, the angels, or the devil. Baptists, secure in their suburbs, their modern churches, their money, don't wake up.

For you those voices may be just the sound of being alone—a wish for a little company. They may be the start or sign of depression, alcoholism, or dementia. They may be apprehension of danger, hard times, or suffering for you or your family. They're all the same, whatever you call them. Just listen for them—but be ready for what they tell you. Anymore, I call the voices that I hear on dark lonely nights Sunshine McQueen.

TWENTY-FOUR

Well into that night and then the next morning, members of the Hardin-Jefferson-Orange County drug task force, deputies from the Hardin County Sheriff's Department, Emily Nguyen and other deputies from the Jefferson County Sheriff's Department, and several Beaumont Police Department detectives questioned us. We told them that Jewel said he had gotten the money to kill Harry from a man he didn't know. We told them Sunshine blew the top of his brother's head off to keep him out of prison. But we did not tell the police about Cody Hudson's offer to us.

Nothing that we said really made a difference. Cody and Jessica were safe. I had done my job for them. The police chose to believe that Sunshine killed his brother in a crazy fit of rage. They chose to believe that Jewel had killed Harry.

First Harry was dead, then another guy no one really cared about was dead. And with him, his defense died. And with his death, a case could be made to catch, incarcerate, and probably execute his really bad-ass brother. With this story, the local law enforcement officials and the prosecutors from two counties had solved the case and earned their tax dollars. To believe Jewel, a known criminal and liar who was dead, was senseless. To investigate further because of three scared people who had interfered with an official investigation was to leave the case in a loose bundle no one wanted. The best course of action, especially when county and city goodwill, confidence, and money are involved, is usually the simplest. The smart or rich criminals don't get caught. Within a week the case was solved, and half of East Texas was looking for Sunshine McQueen, the ultimate bad guy. So justice was done.

A week after the killing, I came home from Nothing To Lose to a phone message from Cody Hudson. "I thank you for your work. I trust now that your work is done. If I have any unsettled debts or payments, please let me know," he said on the machine.

I was tempted to phone the cops and tell them about my fake deal with Cody, to risk my own indictment. But once again, there would be Cody's word against mine. Cody was a respected, well-to-do member of the community, an engineer, a Christian. I was a drunk who took dirty pictures. D. Wayne was a shady guy just a step ahead of the law, the smart kind of criminal that didn't get caught, not like Jewel or Sunshine. Lee was an ex-stripper. She dated D. Wayne. We'd never defeat Cody. I thought about collecting the ten thousand for Jewel's death. I hadn't myself killed Jewel, but I saw to it that he was killed and that Cody was off the hook. I had the receiver in my hand, and my fingers on the buttons—before I became disgusted with myself and hung up.

The Hudsons slept soundly, but not me. I didn't talk to anyone. I put distance between myself and Lee and D. Wayne. We shared some scary secrets, and in talking to them, I might have found myself shouting about injustice and only getting myself into deeper trouble. I wanted to sleep like the Hudsons. I wanted to be a Baptist. I wanted the Lord's forgiveness and his bounty: to live in an all-white neighborhood in a good school district and pay overpriced property taxes and to never again make a raid into the Pentecostal territory behind the Pine Curtain. I'd go to Nothing To Lose and hunch over a beer, then come back to my house. I tried to jog but couldn't get very far. I swore that if I saw Emily Nguyen I'd run (or rapidly walk) away.

Four days after the shooting, I stumbled out of my Toyota truck after a marathon drinking session that started in the afternoon in downtown and ended in a late-night discussion with Lynette and Bruce about what I had seen. Bruce wished out loud that he had been there just to see and scolded me for not taking him along. After all, he reminded me, I had asked him to help me. Lynette gave me a free drink.

In front of my house, my old jogging shoes hit spongy ground and my weak knees barely held me up. I sloshed to the back door, unlocked it, and walked into my dark house. I poured myself some bourbon over ice and walked into the living room, trying to avoid tripping over the stacks of trash that I had accumulated. I simultaneously hit the remote for the

TV and flipped on a small lamp. I sat down to watch some noir-looking movie. Then the darkness behind me seemed to breathe, and I heard a voice. "I ain't never seen that one."

The voice sounded like Sunshine, and at first I silently cussed myself for allowing him to run around and talk in my head. Then out of the corner of my eye, I caught movement and sprang up, spilling my drink. I froze in place. After a beat Sunshine said quietly, "Go on, sit down." I immediately sat in my recliner.

Sunshine was sitting on my sofa. His face was drawn and grimy. "I'll be needing that truck of yours," he said.

"How did you get in?" I breathed.

"You need to learn a little about bolt locks and stuff to keep people out of your house." He looked toward the movie on TV. "Think maybe I have seen that one. They think Humphrey Bogart killed his wife or something like that."

"Whattaya want?"

"I need a car. Police got me connected with the piece of shit Sunbird I was driving, so now I'm in Jewel's truck—with a homemade paint job and stolen license plate. But they probably know about that, too. So I need something they won't know about."

"Why me?"

"You got lotsa questions, but I'm in a good mood, so I'll tell you. I could have real easy killed you or your friends. But as it turns out, I didn't. I figure you owe me."

I reached into my pocket and pulled out my keys. I held them up. He squinted, and I threw them to him. He caught them with one hand.

My mouth had gone dry. I didn't have enough spit to make words. "You want a drink?" I croaked.

"Don't mind if I do," he said. "You stay right there. I'll fetch it myself. I seen where you got yours." He pushed himself up to get a drink but stopped to turn back and look at me. "Good. You just stay planted and watch Bogart. Don't start thinking of no hero shit to do."

I didn't move an eyelash. He came back in with a tumbler filled with ice and my bourbon.

"You here to kill me?"

"If the voices were talking to me, I might. But since this Jewel business is over, they hushed up. God or the devil, one or the other, has forgotten about me." He took a long sip of the whiskey. "You ought to buy a better brand of bourbon." He looked at the TV. "Oh look, I like this part where the police talk to him. Ain't he smooth?" I turned to look at the screen as his unwashed stink drifted through the room.

I was too scared and knew I was too muddled to play him like the Big Bend bear. I wasn't sure that he wasn't going to kill me. But some dogged part of my mind still wanted answers. "You know, you could get the needle."

Sunshine chuckled, then rubbed his beard with his flat palm, like maybe it itched. "You seen what I did. Would a sane man do that? When they get me, I tell 'em about the voices, they'll talk to a prison psychiatrist or whatever it was that examined me, and I get put up for life." He took another giant sip. That smell that was particular to unwashed humans made its way through my nostrils to my stomach, where it curdled my beer and whiskey. My fright kept me from throwing up on my lap. I dared not rush up to puke in the bathroom. Any sudden moves and Sunshine would be on top of me.

"You killed your brother."

"I told you my reasons. You seen the newspapers. Wasn't I right? Now I'm the guy they want to get, the guy going to prison or an early death, not Jewel. You got to admit, I called it right."

"Your mother?"

"She can die easy knowing her good boy didn't go to prison."

"But you *murdered* him, goddamn it."

"Things could be worse."

Spit came back to my mouth. I put my arms on my chair and started to stand. On the way up, I shouted, "Wait a minute. Wait just a goddamn minute. You want to explain to me just how in the hell they could be worse?" I had overcome the nausea from his stink and decided that I was at least going to voice some indignation.

"You and some of your friends could be dead," Sunshine said, and his hard stare made me sit back down. "It could be a lot fucking worse."

I got scared and nauseous again. I slumped in the chair, pulled the lever that pushed the footrest up, and got comfortable. If I was to die, I wanted to have as much comfort as possible before the pain started. "When you shot Jewel and ran out like that, how did you get through the woods? It looked to me like you just ran right through trees."

"I do all right in the woods. The deputies on the TV said nobody can live in the thicket for long. Said they always surface somewhere. Said they always catch the convicts that run off from the prisons and go off into the woods. I do all right in the woods. I can out-wait them there. If I want."

"Where's Jewel's truck? Are you in it now?" I asked, hoping and imagining that, even as we spoke, Emily Nguyen was outside with a bunch of Jefferson County's finest covering me.

"It's parked off to the side of the road in some trees." He reached into his pocket and pulled out the keys and flipped them to me. "Here, even trade." He chuckled. "And you might of got the best deal 'cause yours is older and got all those dents in it."

The keys hit in my lap. "Course, I'll dump yours and steal another up the road. You got insurance, though." I stared at the keys to Jewel's new truck and tried to think my burning stomach into cooling. "I been to see the Hudsons," Sunshine said.

I sat up, the footrest snapping back into place. "What did you do to them?"

"They wasn't home, but I let them know I was there." Sunshine took another long swallow, leaned forward, and put his elbows on his knees. He stared at the TV for a moment and then started talking. "You know, I don't know I believe Jewel or not. I wanted to ask the Hudsons about it. 'Course they could lie. There's just no knowing for sure. I never got much show in life. But then Jewel had even less." He stared at his feet and then at me. He smiled. "There I go feeling sorry for myself. Feeling sorry demeans a man. Makes him small. . . . Still the Hudsons deserve some more grief coming their way." He stared in the direction of the TV but not at it.

"You're not hearing anything, are you?" I asked.

"No, thinking," he said. "I guess you tried to do right by Jewel. You suffered enough. Your nigger friend and his white lady friend suffered enough, too." He looked up at me. His eyes had lost the fire the voices in his head started in his mind. "Everybody's kind of got what they put into poor Jewel's lousy comeuppance. Sufferings been doled out equal." He smiled, and his eyes had rekindled a little. "Everybody except the Hudsons. But they're rich, and can afford not to suffer."

"They can buy enough to insulate themselves," I muttered.

"Yeah, yeah, see. You got it. I kind of thought I liked you. Still, I'm not sorry I beat the shit out of you and your friends. You give me reason for that."

"What are you going to do?"

"Hide as long as I can. Maybe drive around on all the small roads. Maybe go to Mexico. But I'm gonna make 'em have to catch me."

"I could find you a lawyer."

He shook his head. "Why don't you just straight out give me the money you'd spend finding me a lawyer. You got any money here?" He smiled, then his smile left his face. "No, the truck's enough. We're square with that. I figure that makes us even. As long as you quit now."

"I'm quit," I said.

Sunshine swallowed the last of his whiskey, walked to my chair, and shook my hand. "Give my regards to deputy Hurtis Lomax and your friend Emily Nguyen. Who knows, if the voices say so, I might have to visit them again," he said, and walked out of my life, I hoped, forever.

A person who accepts his own death and his and the world's craziness can truly be scary.

⬥

The next morning a cop screaming through a loud speaker begged me to walk out slowly if I could. Still in my underwear, I tentatively stepped out to my porch and saw Beaumont police and Jefferson County deputy sheriff cars lined up in front of my house. Several rifles and a variety of pistols were pointed at me. I slowly raised my hands. Sunshine had taken my truck but had left Jewel's disguised new truck parked in my driveway.

Emily Nguyen was the first to rise up from behind her car. "Are you all right, Roger?" she yelled.

"I'm fine."

"Is Sunshine McQueen in there?" another cop said through a loudspeaker. Emily shook her head and continued walking toward me.

"I'm not dead, so he's not here," I yelled.

"I'm glad you're not dead," Emily said when she got close to me. "He was here, right?" I nodded. "Then I guess I've got to wonder why you're not dead."

"The voices weren't talking to him, so he thought it polite to pay me a cordial visit . . . and he wanted my truck."

"Roger, I just got to say it. . . . I told you . . ."

Out of the crowd of cops, a big, round figure emerged with his palms turned back behind him and with his head bowed as if in reverence. Hurtis Lomax squeezed some words through his nose. "You been lucky."

"Why? Because you cops didn't shoot me?"

Hurtis giggled. "No, because I done some checking. Ol' Sunshine is either bipolar or somehow seriously mentally disturbed. I checked into his prison records and talked to some prison psychiatrist."

"Maybe the voices he hears are real," I said. Emily looked at me like I was crazy. Hurtis chuckled.

"I hope you and him ain't become buddies," Hurtis said.

By noon I was ready to make donations to the Baptist Church. I locked my house, filled out a police report on my stolen car, rented a clunker, and shopped for a new truck. I drove a new Toyota off the lot and straight to Rachel's door.

When the door opened, Amber jumped up and down and clapped her hands. Rachel crossed her arms and prepared to argue my case with me. "So where have you been? You couldn't call? Have you lost your cell?"

I stepped into her and hugged her and held her as tight as I could, even though holding her hurt my ribs. I let her go when I couldn't hide the ache in my side. "When do I start work?" I asked. "My life just changed." I didn't even *camouflage* my new Toyota pickup.

TWENTY-FIVE

For a month I stayed close to Rachel and Amber. My mood and guilt matched the cooling weather. Finally, in late October, a norther passed through and made the weather actually stay cool, somewhere in the seventies, for several days. It actually made us believe that winter might be on the way. Every year at this time in Southeast Texas, we heaved big sighs of relief. We had made it through another summer, and there was enough of our balmy, stormy winter ahead to make us almost forget the next summer. I switched from shorts to jeans.

I was pleasantly involved with Rachel's family and the boring world of lawyers. I traveled around the area getting depositions, sometimes talking to clients or businesses, doing the bidding of those who were surely richer than I, and thought themselves smarter—and better. I got my cast off my hand. My fingers and ribs were stiff, but not achy. It was a protected life.

You know how it is. After stopping by the bar for a couple of beers, you go home and have some of your own booze, your medicine. Feet back in your recliner, you watch movement around you, invest in some small talk, then dinner. You watch the sitcoms, the local news, then the late night shows until you are sleepy and the house has come to a throbbing silence. The movement is gone. So you go to bed to start another day. I got seduced by it. It seemed too easy.

Then induction kicked in. What happened next had no sequence, order, or logic, but taken together it showed me good sense. My thinking and this story about Baptists, Pentecostals, and Sunshine McQueen should have just ended. For nobody in this age and time can still believe that the world makes sense, that order governs, that truth wins out. Except for me. I wanted the case closed, investigation ended. Which it was, but I couldn't close it. My mind made me see the order, and as it turns out, some other people wanted me to see the order and logic, too. Maybe my fate wanted me to start thinking again.

The first incidents started late one night in Rachel's house. Sunshine McQueen came out of hiding and tromped through my dreams. To avoid him, I made myself wake up, and I'd immediately feel I was in a strange place. I turned to feel Rachel's soft breath on the side of my face. I had thought that I was in my own bed in my A-frame, but I hadn't been there in over a month. Even though I still paid Dottie Phillips's rent, I suspected that Sunshine's stink still floated in it, like mildew or dry rot. I rolled to face Rachel and breathed in her hot breath. She didn't wake, but I was wide awake. I felt ill at ease, out of place. She looked content. I could put Sunshine out of my current life with Rachel and Amber, but not out of my mind.

I curled myself out of Rachel's king-sized bed and crept out of the bedroom door and down the hall, past Amber's room. As I got close to the kitchen, I saw just a hint of light.

I followed the light, being careful not to place my foot on any toys and crush them or puncture my foot. The light pulled me into the kitchen and became just a sliver of a light coming from the barely cracked refrigerator door. Next to the refrigerator sat Amber, sucking through a straw from a box of juice. "I'm sorry, Roger," she said when she saw me. "I couldn't reach the lights. And I got kinda scared in the dark, by myself. So I opened the refrigerator."

"What are you doing up?"

She hunched her shoulders and curled over the box of juice. "I had bad dreams. I tried. I really tried to go to sleep, but I couldn't. Am I in trouble?"

"No. I had some bad dreams, too," I said. "A bad man was chasing me."

"Me, too," she said.

And I reached and grabbed her with both hands to pull her up chest high. With Amber in my arms, I went out the backdoor to Rachel's screened-in back porch. Since her backyard faced the fifteenth hole, Amber and I saw the orange streak of the sun highlighting the tops of the distant trees and a very light breeze shaking the long leaves of the palms on the golf course. From somewhere on the course came a frog's croak, and then an early bird started chirping. I placed Amber in a patio chair and sat in a chair beside her. "Since we've both had bad dreams, let's watch the sun come up. Listen to the sounds, Amber."

She listened very intently, heard the frogs, and strained to turn her ear toward the sound. Then her face lit up when she heard the birds. "Those are birds and frogs," I said. She nodded, smiled at me, got out of her chair, and climbed into my lap. She wrapped her arms around me, and after a while the box of juice fell from her fingers and made a sticky puddle behind me. After a few more moments, I felt her warm breath on the side of my face.

My jog would feel good. I had begun pounding out a few blocks around Rachel's house.

Amber's breath on my shoulder felt comforting and could, if I let it, put me to sleep. It felt more familiar than Rachel's breath. I hadn't realized it, but I was at this house more for Amber's sake than Rachel's. If I were to lose this family, Amber would be the real loss for me.

But her breath and her heft on my lap and my night with Rachel were like memories. They were like those quick dreams before waking, vivid, almost real, but not quite. Rachel's family had a pleasant life. But it just wasn't my life. I needed my jogs. I had my deep sleep dreams and memories of Sunshine. I felt sad, wary, and nostalgic.

For several days, I tried to convince myself that I was the type of person who could be good for Amber. I took Amber and Rachel to McFaddin Beach. Even though the weather had cooled, the water was still warm, so Amber and Rachel splashed at the edge of the tide. Later Amber and I took a walk to look for shells.

With Amber's hand in mine, I wanted to be more of a Baptist, some approximation of what Cody and Jessica Hudson had had before sin, fate, bad luck, bad timing, or their own misguided, misaligned all-American values bit them in the ass. I still had Sunshine chasing me through my dreams. But I still couldn't soften up my feeling for Cody and Jessica and those like them. They believed so firmly in their beliefs that they were always disappointed and miserable, because their actions, characters, and desires just never matched their fervent belief in their misguided, misaligned, impossible values. I couldn't forget enough of what I knew to adequately protect Amber, to tell her those gentle lies that would see her securely and undamaged to adulthood.

Amber softly hummed to some tune playing in her head, blissfully ignorant of all that could go wrong as we made our way through the world.

Protecting ourselves, being Baptists, keeping the right religious respectability and social prestige could just get the better of us. It could turn sour, dry up our enthusiasm. Life could become filled with nothing but minor details, the lawn, the cars, the social responsibilities. And some of us just weren't born or raised with the respectability or responsibility that being Baptist made you want. So you courted that sin, bad luck, misalignment in yourself and the world. Those folks were up in the Piney Woods, people like the McQueens, like Hurtis Lomax. Those were the folks at Nothing To Lose. Those were Pentecostals.

"Roger, we're doing a play at school. I'm going to be a pumpkin," Amber said.

"I'd like to see that," I said. "Are you learning your lines?"

"Don't be silly. Pumpkins don't talk."

Amber needed protection and guidance. She needed the safe schools, the concerned parents, the simple values. None of that was my strong suit. I was, unknowingly, just by delighting in her company, perhaps hurting her. "Are you going to come see me be a pumpkin?" Amber asked again.

"Oh honey, of course," I said, but felt bad for knowing what I had to do.

I ran off to Austin and went to see Buck Cronin. I loaded up his gear and drove him down to San Marcos. We sat in an old ice house, Devil's Tavern, with a nice fall view of the Hill Country, and slowly sipped beers while we cackled, bullshitted, and gossiped our way to being young. By the time we got to the point where I told my story about Sunshine McQueen, Buck objected to one of my points. "It's not over," he said.

I stared at the round opening in the bottle of my beer. "The world is a chaotic place. If we expect nice, neat packages with pink ribbons tied up all orderly, we'll forever be disappointed."

Buck wheezed. By now he had an oxygen tank like Ruby McQueen's that he rolled around with him. He took a sip of his drink. Since I last saw him, Buck seemed to have slowed down every sensation to enjoy it as though it were his last. "So you think about dying without ever knowing more than you know now." He paused to look out over the tops of cedar trees, interrupting his own train of thought. "God, this is nice. Thank you, Roger, for giving me this view. And these beers." Then he returned his eyes to me, and his mind to his point. "You ain't going to be able to handle it. You can't let it set, Roger. I wouldn't be able to. Neither can you."

"You were a divorce lawyer, for God's sake. You always let it set," I said.

"And that's why I don't want to let nothing set now that I'm a retired divorce lawyer. Think where you started. Think about who needs the help. Think about what I told you. Harry Krammer. Are you satisfied that Harry Krammer is satisfied? Is his memory satisfied? Are those who give a shit about him satisfied? You can't get a pound of flesh, but you can get a little nearer to the truth. You're still a lawyer. And though we've fucked our profession and our reputation, getting nearer the truth is still what we're supposed to be after."

I hung my head and sipped my beer. Buck beat on me some more: "So why the hell don't you buck up and just ask a few questions?"

"Because it may be illegal, because it could get me into deep shit," I said.

"When's the last time that stopped you?" Buck asked.

"I like my life as it is."

Lightning bugs started to appear. We were in a dry enough climate that we could actually feel some coolness, maybe even a little coldness. In most of Texas, cold is almost romantic.

"You ain't exactly a young man," Buck said as he stared at the stars that were just beginning to appear. "You better try to fix whatever regrets you're going to have. They're a son of a bitch later on, unfixed."

"What's wrong with just letting it hang?" I asked.

"You got more than a little guilt in this. You still have the bribe from Cody Hudson hanging over your head." Buck laughed, then coughed, then breathed deep on his oxygen. He gazed up at the bright stars, savored the cool autumn air mixed with the beer. "We just don't goddamn ever live long enough," he said. "Better set right what you can."

"So why don't you go with me and help me?"

"What help could I be? In my condition?" He coughed as he laughed.

"Why don't you come with me to Beaumont and let me find you a place there. Kind of come by for some drinks and laughs."

Buck sipped his beer and looked around like he was a dog sniffing the air. "Goddamn what I wouldn't give for a cigarette." While I was laughing, he added, "I appreciate your comments, but like I said, I'm going to die here."

On the way back to what was seeming more like home, I stopped at my parents' retirement community. A slight drizzle was floating in the air, but they were at the tennis court, sitting under an umbrella, looking longingly at the slick court, sipping martinis, and seemingly enjoying themselves. Houston's weather was no better than Beaumont's, but my parents had learned to find pleasure in it.

I ran from the parking area to join them under the umbrella. My mother pulled up a chair and said, "Roger, how nice to see you. I thought you had forgotten our phone number." My father poured me a martini.

"Why are y'all sitting in the rain?" I asked.

"We'd rather be playing tennis," my father answered, "but why waste a day." His knees had grown knobby and his thighs thin over the years. I remembered back when I watched him play tennis before I left for college. His ham and thigh muscles bulged against the legs of his shorts. He barrel chest spread the neck of his tennis shirt into a tight V. His stroke didn't look efficient or fluid; instead it was a slap that sent the ball in weird spins. When he had beaten his foe, usually my mother, he smiled with a delight in his body, his sweat, and his peculiar stroke.

"But it's nice to watch the drizzle," my mother said as she sucked up the last of her martini through a straw.

I sipped my martini and thought about myself possibly being retired in this place, instead of in Beaumont. Of sipping a martini through a straw and staring out from below an umbrella at a rainy day. It occurred to me that my parents did indeed have money. This scenario, for me, was entirely possible. "So my inheritance looks pretty good?" I blurted out.

"Well, yes it does," my father said. "Glad you saw fit to drop by and check."

"Roger, I thought that you had a bit more grace than that," my mother said. Her legs were thinner than my father's. Osteoporosis or gravity was curling her shoulders. She shrugged and giggled. "No, you never had much grace. Stumble through. That was you."

"I just meant that, that in a way, I am well off—financial-wise, in a sense."

"Yeah," my father said. "I should think so. I worked hard enough for you to be well off."

"Vernon," my mother said. "Stop teasing him."

"Of course there's your thing about money. If you'd like we could leave it all to charity."

"Why are we being morbid?" my mother asked.

"You know," my father started and cocked a smile and showed it to me, "most families just go on, somehow survive, without money. Our money will go on, but not our family. I hope that you find a good use for our money, Roger." I wasn't sure if I was angry, perplexed, or amused.

My mother looked concerned, not amused. "You know, that will be a problem for you, Roger."

They were right. I was totally unprepared for money. Maybe I should just give it away. I breathed in to ask the question that had been roiling in my mind since I left Buck Cronin. "Did I disappoint y'all? I mean, I know I didn't turn out at all like y'all expected, or maybe wanted. But was I . . ." I stumbled on my own question because I thought that I had an answer to it. Of course I disappointed my parents. Hell, I disappointed me. Maybe that was the wrong question. "Can you tolerate me? Could I still be any damn good?"

My father chuckled. "You could have had more money. But you always had this thing about money."

My mother slapped at my father. "Stop teasing him. He's serious now." She turned her attention to me. She sucked in a tiny bit of air, thought, and said, "You were going down a path that makes parents proud. The kind of path people like to think that their children will follow. But after your marriage went bad, you changed paths." I wanted to sarcastically thank her and leave.

"You said not to tease him," my father said.

My mother swung her head between me and my father. "Maybe you should ask yourself if we disappointed you when you chose that path. We certainly don't understand it. But you did indeed choose it. You didn't just fall into it. And you were faithful to your choice. So your father and I often wondered if you understood us, while we were trying to understand you." As usual, my mother left me speechless and my mind numb.

"I could maybe right a wrong," I blurted out.

"Then by all means, do so," my mother said.

"But be careful," my father added.

✦

Browbeat by my oldest friend, scolded by my parents, when I got back from the glorious fall weather and view in the Hill Country, even though I had all but abandoned my A-frame and the long nights at Nothing To Lose, I pulled into my old driveway and started running down the side of the canal. It was my first full jog in over six weeks, and the aches actually felt good because they were familiar. The cushioning of my feet in the soft muddy ground felt good. The humidity without the heat actually caressed me. I jogged now for some pleasure that I could find in it instead of for penance. But when I finished my jog, Emily Nguyen was waiting for me with a bag of Dixie Creme doughnuts and a cup of coffee.

"Have you implanted some radar tracking device in my head or something? How do you always find me?"

"I try to make a habit of checking up on you, Roger," she said. She pushed a cup of coffee toward me.

"I've cleaned up my life. I do most of my drinking at home or downtown with the lawyers, so I'll take the coffee but no doughnuts, please."

"Yeah, looks like you're losing weight and the cares of the world both. I liked you better fat and worried."

"You got a business proposition?" I leaned against Emily's squad car and felt some of the coolness in the Southeast Texas air. Summer was indeed over.

"I've just got some information." Emily munched on her doughnut and stared at the toes of her black tennis shoes. "The bullet that killed Harry Krammer wasn't from the gun that we found in the apartment."

I slowly sipped my coffee. "And I guess if Jewel McQueen were alive, he could testify that he dropped that gun when he saw Harry dead."

"We probably still wouldn't believe him, but since he's dead, we've just kind of shoved that information into an old filing cabinet."

"So what am I supposed to do?"

"Nothing. I'm just giving you some information. That case is so cold it's frozen. Two counties and the city cooperated to bring justice to one troublesome bad guy and send his really bad-guy brother off into hiding. We tied the murder of Harry Krammer up with a nice pretty bow. We did all of this with a minimum of expense. No expensive trial, no lawyers. Citizens are happy. I'm just having a conversation with you."

"So what? You want me to go after those pillars of the community, the Hudsons? You want me to go after Sunshine McQueen after he nearly killed me three times?"

"Just leave Sunshine to run around in the Big Thicket, just like an outlaw from a hundred and forty years ago. Tell you the truth, I don't think we'll ever catch him. I like him a legend, a boogie man, out there lurking in the piney woods, scaring cops to act right and be careful."

"Yeah, I got him running around in my head at nights."

"You'll get better," Emily said. "But I got some more important news for you."

"You want me to join the sheriff's department?"

"No. You read the vital statistics in the *Beaumont Enterprise?*" Emily didn't even wait for me to say no. "Cody and Jessica Hudson filed for divorce. That's pretty fast, don't you think? They filed before they even separated. He's in the house, and she's got an apartment. I'm surprised you didn't know that. That kind of information is in your field of expertise."

"That's not my line of work anymore."

"I'm just hoping that, if you find out something, you might have another conversation with me and let me know. Just because I'm interested."

I sipped my coffee and stared at the dirty water in the canal. "I'm changing my life," I said.

"You don't sound convinced of that."

"Well, shit. Just . . . well, shit. I don't owe anybody anything. In fact, at my age and past, all I owe is me. It's time I started thinking about a quiet, comfortable life."

"You do what you want now that you're the new Roger. That old Roger seemed a little antagonistic to me, but somehow nobler for his bitterness, even if he did have some shady dealings with Cody Hudson." I stared at Emily, no doubt with my mouth open. "You once said I'm smart and work harder than any three white men." She left me staring after her as her patrol car kicked up gravel on my ankles.

Within a day, Lee called me. I had tried to erase her, D. Wayne, and Buttermilk from my mind because of the dreams of Sunshine that they might conjure up. But I went to see her anyway, in her dilapidated mansion in Old Town. Balanchine was there to first growl at me then drool on me. Lee had the gin prepared for me on the small serving table on her screened-in porch. I asked about D. Wayne. He wanted to forget about Sunshine, the same as I did, for Sunshine was an insult to D. Wayne's courage and male stamina. Good for D. Wayne, I thought, to recognize his own limits. Buttermilk's jaw wasn't healing right, so the doctors had to rebreak one side to make his mouth work properly.

"I went to see Mrs. McQueen up in Kountze," Lee said. She had on a sheer negligee-like gown that ran from her shoulders to her ankles. I could see her trim body wrapped with a spandex exercise suit as it pressed into the sheer, clingy cloth. She exhaled from her one cigarette of the day. I looked into my glass, gulped down the gin and tonic, and poured myself another.

"The woman cried," Lee exhaled some smoke. "I told her that her son did not commit the crime that he was accused of. I told her all that I knew. She cried and said now maybe her boy could go to heaven instead of hell. You going to let this alone?" she asked.

"He's only innocent of one crime," I said.

"What about you? I know one crime where your innocence is in question—by two other participants in this crime. You could maybe fix this crime."

"You told me D. Wayne wants to let it alone."

"I'm asking about you."

I shoved Balanchine's head out of my lap. "The bullet that killed Harry wasn't from Jewel's gun. And Cody and Jessica Hudson filed for divorce."

Lee digested this for a moment. "Mrs. McQueen let me go through Jewel's things," she said. "He had three uncashed checks from Jessica Hudson." She blew smoke out between her lips.

As I hung my head, she continued, "Greg Giddings, the principal, remember him? He's willing to help. Your friend Emily Nguyen called me. She's willing to help. You know the Hudsons, Roger. You can do this. You've got to help."

I met Balanchine's soulful eyes with my own and thought of Amber. She needed more protection than I could even believe in. Rachel would never understand why I fell into the life I had. To her, all I ever had to do was simply pull myself up out of my situation by my bootstraps—or in my case, my jogging shoelaces. To her, all I had to do was to forget what I knew.

I couldn't blame her though. Her little family would be better off without me. Balanchine cocked his head, and I cocked mine to look into his soulful eyes. Then I lifted mine to look into Lee's eyes. "Harry's not resting yet," Lee said. "You should do this for Harry."

"And for Sunshine, Jewel, and Ruby McQueen." Lee and I smiled and nodded in unison. "What do you want me do?" I asked.

Lee had a plan. I did, too. I told her I saw this bear in Big Bend while I was trying to pee.

TWENTY-SIX

I walked into Nothing To Lose feeling as though I had crammed wads of tissue up into my nose. I wanted to heat up the tip of an ice pick and jam it up a nostril to loosen up the congestion. We had four cool, clear days. As punishment, the fall grasses excited my allergies.

My voice had just come back, so I could talk. But I wheezed. "You sound terrible," Lynette said when I told her hello. "Glad to see you after so long, but why don't you go home," she said.

Things hadn't changed much. Leroy and horse-faced Shirley were back from their vacation together and were showing off her engagement ring to Edmore and Ridley. Ridley just nodded, and Edmore got out the perfunctory, "That looks real nice."

Big Billy sat at the end of the bar staring into a drink. "How the hell are you doing, Roger?" he yelled, way too loudly. The professors who had gathered with their hangers-on sat at a table next to the dance floor. Because of what I intended to do, I envied them all the more.

I sat at a seat down from him, but Zia found me. "Hey, you know what, no more nasty, sexy, fuck movies and key fobs. I'm selling the pre-owned cars now. What do you know, huh?"

"Congratulations," I said.

"Who'd have thought I'd be so good in the car business? Sold four already, to people with no money, so they get real high interest to get the used car; I get a commission; and when they can't make payments, I get the car repossessed and sell it again. So I am thinking why was I ever in the fuck-book and fuck-toy business to start with? Who'd have known, huh?"

Lynette put a beer in front of me and cut Zia off by talking to me. "So you haven't been in in awhile. You take the cure or what?"

"I thought that I'd change my life and get respectable."

"Why would you want to do that?"

"I was scared," I said. "I still am."

Lynette's smile dropped, and she reached out to pat my hand. "Most people drink when they're scared. You try to stay sober." She leaned on her elbows across from me. "I don't imagine that you'd want to bore me with the details. But say you did, I'd be happy to listen awhile."

"I may bore you yet tonight," I said.

Bruce was the first to show up. His jaw had mostly healed, so he could drink without a straw and talk without squeezing his words between gritted teeth. His hair was longer, and he had been to a barber. His earrings and studs were gone. He wore a polo shirt, khakis, and some European shoes. He must have found a stray *GQ*. "She here yet? They here?" he asked.

I had gotten Bruce to call Jessica Hudson and ask her if she wanted some newer, fresher-cut cocaine. He told her that he got her number from Jewel McQueen, before he was killed, of course. She was coming by Nothing To Lose to pick it up. Bruce was excited, and he bounced up and down on the balls of his feet. "Thanks, Roger. I mean thanks. Especially after all the beatings I took. I think maybe I'm pretty good at this."

It was my first beer of the day and it gave me that cold bite at the back of my throat that made me feel better. I wished, though, that with my allergies and the wadding up my nose, I could taste it. "Just relax," I told Bruce.

"You don't sound so good," he said. "You want me to talk for you?"

"Just do what we rehearsed, okay? Just do your job."

Lee, D. Wayne, and Buttermilk walked in next. Lee wore tight jeans, high heels, and a white shirt with a pearl or imitation pearl necklace. She seemed classy. D. Wayne had on his shiny black pointy-toed boots, a black felt, curled-brim hat, cocked at an angle, and a leather vest over a white shirt. When he stuck his hand out to shake my hand, his gold bracelets clanged. "I don't like to admit it, but I kind of missed your sorry ass and your sorry wise-assed mouth," he said. "Lee tells me you went straight."

"I tried," I said and gasped for air. Lee looked at me for an explanation. But I did not have the time or temperament for one at the present moment.

Buttermilk walked up to me, and I shook his hand. "How's the pussy eating going?" I asked, and I thought at first that he would slug me. But he smiled and showed me the braces that held his splintered, re-fractured jaw in place.

Through his teeth, he said, "I'll be whipping your ass again once this heals. Whipping your ass always makes me feel better."

Then Greg Giddings walked into the building, spotted Lee, walked to her, and hugged her. When he joined our group, I asked the obvious, "Are you sure you're up to this?"

"You got them damn allergies, too, don't you," he said in a nasal voice. "I'm in this." For what I had planned, I didn't want Emily Nguyen anywhere even near, for her sake. I had a lot of doubts about inviting Greg Giddings, but I figured I owed him. I had already done him one favor. I had asked Emily Nguyen to give me the flat football that Greg had dropped when he and Harry played for the Black Mollies. "This morning I got this flat football that Harry had displayed in his living room. You once asked me if you could have it. I boxed it up and mailed it to you at your school."

"Thank you," Greg said and held out his hand for me to shake. After I shook his hand, Greg looked at Lee. "Stacy said she can't make it."

"Of course she can't," Lee said.

"But she would like to know what we find out," Greg said.

"Of course she does," Lee said.

"I'll trust that one of you will talk to her. I don't necessarily want to make her nervous just by being close to me," I said.

D. Wayne pulled a wad of money out of his pocket and began to conspicuously count it. "Let me get a round. This is a glorious occasion."

The beer cooled my raw throat and the tickle at the back of it that just would not go away. I growled. "Do we need to go over who is doing what?"

"Drink your beer and loosen up. It's almost showtime," D. Wayne said. "All the talking you're about to do is just going to make people nervous."

"I'm nervous already," Buttermilk said through his clenched teeth.

Bruce eyed Buttermilk, and Buttermilk nonchalantly dropped his eyes on to Bruce. "I hear we got our jaws broke by the same guy," Bruce said. Buttermilk gave no notice. "Mine's healed," Bruce said.

"It could be broke again, you keep comparing jawbone strength," Buttermilk said.

"Just saying, I know what it's like sipping barbeque through a straw."

Buttermilk nodded his head. "I'm afraid it's damaged some of my taste buds."

Before we could go on, Jessica Hudson stepped into the bar. She looked around, and I turned my back. She was early. Pulling my baseball cap low, I hurried to the back door and stepped outside with Lee and Greg Giddings behind me. We followed each other down the steps, then we all leaned against the railing that had just been reconstructed on the deck. For several days, I could almost smell the pollen hanging in the air. But now, a gentle mist was washing the air. In a day or two, the typical Beaumont weather would relieve my allergies.

"So, we all know what to do?" Lee asked and smiled at me and Greg.

"Hell of a time to ask," I answered. When the back door pushed open, we watched Jessica being led down the steps from the bar by Bruce. Lee's face twisted into a scowl. When she saw me, Jessica's face swiveled between me and Bruce, and then Bruce stepped back in and locked the door. She was stuck with the last people in the world she wanted to see.

"Mr. Giddings," she said. "What are you doing here, with him?" she asked. She was making an effort to sound pleasant, in control, but she looked like hell.

"I'm just listening," Greg Giddings said. "You probably remember that I was a good friend of Harry's."

"As was I," Lee said.

"You, you," she said, pointed at me, then turned, grabbed the doorknob, and started yanking at it.

"Jessica," I tried to purr, but coughed. Both Lee and Greg looked at me. "The bullet that killed Harry was not a bullet from Jewel McQueen's gun. When he died, Jewel McQueen had several uncashed checks that you had written him. The Jefferson County Sheriff's Department now has this information. They are going to talk to your soon-to-be-ex-husband. Do you have any idea what he will tell them?"

She turned around and almost purred at me. "How can you do this?"

"Mrs. Hudson," Lee said. "I was a friend of Harry's. If you will just tell us what you know, I swear I will never tell the police."

"I was Harry's best friend," Greg said, then added, "as Harry no doubt told you. He kept me up on his life. What he did. Who he did. If you tell us, now, what happened, we will let it stay here. We won't go to the police. I'll try to help you in the school district. I'll see if I can keep you from getting fired if this goes to court."

Jessica gasped, hugged herself, then raised a finger to her mouth and rubbed her front teeth. "We don't know what your husband has told the police, or what he will tell the police, but we want to hear from you what happened. In exchange, we won't go to the police. They'll have to find it out on their own."

"You can't do this to me. How can you sleep at night?"

"Same as you, I guess."

Her eyes darted from one of us to the other. I felt as though I should feel sorry for her, as though I should shift sides yet again. "I'm a teacher, a mother, a Christian. You can't do this to me. You can't treat me like this." When she finished, I wanted to stay on the side I had chosen.

"As a teacher, you ought to value the truth. That's what we want," Greg Giddings said.

"I want to know what to think of Harry," Lee said.

"I want to know what to think of what happened to him," Greg said.

"I want to nail you and your husband to a post out in front of your suburban estate if you don't finally tell me what happened," I said.

Jessica sucked in for air and just screeched. She reached into her purse and fumbled around for a while. "Would you like some of this?" I reached into my light jacket pocket and pulled out a baggy with some highly diluted cocaine. Greg and Lee both jerked their heads toward me. This hadn't been a part of the plan. But Bruce was now a partner of sorts. "This is what you came here for," I said, coughed, and tried to pull some air in through my mouth at the same time that I tried to push words out. "Now an administrator has seen me offer this to you. Now he knows why you are here. What kind of a teacher does that? What kind of administrator would he be if he turned a blind eye to it?" I coughed again, so I turned my head while I held the baggy just in front of her face. "But he's willing to overlook it. He's willing to let you stay a schoolteacher, a mother, and a Christian—if you just shed a little light."

She stared at me. I could feel Greg's eyes on my back. I had pushed him too far into a corner. But this is what they wanted. Only D. Wayne and I knew what steps to take, knew how to do this.

Jessica started shaking her head. I opened the baggy, dipped my finger back into some powder, and held my white-coated finger in front of her. She stared at me as though I were her abstract Sunday School devil suddenly made incarnate. "How can you?" she asked. Then she licked my finger.

I dipped my finger into the baggy and held it in front of her. "Want some more?" I asked. "Who knows what Cody has told the police," I said.

"Maybe this has gone a little too far," Greg said.

"Shut up," I snapped back at him.

"Roger," Lee said.

"I've been beaten to shit, seen two of my friends beaten to shit, and I've seen a poor shit with a Christian momma killed. I don't want nobody's pound of flesh. I just want a little light to shine on these dark, squirrelly events." I waved my finger in front of Jessica. Once again, she licked my finger. Then she grabbed the bag.

She dipped her own fingers into the cocaine and licked them. Lee and Greg stepped up to either side of me. "You didn't say you were going this far," Greg whispered.

I wanted to turn to face him and start cussing him for being one of the people who pushed me into humiliating and abusing Jessica Hudson. I wanted to cuss the series of supposedly random incidents that pushed me into doing what I really was capable of doing. I wanted my head cleared of *all* congestion. "Roger!" Lee said sternly. I focused back on Jessica.

"I guess, I guess, Cody must have hired Jewel to shoot Harry," Jessica said.

"How did he know Jewel? Where did he ever meet Jewel? How did he contact him?" I shouted without breathing.

"But Jewel said he didn't kill Harry," Lee said. She eased past me toward Jessica. As Jessica licked another finger, Lee stepped up next to her, turned to face us along with Jessica, and put an arm around Jessica's shoulder. "Come, Jessica. Come on honey. You knew Jewel. You knew him. Who got him to go over to Harry's house?"

Jessica stamped her foot. "Cody did."

"How much did Cody pay him?" I asked.

"I don't know."

Lee cooed to her, "Come on, why did you want to kill Harry?"
Jessica pulled away from Lee. "I didn't kill anybody."
"Who did?" Greg asked, because he just couldn't help himself.
"I don't know," Jessica said. Then the backdoor opened.
Bruce led Cody Hudson out onto the deck. D. Wayne and Buttermilk followed behind him. Bruce had called Jessica with the coke deal. I had called Cody and told him that I had information about the ongoing and secret investigation of the Jefferson County Sheriff's Department and the Beaumont Police. I told him that I now wanted the payoff for Jewel's death and that, if I got it, I wouldn't talk to the police. We had timed it so that when he walked in, I would be outside with Jessica. D. Wayne, Buttermilk, and the new, intimidating-looking Bruce were to keep him waiting. We had even told Lynette to let us have our privacy out on the deck.
Cody looked at his wife. "Jessica, what are you doing here?" Then he looked at me, "You son of a bitch," he said. Buttermilk and D. Wayne caught him before he could get up to me.
I slowly walked toward him. He twisted within D. Wayne and Buttermilk's grasp. "You can't whip all of us. Especially not that mean son of a bitch holding you. That mean fucker went punch to punch with the meanest, toughest human being I've ever seen. That would be Sunshine McQueen, Jewel's brother. I still get nightmares about Sunshine. Buttermilk, there, wants another chance at Sunshine's ass."
Cody looked over his shoulder at Buttermilk and stopped struggling, but Buttermilk still kept a light grip on him. "Now, I've made a deal with your wife. We'll be scarce. We won't say anything to the police, but you got to tell us the truth."
Cody looked at me, then at his wife. He thought for a moment. "I've got your money in my car. I didn't dare bring that kind of money in here. Just take your money and leave us alone."
Jessica stared at her husband. "You can keep your money," I said.
"Now, let's think this through," D. Wayne interrupted.
"D.," Lee scolded. "We've been over this. It's not about money. We won't taint it with money."
"It's ten thousand dollars."
"This is too much information. I'm not hearing this," Greg Giddings said.
"What money?" Jessica asked her husband.

"It was for you, dear. To protect you," Cody pleaded.

I looked at Jessica, then at Greg Giddings. "You see, Cody here, when he last met me, offered D. Wayne and me ten thousand dollars to kill Jewel. That's why he's here. To pay up."

"Oh, my God," Greg Giddings said. "I'm not hearing this."

"Sorry, Greg. There was no other way," Lee said.

"You did that?" Jessica said, almost lovingly, to her husband.

I turned my gaze and full attention to Jessica. She pulled her head away from her husband to look at me. "We didn't kill Jewel. But we got him killed. Still we don't deserve the money. Except for D. Wayne there, we couldn't live with ourselves if we took it."

"Oh, there's another one of us could live with hisself and that money," Buttermilk said.

"But now we're all bound up real tight," I continued, looking at Jessica. "I was tempted to tell the police about Cody's offer, but D. Wayne, Lee, and I could never have proved our offer was fake. We could never have gone to court. We couldn't beat two respected citizens. But now that the police are snooping around, we might all be in a little trouble. So what I want now for our past and future services, especially if I'm going to continue to shut up about that money in Cody's car, is a little truth."

Cody stepped toward me, and Buttermilk and D. Wayne stepped right up with him. "You've got everything pretty well figured out already," Cody said.

"Not about Harry. I want to know how Harry got killed. Your wife's version is that you hired Jewel to kill Harry."

Cody lunged again, but Buttermilk and D. Wayne caught him. His face turned red as he struggled. "What kind of ethics do you have? What about your profession? I hired you. I goddamn hired you."

"How do you sleep at night?" Jessica yelled at me.

"Same as you do—or don't, I guess," I said. Lee glared at me as though I were botching this. I probably was. I had never really performed in a court. I had never even practiced. All I had were the lessons and advice of Buck Cronin.

Cody relaxed, then turned his attention to his soon-to-be-ex-wife. "Jessica, what did you tell them?"

Her eyes clouded. Even in the soft light in the mist, I could see her mascara run. "Nothing. Nothing, dear."

"She said you hired Jewel. Jewel says he never shot Harry. That leads me to think maybe you shot Harry. Look Cody, the jealous husband is always the first suspect—unless there's a wayward drug dealer and his brother to blame."

D. Wayne, even though he was supposed to leave this to me and Lee, spoke up. "You got the balls to tell us this was all some kind of coincidence?"

"Looks like it," Cody said.

"Say that again. Say it once more," D. Wayne said.

Greg pushed his way through us to the backdoor. Bruce stood his ground as the guard to the door. "Do this without me. Do what you have to. But do it without me. I can't go where you're leading."

"Pussies are leaving," Buttermilk mumbled. I nodded toward Bruce. Bruce opened the door, and Greg hurried through it, giving a sympathetic glance to Lee and a scowl to me.

"We didn't do anything," Jessica screamed. "We didn't do anything. How could we? I mean this is not supposed to be happening. None of this was supposed to happen."

"Shut up, Jessica," Cody said.

"Honey, honey," Jessica cried. "Oh shit, Christ." Jessica looked at the baggy of diluted cocaine in her hands.

"Look at you," Cody yelled at his wife. "Back with that shit. Let me go. Let me go," he said.

Almost obediently Buttermilk and D. Wayne let him go. He walked up to Jessica and snatched the baggy away from her. He threw it to the ground. "Oh, man," Bruce muttered. "Don't just spread it on the ground like that."

"What did he tell you?" Jessica shouted to me. "What did he say?"

"I'm not in on this," Cody shouted to his wife. "What the hell are you thinking? Shut up."

"You said not to confess. You said to be quiet. You said there had to be a solution," Jessica screamed and cried both. I lifted my head.

"Shut up," Cody said.

"Okay, okay." Jessica squared off in front of her husband. He looked for a moment as though he would hit her. But then, almost together, some great tremor that only they could feel shook them both.

"Honey, oh honey," Cody purred, and Jessica convulsed, then screamed.

"So what happened?" I asked, the only one prepared to be the ultimate asshole.

Jessica cried. "Okay, I killed him," she screamed and looked at each one of us. Her eyes settled on me. "You gave those damn photos to my husband." She shifted her gaze to Cody, "And he gave them to me." She shifted her gaze to me, and her voice sounded like she was pleading. "When I showed your photos to Harry, he said he loved me. He said he was going to tell my husband he loved me and wanted me to leave my husband. I couldn't have that. I couldn't take that. I couldn't destroy my family." She stared at Cody, and he started to cry. "I'm a teacher, a mother, a Christian. I couldn't have that. So I don't know how, but I used the gun Harry bought for me from Jewel, and I shot him—while he was going to the bathroom."

Buttermilk stared at her with a quizzical look. Jessica caught his stare. "While he was peeing."

Cody moved closer to her and held her. "You don't have to go on."

"He was bleeding but he wasn't dead. So I shot him again." Lee turned away from the two of them. D. Wayne went to her. Only Buttermilk and I looked on. "And I forgot to get those damn photos. I left them there and forgot all about them."

"Cody," I said. "You want to tell me anything, or you want me to guess?"

"You're pretty good at guessing," he sneered and pressed his wife's face into his shoulder.

"You offered Jewel what? Ten thousand dollars? Five up front and another five after? You knew he was a fuckup. You knew the police would suspect him. You even wanted me to find him so the plan could work itself out. Jesus, he even dropped his own gun when he saw Harry dead. And that wasn't the gun that killed him, and still he's the suspect."

"I've got a lawyer. This will never hold up in court. This is coercion pure and simple. I could countersue you."

"Bring it on, motherfucker," Buttermilk mumbled.

"There's not going to be a trial." Both Jessica and Cody looked at me. I tried to pull some air in through my throat and clogged nostrils so I could explain. "I lied," I said. While they stared at me, I forced out more words. "It's a closed case, and it's not going to be reopened. Neither of you two are going to be indicted. You got away with murder. Seems we all got each other by the short hairs, but there's nothing we can do about it without getting everybody in a world of shit. No reason to divorce. In fact, stay together," I said, almost out of kindness.

"You son of a bitch," Cody growled.

"We are not bad people," Jessica whimpered.

"All we wanted to do was to see why poor Harry Krammer got killed and to tell some other poor shit's mother that her boy was innocent of at least one crime. Go home and go to sleep. When your dreams wake you up, they'll be from guilt rather from fear of getting caught," I added.

"You people are no better than us," Cody said.

"Not really," D. Wayne said with his arm around his woman.

Bruce held the door open as Cody escorted his wife back into the bar. Bruce went to the spilled cocaine and tried to salvage what he could, but the rest of us filed in after the Hudsons. They went out the front door, just as the disgusted Greg Giddings had done. We all sat at the bar, no one saying anything until Bruce joined us. "Pretty cool," he said. "You know, Roger, you were right. I think I could be a private eye. That's my calling. How do I get started?"

"Someone slap him," D. Wayne said.

"Come on. We all wanted this," I said.

While I was thinking, D. Wayne opened his wallet and pulled out several bills. He handed them to me. "Even though you don't want Cody's money, I suppose you want what Lee promised."

I looked at the cash in my hand. The outer bill was a hundred. I didn't look to see what the others were. "It ain't exactly necessary now."

"I pay my debts. And I pay a few of Lee's too. That's what I figure Lee owes you."

"I was thinking of giving a discount," I said.

"I took that into account. It's a little light."

I folded up the money and put it in my wallet. I found myself nodding and saying, "Feels hefty enough."

TWENTY-SEVEN

After three of Lynette's heavy-hand drinks, the second act of my drama for the night walked in the door right on time. Rachel came in and immediately sniffed at the smell of cigarettes, piss, and stale beer. Welcome to my world.

All of my friends were quietly drinking, waiting for some last scene that I only hinted at. "Oh my God," Lee whispered to me when she saw Rachel. "Roger, what have you done?"

I pushed myself up from the barstool and walked to Rachel. "Roger, Roger," she said with a hint of disgust. But she rose on her toes to kiss me on the cheek. The next morning my penitent jogging would be back.

I took Rachel's hand and pulled her behind me. I went through the back door to the deck and stepped into the mist. "Roger, it's raining," Rachel said.

I let go of her hand and stepped away from her. The mist would keep the allergens out of the air. In a day or so, I would breathe again. But now I snorted and fought against the moisture in my eyes. "Rachel, Rachel, honey. You don't like this place do you?"

"No, I don't," she said.

"I don't know if I do either, but I belong here, with those people."

"They're disgusting," she said.

I hung my head. "Maybe so, but I can't leave them. I wish I could."

Rachel stepped up to me, "There's counseling. You could go to a clinic. You can beat this," she said.

"No, no, that's not it." I stared up into the mist. A slight breeze was starting.

"I've let you back into my life. I've let you into our life again. Don't screw that up, Roger. You've come so far."

"Rachel, dearest, honey. You want a straight and narrow life. You want safety. You want the odds in your favor. You want the world to be pushed outside of your door."

"And there's something wrong with that?"

"Exactly," I said. "Me, I want deep down, maybe, or damn near, what you want."

"Roger, you've been drinking."

"I've always been drinking."

I wanted to see a short skirt wrapped around her taut thighs, but instead I saw her shapely legs outlined by her tight jeans. The mist had pasted strands of hair to her face. Her lipstick was smudged. The slight breeze lifted just a few unsoaked wisps of hair. My mind conjured a thought: I could change; I could be what Rachel saw me as. "Rachel, you're a Baptist."

"What?" she said. "What? I'm Baptist? You know I was raised Catholic."

"You want the socially-sanctioned, safe, secure, guarded, gated life and community. But I'm a Pentecostal. Voices talk to me. But they talk in tongues, and I can't make sense of them."

"Your voices come from a bottle."

"I won't call. I won't bother you. I won't go by Amber's day care."

Rachel nodded nobly. "Okay, that makes sense then."

"Aw, hell. Sure I will. I say I won't now, but I will. And I hope you'll be tolerant and help me with this when I get tiresome and obnoxious. When I call you crying because I think I've made a mistake. When I try to say hello to Amber through a picket fence at her school or day care."

"This conversation is a mistake." I couldn't tell in the mist and dark if she was crying or not. I wished that she was. I think that I was. "Leave it to you, to come up with some convoluted explanation. Why couldn't you have just left? Why did you have to come back to me and my family?"

"You were right about one thing. I've hurt Amber. I didn't think of her. She needs someone different from me. I shouldn't have let her get so used to me. I shouldn't have let myself need her so much." As soon as I said that, I was pretty sure that I was crying. Liquor is never good for such scenes. But every time we get ready for one, what do we do but drink?

"So you're breaking up with me, Roger. You beg to come back. I make sacrifices. And now this. I hope you don't call back. And when and if you do, I'll hope that you'll forgive me when I hang up on you."

"I'll be at Amber's play because I promised her I would. I want to see her be a pumpkin. And maybe sometime, after some time, I could talk to Amber."

"No, don't do that," she said. "Stay away from us."

Rachel, more than me, had the courage and the clarity of mind to end on a dramatic note rather than letting the discussion get even sloppier. She went back into Nothing To Lose, and then, no doubt, through the front door.

I stayed outside and tried to breathe the rain into my clogged sinuses. The cool weather promised a winter. In the middle of winter, when everyone in Southeast Texas was just grateful that it wasn't summer, as always, I would be wary of the approaching summer, because I remembered the last one. In the midst of August, in the most unbearable oppressive humidity that just stole your breath, I would look forward to winter.

But that early fall night, I looked up and saw the black rain clouds behind the swaying pines in the gray rain. There were things to feel here, to enjoy. In a day or two, my allergies would be gone, and I'd be breathing easy through a clear nose and with healed ribs while I jogged down my canal. Maybe Emily Nguyen would be waiting for me when I finished, with some Krispy Kreme doughnuts and a cup of coffee. We'd talk about how the Hudsons used the way the world was to get away with a murder. Maybe Emily would have a new case.

When I turned to go inside, the back door was open and Lee was standing in its frame. "I kind of overheard what you said," she said. "But I've got to disagree. I think you're just what that little girl needs. I think you'd be a fine daddy."

She seemed to soothe me just with her gaze. "I sure want to see Amber's performance as a pumpkin," I said.

Lee turned her dancer's smile, her grace, and her charm on for me. For a moment, she was my girl. "Let's go back to your friends in the bar," Lee said.

"You know, we drink too much; we're trashy; we're welfare mothers; we're irresponsible; we're pregnant teenagers; we heed our incessant hormones instead of listening to our good sense; we blew our best chances years ago; we just can't see what's best for us."

Lee took up the chant. "We're titty floppers; we're artists; we're agitators; we just can't accept what they say is good for us. We're a burden on society, yet we push it on and give notice to how it's fucked up."

"If we'd just had more money, more social prestige. If we had more luck. If we were smarter."

"But sometimes, a few of us just skirt around the edges of being wise."

I smiled at her, kindhearted Lee. "But still we're better off than the Hudsons," I said. "I kind of pity them."

"So maybe they'll become one of us. And we, those like us, just need to help each other and let ourselves be helped."

She held her hand out in the dark. I grasped it. Lee led me inside to Buttermilk, D. Wayne, Bruce, and Lynette.

After several more bourbons with my Pentecostal friends, I thought I heard Sunshine's heavy breathing as he ran through the Big Thicket, evading cops and his past, or maybe it was the squealing tires and churning engine of my pickup as Sunshine drove it down back roads across the country, as he tried to both outrun and catch the voices in his head.

Jim Sanderson has published two collections of short stories, *Semi-Private Rooms* and *Faded Love* (Finalist for the 2010 Texas Institute of Letters' Jesse Jones Award for Fiction); an essay collection, *A West Texas Soapbox*; five novels—*El Camino del Rio*, *Safe Delivery*, *La Mordida*, *Nevin's History: A Novel of Texas*, and *Dolph's Team*. In addition, he has published over sixty short stories, essays, and scholarly articles. Sanderson serves as the chair of the Department of English and Modern Languages at Lamar University.